FOREVER BLACK

Elise Noble

Published by Undercover Publishing Limited

Copyright © 2017 Elise Noble

R4

ISBN: 978-1-910954-14-0

Edited by Amanda Ann Larson

Cover art by Abigail Sins

www.undercover-publishing.com

www.elise-noble.com

For my mum.
If you could just skip over chapter 29...thanks.

PROLOGUE - PART 1

"YOU KNOW IT'S love when your feelings don't
leave, even if the person does."

It started off as a better than normal day. I'd go so far
as to call it good, because when I finished my session
with Alex—the ex-Spetsnaz sadist my husband had
lovingly appointed as my personal trainer—I managed
to walk out of the gym rather than having to crawl.

"You should do more squats," Alex said, following.

I flipped him the bird. "I have a meeting."

Speaking of my husband, he was due back from
California later that morning. He'd flown there to
review staff performance at the LA branch of
Blackwood, the security firm we ran along with two
close friends, Nate Wood and Nick Goldman.

We'd flipped a coin for the trip, but I'd called tails
and ended up spending two nights in New Jersey.

My phone chirped as I pulled a smoothie out of the
fridge, letting me know Black had touched down in
Virginia, just in time for our lunchtime appointment
with a potential new client. Black hadn't elaborated on

who. That meeting couldn't be over fast enough for me, because in the afternoon, to turn a good day into a great day, the two of us were heading off to our chalet in France.

According to the weather forecast I'd checked over breakfast, there had been fresh snowfall in Chamonix overnight, leaving a couple of inches of beautiful powder. Happy days. Work had been crazy lately, and the thought of a few days of skiing without ringing phones or meetings or emails or people asking me what to do was bliss.

"I've put clothes out on the bed for you."

Bradley, my assistant, wandered past carrying one of those little books of paint swatches. Now what was he planning? Last time he got it into his head to decorate, he'd created a replica beach at the edge of my swimming pool, and the sand got on everything, not least my nerves.

But when I got to the bedroom, I couldn't criticise his choice of outfit. A practical yet elegant trouser suit, single-breasted, black. I'd never cease to be amazed at the way he always bought me clothes that fitted perfectly without me ever trying them on. On the rare occasions I did go shopping myself, I couldn't manage it, even if I spent hours in the fitting room.

Black called me as I hopped up and down, trying to put on a pair of knee-high stockings. I laddered one, gave up, and answered the phone instead.

"All right, Chuck?"

I could picture his scowl, and it made me smile. His given name may have been Charles, but he hated it, and ever since I'd known him, he'd been Black. His surname and now mine as well.

"Still feeling bitter about your trip to Newark?"

"Whatever gives you that idea?"

He sighed, something he'd done a lot over the years. "I'm in a cab, and I should get there for twelve. Are you on your way?"

"Just pulling out of the driveway right now."

"I don't hear a car engine."

Trust him to be so observant. "Would you believe I'm driving quietly?"

"Just hurry up, Diamond."

Satnav said the drive to the Green Mountain hotel on the outskirts of Richmond should take thirty-five minutes, but if I paid lip service to the speed limits, I'd shave ten minutes off that. The sun shone from a blue sky as I walked to the garage, whistling out of tune. It would be rude not to take my Viper out for a spin, wouldn't it?

My good fortune held when I reached the hotel without hitting any traffic or getting a speeding ticket. Five minutes to spare, not bad. Where was Black? I couldn't see him outside, so either he'd gone in already or he hadn't arrived yet. My competitive streak hoped for the latter.

I winced as a woman pushing a buggy clipped the mirror of a Ford Taurus parked a few feet away. No way was that happening to my baby, which was not only shiny but also a present from Black. The corner of the lot beckoned, well away from toddlers, careless elbows, and swinging handbags. A minute later, I'd swapped out my trainers for high-heeled instruments of torture and made it to the hotel entrance. The decorative clock above the door told me I was bang on time.

Congratulations, Emmy. Take a bow.

A battered yellow cab drove into the parking lot, and I paused with one foot over the threshold. Was that Black? Oh, please let that be Black.

The car pulled up at the kerb, and sure enough, he was in the back seat. My lucky day. He reached one tanned, muscular arm out to pay the driver, and it was my turn to sigh. How did he go brown so quickly? It took me a week to get a healthy glow. Fifty bucks said he'd been doing too much surfing and not enough work.

We'd be having words about that. If Black planned on slacking when Alex had made me run seventeen miles yesterday, he had another think coming.

Black needed a haircut too. He'd said that three weeks ago, but clearly lazing around in the sun had taken precedence and now his hair was curling over his collar. I'd just stepped forward, trying to think up some pithy remark about him being a beach bum, when movement to my left caught my attention.

Thirty yards away, the side door of a white van slid open. The "Flowers 2 You" logo emblazoned on the side in Pepto-Bismol pink peeled around the edges, but that wasn't what bothered me. The door was opening all on its own, or at least it seemed to be. Where was the delivery guy?

That picture wasn't quite right.

Something poked out from the gloom inside. A cylinder with a bulbous tip. Dark grey or green, perhaps. As I focused, the figure of a man inside became clear, holding...

Holy fuck! He was holding a fucking RPG launcher.

"Black! Blaaaaaaaack! Get out!"

The world moved in slow motion as I spun and ran

towards the car, but my bloody heel broke and I went down on one knee. I scrambled up just as Black turned his head and looked at me, probably wondering why the hell I was making so much noise. As our eyes met, a streak of flame flew past me and hit him.

Dead centre.

He didn't even see it coming.

Glass shattered all around as the car exploded into a ball of fire, then to make doubly sure nobody walked out of it, a second grenade followed the first, causing the flames to jump even higher.

It took a second for my brain to register what had happened, then Black was gone. Nobody could have survived the inferno raging in front of me. The blaze was so intense I couldn't even see his outline, and there was no sign of the driver either. My heart beat in a crazy rhythm, a stubborn refusal in Morse code to accept what my head knew was true.

Two lives had just been lost.

Three, if you counted mine.

A blur of pink and white shot past as the van peeled out of the parking lot, and the training Black had spent the past thirteen-and-a-bit years drilling into me took over. I didn't have time to think, and I didn't have time to feel. That would come later. Right now, I gave chase. My first thought was to run for my car, but the huge expanse of tarmac between it and me quickly put an end to that idea. Instead, my gaze landed on a kid sitting astride a Yamaha R1 motorcycle. He'd stopped to stare at the fireworks, eyes wide behind his visor.

"Get off!" I yelled, belting in his direction.

He took one look at my hand and leapt to the side. Why the horror? I glanced down myself and saw the gun I was carrying. When did I get that out of my bag? I shoved it into my waistband to free up my hands then caught the bike before it toppled to the ground. The engine was still running, and I revved it, leaving a black streak of rubber as I accelerated after the van. By the time I hit the road, I already had my red phone, the one I used for emergencies, clamped against my ear.

One ring, two, then Nate picked up.

"Black's dead. I'm going after the shooters. Send help."

I didn't wait for his reply. I didn't need to. Nate knew I'd never kid about something like that, and he'd track my phone to find me. No, I only had one job to do now, and that was to catch the van. It already had a good head start, and if the driver had taken one of the multitude of small tracks that branched off the main road, there was every chance I wouldn't find it.

I sped along the highway, putting myself in the shoes of a fleeing murderer. Left? Right? Straight on? *They'll want to disappear.* The tyres squealed as I took a left-hand turn towards Richmond. *Please, say I've guessed right.* A minute later, I flew over the brow of a hill and spotted a van ahead in the distance. It might have been travelling fast, but the bike was faster.

Was it the right vehicle? Or just a plumber running late for a job?

I'd memorised the licence plate as the bastards drove away from the hotel, and those digits burned in my mind as I leaned into the bends, my one goal to get close enough to confirm my suspicions.

What if I was right?

Well, I'd hang back and wait for the cavalry to arrive. For once in my life, I hoped the cops would get there before my own guys. Team Blackwood would have murder on their minds, and I didn't want any of them going to prison. Not only that, I wanted Black's killers alive for questioning, and after I'd found out what I needed to know, I planned to peel their skin from their bodies, piece by fucking piece.

And I'd smile while I did it.

Why? That was the question I wanted to ask. Why had they killed my husband? Something told me this was bigger than just two men.

But you know what they say about best-laid plans? Yeah, that happened. The arsehole driving must have looked in the mirror, because the back door of the van opened and a hail of bullets came at me, that shooter hanging on so he didn't fall out. I returned fire, aiming wide. I wanted to stop him temporarily, not permanently. That would come later.

The fucker disappeared from view, and I thought my warning had worked, but it turned out he'd just gone to get the grenade launcher. It looked like Lady Luck was at home with her feet up while Mr. Murphy, of Murphy's Law fame, rode pillion.

The asshole let one fly at me, and I swerved to the left, swearing under my breath as the grenade took out a tree at the edge of the road. I eased off the throttle to put some space between us, but rather than speeding away, the van mirrored me. The gap closed, and door guy started up with the pistol again.

Well, it wasn't the first time someone had tried to kill me, and I was good at playing that game too.

My first shot hit to the left. Another squeeze, red blossomed across his shoulder, and he stumbled back inside. Then I shot out the right rear tyre. *Slow down, asshole*. Trying to balance the bike and shoot and dodge flying bullets while zipping along at a hundred miles an hour didn't look good for my life expectancy. One wild fishtail and I'd be joining Black in hell.

The good news was, my plan worked. But unfortunately for the men in the van, it worked a bit too well, because when the tyre popped, the van swerved right, left the road, and hit the side of a bridge. I slammed the brakes on, barely keeping the bike upright as it went into a skid. As soon as it stopped, I leapt off and ran towards the wreckage in a crouch, hugging the treeline so they couldn't get a clear line of sight.

I tried the driver first, but someone should have told him to wear a seat belt because his brain had created a Jackson Pollock masterpiece on the inside of the cracked windscreen. Not only that, his bowels had let go, and the stench of shit mingled with smoke as the first flames licked out of the engine bay.

With him a lost cause, I ran to the back. Had asshole number two fared any better? The door swung in the breeze, and I approached cautiously. Would he be in any state to fight back?

No, was the short answer. He lay motionless among piles of broken flowers with a tyre iron protruding from his stomach. Fuck. Blood bubbled from the wound, leaving a scarlet trail as I dragged him out onto the damp grass verge. Just in time, because the fire had taken hold in the cab by then, and the flames were spreading fast. The smoke made me cough as I checked for a pulse. Nothing. I fought down the bile rising in my throat, made sure his airway was clear, then started chest compressions and mouth-to-mouth resuscitation.

Why, you may ask, did I try to save my husband's killer? Good question. Let me tell you, I'd have liked nothing better than to give him a good kicking and leave him to rot, but I only had one connection between the man who pulled the trigger and the person who hired him, and right now, that connection's life was seeping away into the muddy grass at the side of the road.

How did I know he was a hired gun and not just some lone wolf with a grudge? I didn't at that point, not for sure, but I'd had enough experience in the business to suspect it was the most likely scenario.

Rarely did two amateurs carry out a hit as organised as that one. The men knew who Black was and where he would be, and the killing itself had been dramatic but precise. Not to mention they had access to some pretty nasty weapons. If I hadn't been there, they'd have made a swift exit in their no doubt stolen van and be heading straight to the nearest bar in a non-extradition country to celebrate a job well done. So I figured they had to be professionals.

And professionals got paid. I wanted the person holding the purse strings.

To me, these men were nothing. *Nothing*. Just tools hired to do a job. For them, it was nothing personal, and I could identify with that. So, seeing the bigger picture, even with grief starting to set in, I did what I could to make the asshole breathe again.

Several cars stopped, and their occupants gathered to watch, hovering in front of the trees. Ghouls. Not one of them offered to help. They just wanted to get their sick kicks by watching someone else struggle, and I almost emptied a clip at them.

After what seemed like forever but was probably only a few minutes, Nick arrived. His Ferrari was swiftly followed by blue lights then red as cops and an ambulance turned up too.

Nick took hold of my arm and gave me a gentle tug. I tried to shake him off, but he pointed at the medics fast approaching behind him. They could take over now. I let him pull me to my feet and got in a sharp kick to the bastard's side before I stepped back.

"Breathe, you piece of shit."

The emergency crew did their thing while Nick carried me to his car. In one of those strangely irrelevant thoughts, I noticed his hair was wet and smelled of shampoo. How many more lives would be disrupted before the end of the day?

"Sorry I dragged you out of the shower."

He gave me a "What the fuck?" look then deposited me in the passenger seat, my legs haphazardly stuffed into the footwell. I'd started shaking when he wrapped me in the blanket he always carried in the trunk.

"It's okay, baby. It's okay."

He perched on the door sill and drew me close, stroking my hair.

"It's not okay, Nicky. It won't ever be okay. He's dead."

And I might as well be.

PROLOGUE - PART 2

NICK DREW BACK and tried to look me in the eye, but I couldn't meet his gaze.

"You don't know for sure that Black's dead."

He clearly hadn't been to the hotel and seen the carnage outside reception.

"Yes, I do. Nobody survived that explosion. Trust me; I know."

Nick went quiet. Any words he could have offered would have been inadequate. Instead, he tucked me in his arms, shielding me from onlookers and two dozen cops who didn't have an ounce of tact between them. One tried to approach, full of questions, and got the sharp end of Nick's tongue.

"Back off and leave her the hell alone. She's not speaking to you today."

The guy from the back of the van was loaded into the ambulance and shipped off to the hospital, but I barely noticed. Even the fire brigade who came to extinguish the burning vehicle hardly registered. The only thing I was vividly aware of was the burning smell of human flesh from the barbecued driver. That stayed with me for weeks afterwards.

"Nate's at the hotel," Nick said, after a brief phone conversation. "Do you want to go there?"

I couldn't. I didn't want to see the mangled, charred

wreckage of the car my husband had burned to death in, especially since it would be accompanied by the same stench.

"Can you take me to the hospital instead?" I wanted to be first in line if tyre-iron guy survived.

But he didn't.

"Massive internal injuries, I'm afraid," the bespectacled doctor told me, feigning sympathy. "He was gone before we got him out of the ambulance."

I sank onto a hard plastic seat in the waiting room, my mind black. Empty. In less than half a day, my whole world had twisted into a nightmare I'd never wake up from.

Nick must have taken me home although I had no recollection of the journey. By the time he carried me upstairs and put me to bed, I'd gone numb. His lips moved, but I heard nothing. I couldn't speak; I couldn't move; I couldn't think.

That night, I relived the explosion. Over and over and over and over. I lost count of the number of times I woke up screaming. Nick stayed with me, fidgeting on the sofa by the window, undoubtedly ready to make a swift leap off the balcony if the need arose. A long time had passed since he spent a night in the same room as me, and on the last occasion, I'd sent him on a trip to the hospital. It was a testament to how worried he must have been that he stuck it out. I did notice he had a Taser in his lap, though, just in case.

Things only got worse the next day when the police arrived. I couldn't get out of bed. If I stayed buried under the covers, perhaps this horror story would turn out to be a bad dream. My three closest girlfriends, Dan, Mack, and Carmen hovered at my bedside, at least one of them there at all times, never leaving me alone. Dan had the hugs, Mack had the tissues, and Carmen had the gun.

There was a soft knock at the door, and Nick slipped inside.

"There's a couple of detectives downstairs."

"So?"

Let them stay downstairs. There was no love lost between me and the local cops.

Nick sat on the edge of the bed and squeezed my hand. "Baby, they can't identify Black by sight, and his teeth were too badly damaged for dental records to be an option."

"It's him. I know it's him. I was right there, Nicky."

"I understand, Ems. But they say they have to be sure. They want a DNA sample."

Black and I had always guarded our privacy fiercely. Neither of us had fingerprints or DNA on file. On the rare occasions they did pop up, Mack simply hacked in to whatever system they'd appeared in and erased them. But he was dead now, so what did it matter?

"Fine. Give them the DNA. Then tell them to get lost."

While Nick went to Black's room to hunt for a hair sample, I rolled over and curled up again.

Don't think; don't think; don't think; don't think.

But the police wouldn't leave. Nate stood outside my door like a guard dog for the rest of the day, and every so often, I heard an angry exchange of words. Eventually, though, after ensuring I was suitably lawyered up, he had to allow the police to question me.

"Just stick to the bare minimum, Ems."

"Do we know anything new?"

"They've identified the dead fucker from the hospital. A wanted hitman, and the driver too. The pair of them had a collection of outstanding warrants from here to California."

So I was right.

"Any news on who hired them?"

"The money trail's a dead end. The cops found two hundred thousand in cash when they searched their hotel room, but it could have come from anywhere."

"Two hundred? Is that all?"

How could Black's life have been worth so little? My rates started at five times that.

Nate rubbed his temples. "I know. It's insulting."

"Have the cops found anything else?"

"Not exactly." Nate walked over to the window and stared out.

"What's that supposed to mean?"

"It means the lead investigator keeps spouting shit about statistics. That it's always a victim's nearest and dearest who's most likely to have killed them."

Realisation dawned, and I sat up. "They think it was me."

He nodded, and anger flashed in his eyes. Not at me, but at the police.

On paper it fitted. I had the connections, I had the money, and I stood to gain a massive financial benefit from my husband's death. But what the idiots obviously didn't understand was that I'd loved my husband, and as a part of me died when he did, I was hardly likely to have helped him on his way.

I explained this to my lawyer, Oliver, as well as the fact that I already had more of my own money than I could ever spend and so I didn't need Black's as well.

Not to mention that if I *had* wanted something ridiculously expensive, like a new jet or perhaps a small country, I'd only have had to ask and he'd have bought it for me.

The other thing, which I didn't put into words because it wouldn't have helped the situation, was that if I'd wanted Black dead, which I didn't, then we wouldn't have been having this conversation. Why? Well, firstly, I'd have done the job myself, and secondly, nobody would've suspected it was anything but a terrible accident.

Between them, the girls got me out of bed and semi-presentable. Call it zombie chic. The police had made themselves at home in my dining room, papers and candy wrappers strewn everywhere. A steaming mug of coffee sat next to one of them, right on the polished oak table. If Bradley saw that, Black's wouldn't be the only murder they had to look into. I sat there for over an hour, confirming only my full name and address while my high-priced pit bull of a lawyer ran circles around a pair of detectives and an assistant DA who appeared to have barely graduated from law school and was extremely nervous to boot.

Luckily, despite the cops' conviction I had something to do with my husband's death and the media christening me the Black Widow, my friends didn't doubt me. I couldn't have asked for a more loyal or amazing bunch of people in my life, and they had my back. *Always* had my back. So while I wasted my time listening to Oliver snap "don't answer that" and "that's completely irrelevant," they started the hunt for Black's true killer.

Sadly, they didn't get very far.

The van had been stolen from a long-term airport parking lot three days previously. Professionals that they were, the hitmen had even bought a few bouquets to maintain their cover story as they drove it around. Unfortunately, they'd also covered up the money trail, and so far, we hadn't found large payments into any accounts connected with them. We couldn't trace the origins of the cash either, although the assholes certainly lived well enough.

Their upstate New York homes were far too nice to be afforded by the insurance salesman and freelance piano tuner they claimed to be, and neither had family money. We found swimming pools, a vintage Rolls Royce, and enough art to make any respectable gallery weep.

But no leads to their employer.

My clients lent their support as well as my friends and colleagues. The FBI sent a couple of agents to assist in our investigation, the NSA searched through their archives, and the CIA offered to help overseas. Although, as ever with the CIA, they had an ulterior motive. They wanted to get me back on track as soon as possible so I was available to do their dirty work.

They knew that, I knew that, and they probably knew I knew that. They didn't care.

When I did go back to the office, three days after the explosion, I wandered around in a trance. Going through the motions. I checked emails, made phone calls, and spoke to people, but although the wheel was turning, the hamster was dead. With Black reduced to a letter of condolence confirming the DNA match, I didn't want to work, but I needed to. Work was what I had left.

Thanks to the FBI, I'd been cleared of any wrongdoing in the van chase. I'd called in a favour and they'd pulled rank, putting pressure on the local cops by claiming an interest in the case. One of their agents stepped in and got everything closed down sharpish. The police were still sniffing around Black's murder, but Oliver was earning his money there.

Meanwhile, my team put their all into trawling through Black's cases, starting with the most recent and working backwards, searching for some kind of connection between his life and his death. The control room ran 24/7, fuelled by caffeine and a determination to see justice done, but ultimately their efforts were in vain.

There was nothing, not a hint of a clue and no trail to follow.

At least, not until the day of Black's funeral when I received the phone call that tipped me over the edge and sent me running to England.

Chapter 1

THOSE WHO KNOW despair once knew hope...
Those who know loss once knew love...

The voice of the man who'd ordered my husband's death echoed in my ears, as did the crack my phone made when I hurled it against the wall after I hung up on him.

As if killing Black wasn't bad enough, now he had to call me and gloat over it? And not only that, if I tried to do anything about the state of affairs, he'd start taking out the other people I cared for. The situation made me want to break bones. His bones.

But that was out of the question.

As I stormed out of the control room and down the corridor, memories of Black's death flew through my head, as crystal clear as if it had happened yesterday. And I was mad. Mad in a way I'd never been before.

Employees scattered like bowling pins as I marched along the hallways. One glance at my face and they decided keeping quiet and getting out of my way was the best approach to take. A wise move.

I needed to get rid of my anger before I took it out on someone who didn't deserve it, and a punchbag seemed the best way.

A handful of guys looked up when I walked into the gym, their expressions quickly turning confused.

"Just leave, would you? I need this place to myself."

They filed out as I taped up my wrists, hands, and ankles—I may have been furious but I wasn't stupid—and I spent the best part of an hour punching and kicking a heavy bag into submission.

By the end, I'd collapsed in a puddle of sweat, but at least I felt calmer. Movement caught my eye as Nick and Alex appeared in the doorway. Nick looked a little bit nervous.

"Glad I wasn't on the receiving end of that," he said.

Alex, ever the critic, told me in his thick Russian accent, "Make sure you keep your head up, and your left arm was too straight on your hooks."

Thanks for that.

"I wasn't exactly worrying about my form."

"Just saying. Apart from that, you did all right." High praise indeed from Alex.

Nick walked over and sat on one of the weight machines.

"Nate said you had a call from Black's killer."

"That's right."

"And?"

"And nothing. I have to put it out of my mind because otherwise it'll make me so angry I won't be able to think straight."

"I'm surprised you don't want to retaliate."

"You think I haven't considered it? Believe me, the desire for revenge has been eating away at my insides like cancer. And if it was just me that my decision affected, I *would* go after him. I'd hunt him till my dying breath. But it *isn't* just me. He threatened everyone around me last time, and he did it again today. I couldn't carry on with your blood on my hands. There are enough days when I don't care whether I live or die as it is."

"So that's it? You're going to let him get away with murder?" Nick managed to mix disappointment and incredulity in two short sentences.

"If it means you and Nate, Carmen, Dan, and Mack get to live long and happy lives, then yes, that's precisely what I'm gonna do."

"Every single one of us would be right behind you if you made a move to find him, you know that, right?"

"Yes. And believe me, your loyalty means everything. Which is exactly why I'm sitting on my hands. I'd rather have you alive and loyal than dead and loyal."

"What if he does the same thing to somebody else's husband? Or son? Or brother?" Nick asked.

"You think that hasn't crossed my mind either? The way he is, he's done it already, many times over. And there's no doubt in my mind he'll carry on doing it. But while that's a tragedy, as long as none of his victims are you guys, I can live with it. Am I being selfish? Undoubtedly." Nick held my gaze, and I knew my words didn't please him. "And for fuck's sake, stop putting me on a guilt trip, will you? I've been doing enough of that myself."

"Well, someone's got to say it."

"You've said it. Now lay off." I turned my back on him and half-heartedly started on the bag again.

"I can't. I've talked to the others and we all feel the same. It's our decision as much as yours."

I fixed my eyes on the wall beyond Nick and sighed with a heaviness that matched my heart.

"I never wanted to have to say this, but I'm now the majority shareholder in this company, so if you want to commit resources to the problem, it has to go through me first. And I'm telling you we're not pursuing this."

There I was, living up to my reputation of being the world's biggest bitch.

"I never wanted to have to say this, but I'm disappointed in you."

"Fine, join the club. You're not the only one."

I sat down on the nearest weight machine as Nick stomped off. Well, to put it more honestly, I collapsed. His words hurt me. Deeply. But no matter, I was sticking to my guns. I couldn't feel much worse than I had before, so if everybody decided to be angry with me then that was just the way it was. At least they were alive.

Instead of dwelling on things I wasn't willing to change, I threw myself into the drugs case I was working on and stayed away from Blackwood as much as possible. I ran the investigation out of my home, Little Riverley, and cultivated the image of a lone wolf. For the most part, people stayed away from me. It didn't take a genius to work out Nate had told them what happened, and they'd all sided with him and Nick.

The only people who weren't annoyed at me were Bradley, who shied away from any form of conflict unless it was on a reality TV show, and Tia, my ex-boyfriend's sister who didn't know the whole story anyway. She'd called me from England a few times, moaning about life in general and exams in particular. Just having her talk to me as if I was a normal person cheered me up more than she could have imagined.

"Exams are so pointless. What use is a polynomial function in the real world?"

She had me there. I didn't have a clue what a polynomial function was, and I didn't feel I was missing out on anything because of that.

"No idea, but you need to get good grades to go to university."

"I don't know if I even want to go to uni. You didn't go, and you've done all right."

"Don't say that in front of Luke, whatever you do. He'll think I've been encouraging you to abandon your education."

I nearly added, "And I'm in his bad books at the moment already," but I managed to stop myself. Information on a need to know basis only. Her brother, Luke, was dating my friend Mack. Mack was pissed about my stance on Black's killer, so by extension, Luke wasn't happy with me either.

"Okay, I won't. But I'm not sure I want to spend three years of my life stuck in more lectures."

"Promise me you'll at least try hard in your exams and keep your options open?"

"Fine, I will." Tia didn't sound particularly convinced.

"Look, if you get straight As, and Luke agrees, I'll think of something fun for us to do afterwards. How about that?"

"Like a trip or something?"

"Yeah, something like that."

"Got to go. Need to study."

Tia hung up in a hurry. Bribery worked wonders for politicians, so why not a teenager? Hopefully, she really would put some effort in.

I know I did. I worked bloody hard that week, seething about my husband's killer the entire time. In my head, I'd christened the fucker Blanco—the anti-Black—and I imagined him as an over-the-top movie villain. In my quieter moments, I fantasised about dropping a house on him and seeing his feet shrivel up under the edge.

At least the DEA didn't seem to care about what I wasn't doing to catch him. In fact, the DEA didn't seem to care what I did at all as long as I got them results. Over the next seven days, I took out three dealers, one supplier, found a decent-sized stash of bad coke stored in what looked like an ordinary suburban house, and gave them a fair few leads to the next step up the food chain.

I also got shot at twice, attacked with a machete once, twisted my ankle jumping from the second floor of a building, then got hideously drunk in a bar with my new DEA buddies at the end of it.

After waking up with a headache that convinced me the devil himself was holding a party in my skull, I decided perhaps I deserved a day off.

What's more, it was my official birthday, as per my passport and the genuine fake birth certificate Black had supplied me with when we first met, and how better to celebrate than by spending the day in bed with the hangover from hell, feeling sorry for myself and pretending the world outside didn't exist? Thankfully Alex had the day off, or he'd have thrown cold water over me then dragged me out for a run. I knew this because it had happened before.

As it was, I managed to sleep until almost noon before Seth in the guardhouse woke me up. My phone blared with the sound of Pearl Jam's *Black*, which I'd set as my ringtone after drinking most of a bottle of wine.

"There's a guy here with a package for you."

"So? Can't you bring it to the house?"

He ignored my tetchiness and kept his tone professional. "He's insisting you come and sign for it yourself."

"Fine. Whatever."

I rolled out of bed, groaning as I pulled on a pair of jeans and a sweatshirt. Shoes. I needed shoes. One of my favourite Converse had a hole in it, but they were comfortable so I didn't care.

The guardhouse lay three hundred yards from the main house, and a swarthy-looking man hovered outside it next to a black Mercedes, top of the range. He stood about six feet four, and his black outfit matched his neck tattoo nicely. Not exactly your usual courier, and a complete contrast with the package he held out to me, which was wrapped in pink paper and adorned with bows and ribbons.

He grinned, well, sort of. On him it was more of a grimace, and sunlight glinted off a gold tooth.

"Boss said I had to give this directly to you."

I held out one hand. He placed the box in it then got into the car and drove off without another word.

Seth raised an eyebrow.

"Just a birthday gift from an old friend."

He nodded as if it was the most natural thing in the world for a dude who looked like he'd escaped from prison to turn up with a froufrou little parcel for me. Mind you, after some of the things Bradley had brought through those gates, I suppose nothing surprised him anymore.

Back in my bedroom, I unwrapped the box. Inside, a stunning necklace lay nestled in plum velvet, platinum, an infinity symbol that glittered under the ceiling lights. One half was studded with white diamonds, the other with black. Stunning, unique, and no doubt expensive.

The card that accompanied it came in a pink envelope, and I slid it out. Nothing special, a cake with candles and *Happy Birthday* written above. A note fluttered to the floor when I opened it.

Dearest Angel,

I hope your heart is starting to heal after your loss. Somebody once told me that time was a great healer, and although when she said it I didn't believe her, over the years I found it to be true. I hope you are able to find your closure as I found mine. If there is any assistance I can offer, I will always be here.

E

No sooner had I finished reading when Seth called again. "Emmy, some guy's arrived with a car, and he says it's for you. You didn't mention anything about a delivery?"

"Nope, I haven't ordered a car. What kind is it?"

"Uh, it's in a truck. Hang on." Voices mumbled in

the background. "A Corvette, apparently. A Stingray."

"Sorry, I still didn't order it. Kind of wish I had, though."

After more muffled chatter Seth came back. "The delivery guy insists it's for you."

"Can I speak to him?"

"Sure."

After some fumbling, the phone was handed over.

"I understand you have a car you're trying to deliver," I said.

"Yeah, that's what I keep trying to tell these clowns. The paperwork specifically says it needs to be delivered today, to Emerson Black, at this address, at twelve thirty in the afternoon. The guy even paid extra for that."

"What guy?"

"Says Charles Black on the paperwork. Address just down the road."

"When was it ordered?"

I heard rustling as he checked. "Last October. Right after the new model was announced."

Shit. Black had bought me a car. A heaviness settled in my chest as I recalled sitting in our office a month before he died, sipping coffee while watching an internet clip of the latest upgraded Corvette. I'd jokingly said I'd have a black one with a dark purple leather interior. And because Black was Black and he didn't mess around, I bet he'd called to order it the moment I'd stepped out of the room.

"What colour is it?"

"Black."

"And the inside?"

"Nightshade leather, special order. I think that's a

fancy term for purple."

I leaned against the cool wall, blinking away the prickly feeling from the corners of my eyes.

"Okay, it sounds like it might be for me after all. Can you put the guard back on, please?"

When Seth came on the line again, I told him to let the truck driver in, and I'd go down to meet him. *Pull yourself together, Emmy.* I put the necklace and card away in the safe hidden behind a painting in my room then went back outside.

In the driveway, I struggled to keep my emotions in check as my beautiful new car was lowered out of the truck. So shiny, and they'd even put a big bow on the top. Ever had a vehicular orgasm before? Let me tell you, they're a wonderful thing.

Still, I had to unclench my fists as I signed for the delivery. Black should have been standing by my side, and right now, I missed him more than ever.

"Cheer up, lady," the driver said. "Anyone else getting a new Corvette would at least have a smile on their face."

"Yeah, probably."

He shook his head as he climbed back into the truck, no doubt thinking what a spoiled little bitch I was. Black had always tried his best to make me happy, never the easiest job in the world, and even from beyond the grave, he was still having a go. Another wave of grief hit me as I realised this really would be the last birthday gift I'd ever get from him.

To be on the safe side, because Black taught me to be paranoid, I checked the car with Nate's electronic gizmos. Clean. And when I ran a mirror around underneath, all I found was a small tag that said *Good*.

Another of Black's special requests, no doubt, and his way of congratulating me for remembering to do my job properly.

Now what?

Well, the car had been delivered with a full tank of fuel, and what better way to cheer myself up than to go for a blast? I shoved the bow into the passenger footwell, hopped in the driver's side, and took off.

The sun was shining, the roads were clear, and the car was awesome. The only thing missing was Black. If he'd been alive, he'd have been right next to me, arms crossed as he muttered, "For fuck's sake, Emmy, brake!"

After a couple of hours of aimless driving, I returned home with an ache in my chest that even a wild ride in the countryside couldn't get rid of. Not that I'd truly expected it to. Upon checking my garage, I evicted an Explorer so I could park the Stingray beside the Viper. With Black's Porsche Cayenne next to that, I had one mean-looking line up of cars, but even that failed to bring me any joy today.

I was all ready for episode two of my pity party, which involved a box of Belgian truffles and a bottle of red, when I found Luke waiting for me outside the house, leaning against Mack's car.

"Hi," he said.

"Hi yourself." What was he doing here?

"Uh, I was wondering if I could ask a favour?"

"You can ask."

"Can I come in?"

I shrugged and swung the door open, and his footsteps echoed on the tiled floor as he followed me to the kitchen. I could hardly start on the wine and chocolate so early in the day with company, so I set about pouring myself a bowl of muesli instead. If nothing else, it would absorb the alcohol I planned to have for a late lunch.

"Your lawyer's drawn up the papers for the building lease, but they need your signature. I'm trying to get things moving, so I hoped you'd be able to sign them now."

Luke was opening a new branch of his company in the States, and yours truly just happened to own the empty office he'd be basing it in. "No problem. Where are they?"

"In the car. I'll get them."

Luke returned with the lease agreement, and I settled down to read over it. Not that I didn't trust Luke and my lawyer, but Black had always taught me to be thorough. Everything was fine, so I signed and handed it back.

"Tia told me it was your birthday today."

"Yeah."

"She made a present and asked me to give it to you."

Made a present? Nobody had ever made me a present before. Paid someone else to make it, maybe, but not made it themselves.

Luke held out a parcel wrapped in purple tissue paper, complete with a fancy ribbon.

"Thanks."

Well, it didn't rattle. I tore off the tissue paper and found a white T-shirt with a picture of a Barbie doll dressed in combat gear and the words "I'm a bad girl" written across it. Maybe not what I'd normally wear, but I loved it.

"They were doing screen printing in art at school," Luke explained. "Apparently, she wanted to write 'Badass bitch' on it instead, but the teacher wouldn't let her."

"I don't suppose you'd have been happy either. You're always moaning about her choice of words."

"I'd have had to make an exception this time, seeing as you are. And besides, I'm fighting a losing battle when it comes to Tia's language."

"It could be worse. Hey, if you'd seen me as a teenager, Tia would seem angelic in comparison."

"You're probably right there."

Luke tucked the papers into a folder but made no move to leave. Why was he hanging around?

"Okay, I've signed the lease, and you've dropped Tia's present off. Is there anything else or can I get back to what I was doing?"

Important things, like finding a bottle of Cabernet Sauvignon and more headache pills and sitting in the hot tub for a couple of hours.

"Uh, the others were wondering what you're doing for your birthday?"

"As I feel like shit, I'm staying in with a pizza."

A big pepperoni pizza, dripping with cheese. If Toby, my nutritionist, dared to utter a peep, he'd lose parts of his anatomy. I wasn't planning to tell him, but somehow he always seemed to find these things out.

"Do you fancy some company?"

"Whose?"

"Everyone's. I think they're all feeling bad about the disagreement last week. I know Mack's upset you're by yourself today."

"Well, I'm not changing my mind."

"Nobody expects you to. Now they've slept on it for a while, I think they can see your point of view even if they don't agree with it."

So, Luke had been sent to test the waters. A sacrificial lamb, if you like. I didn't want to come across as being overjoyed, but secretly, I was thrilled at the prospect of my friends visiting. I'd been missing them like crazy, and I hated it when they were mad at me.

"In that case, tell them they can come over if they want."

Finally, Luke smiled, a mixture of happiness he could leave and relief that I'd agreed to the plan.

"Great. See you later, then."

I gave him a little wave as I backed into the house. Feeling lighter inside, I decided to go out for a ride on my horse, Stan, instead of wallowing in self-pity in the Jacuzzi.

Maybe it wouldn't be such a bad day after all.

CHAPTER 2

SOMEONE MUST HAVE mentioned the word "party" to Bradley, because he rocked up at four o'clock laden down with bags, boxes, and half a liquor store. The suspension on the hot-pink pickup he was driving groaned under the weight.

"Bradley, which part of 'a quiet night in with pizza' didn't you understand?"

I loved Bradley dearly, but sometimes his positive outlook made me want to eat a bullet.

"Don't worry, we're still having pizza. I pre-ordered everything on the menu except the one with pineapple. We're not having pineapple again."

Last time Bradley put pineapple on my pizza, I'd taken it out the back and fired ten rounds dead through the centre of it. Good to see he'd got the message.

"So what's in the truck?"

"I just brought a few extra bits and pieces. Party poppers, balloons, a cake. And games. We can't have a party without party games."

"Yes, we can. I'm not playing strip poker again."

"Oh, don't be so boring. We can just play beer pong and Twister. Now, will you help me carry some of this stuff?"

Twister. Great. My temples throbbed again, the steady pulse of a Bradley-induced headache. I picked

up a grocery sack containing nothing healthy at all and
carted it into the kitchen, then went back for another.
How much had he bought? There couldn't be more
than ten people coming, surely?

At least I got a reprieve from carrying duty when
my phone rang. Saved by the bell. It was Tia checking
I'd received her present.

"Sure did. Thanks, honey."

"You're so welcome! I can't believe I'm missing out
on a party. Exams suck."

"How about I fly you out when they're finished?"

Luke seemed to be in Virginia for the foreseeable
future, so I didn't see how he could object.

"That would be awesome!"

"You've got to study first, though."

"I'm already gone."

Tia went back to her books, and by seven thirty, my
movie screening room had been turned into a riot of
confetti and streamers. People began to arrive, starting
with Nate and Carmen. No surprises there. Nate was
never late for anything. He had one of those radio-
controlled watches, and he lived by it. Of course, since
he'd designed the thing himself, it also contained a GPS
transmitter and a miniature radio, and if you set the
alarm for 11:06, you had fifteen seconds to get out of
the way before it blew a really big hole in something.
He gave me a slightly awkward hug, and Carmen
squashed the breath out of me.

The others trickled in over the next half hour. Mack
and Luke, Nick, Dan, Alex, and Jed, plus Logan and
three others from Blackwood—Evan, Jack, and
Malachi.

Bradley had ordered enough pizza to feed a

battalion, plus fries, onion rings, wings, and dips. It was a good thing Toby had left two days ago to visit his sister in Idaho because he'd have had a heart attack at the sight of that lot.

"How many people did you invite?" I asked my darling assistant.

"Just the people here, plus Gage, but he got held up in the office."

"We've got two pizzas each."

"People get hungry."

Food and drink covered every surface, and we barely made a dent in it. I took a couple of deep dish pepperonis and a plate full of other snacks out to Seth and Mick in the guardhouse—at least that was a bit more of it gone.

Nate stretched his arms above his head, leaning back on one of the sofas. "Time for a movie? I can't eat another mouthful."

"No!" Bradley said. "We haven't even started the cake."

"But—"

Too late; he'd gone.

To give him his credit, the cake he wheeled in five minutes later was a work of art. Three enormous layers covered in waves of milk, dark, and white chocolate topped off with glitter. Almost too pretty to eat. The top tier held thirty-three candles, and Nick handed me a fire extinguisher.

Asshole.

"Make a wish," Bradley cried.

I did. A crazy wish for the only thing I wanted, which was also the one thing I could never have. Black.

Everyone at the party had brought me a gift, and

Bradley lugged in a box of colourful packages he'd collected from people at the office for my parcel opening session after dinner.

"Thanks, guys. These presents are really... interesting."

"For the girl who has everything," Jed said, holding up the cuddly amoeba he'd chosen.

There was little point in buying me expensive presents. I could already afford anything I wanted, so people went with silly stuff instead. Heated gloves from Nate, a woolly hat with cat ears from Bradley, and a T-shirt with the slogan "I fight better in heels." Only Carmen gave practicality a nod with a new scope for my AR-15.

"Now is it time for a movie?" Nate asked.

Bradley folded his arms. "No, Twister."

Oh, good grief. "Bradley, if we try to play Twister right now, we'll puke."

"Why do I even bother? You're all a bunch of party poopers."

"How about we play later?" Dan said, playing mediator. "You can have the first spin."

Bradley gave a little huff and settled into his favourite seat, the one with twelve cushions and a fluffy pink blanket. Guess he didn't want to clear up vomit, and with any luck, he'd forget about his games if we fed him enough popcorn.

Meanwhile, Nick had found a football game, and although it wasn't my thing, I didn't want to rock the boat seeing as the others seemed keen. Relief that the evening hadn't been too awkward tempered my boredom—nobody had mentioned last week, and I wasn't about to.

I should have been happy.

Well, not happy exactly, but at least relaxed and enjoying a pleasant evening with my friends. But I couldn't shake the prickly feeling at the back of my neck, a sense of foreboding that something wasn't quite as it should be. I'd had these niggles before, and Black always encouraged me to listen to them.

More than a few times they'd been right on the money.

Looking around, I saw I was the only one getting antsy—the men were focused on the football and Carmen and Mack were engrossed in their guys. Dan sat on Nick's lap, her attention split between the TV and a huge bowl of M&Ms. Even Bradley had given up his sulk and started cheering on the dudes in tight trousers.

I slipped away and went for a mooch. The house was secure, and the perimeter alarms flashed green. When I called down to the guardhouse, Seth reported all was quiet. I heard the game buzzing in the background and a cheer from Mick. In the control room on the ground floor, I stopped and scanned the monitors, clicking between the cameras that kept watch over the estate. Everything seemed peaceful, nothing out of the ordinary.

The only thing that wasn't calm was my sixth sense, which poked at me like a toddler with ADHD.

Hold on. What was that?

I'd got halfway out of the door when I glimpsed movement on one of the screens covering the woods behind the house. A deer ran along a trail, caught in a beam of moonlight that filtered through the trees. I nearly wrote it off, but with the way I was feeling, I began to wonder what startled the deer in the first place. They lived all over the estate, and I was used to seeing them when I rode Stan out there around dusk, which meant I knew they only ran like that when they got scared.

The monitor showed nothing else except fuzzy darkness. Twisted outlines of trees swayed against a grey sky, and a layer of high clouds masked the stars. I'd just reached forward to switch the camera to thermal imaging mode when Michael Jackson's "Bad" played.

I looked down at my red phone, the one I kept for emergencies only, and the display showed an unknown number calling.

No way.

No way could that bastard be calling tonight.

Not on my birthday. Not when I was supposed to be having fun.

Yeah, technically I didn't know it was him because I hadn't answered the phone yet, but I *knew*.

I just knew.

Which was why when I answered, rather than my usual "Yeah," I greeted him with, "What the fuck do you want?"

The electronic voice came back at me. "Is that any way to greet the man who holds your life in his hands?"

"I'll ask if I ever speak to him."

"You've got a lot of fight for such a delicate thing. It's a shame you don't have some obedience instead. I was generous. I gave you two warnings, but you just couldn't hold back, could you?"

"I have no idea what you're talking about."

Except in a moment of clarity, I suddenly did. *The*

drugs. It had to be the drugs. This guy had money, he had connections, and when he killed Black, it was with a flair for the dramatic, a trait not uncommon among drug lords who wanted to send a message telling everyone not to fuck with them.

So while I'd insisted I wanted everybody to avoid any trouble, I'd spent the last week inadvertently stirring it up all by myself. Fuck, fuck, fuck indeed.

A distorted cackle came down the line. "I wish I could say I believed you, but I don't. Happy birthday, Ms. Black. I hope you like your surprise."

Everything came together in my head. I had something in the woods and a pissed off drug lord with a penchant for heavy weapons on the phone. Fifty bucks said my latest birthday surprise wouldn't come neatly wrapped in a gift box.

But no matter. I was going to dish out a few surprises of my own. Happy birthday to me. I reached out to the keyboard in front of me, starting to type even as I answered.

"A surprise? For me? How thoughtful. I'm sure I'll love it." I wanted to keep the asshole on the phone if possible. One, I'd just started a trace, and two, I had a feeling that as soon as he got off the line, he'd press the "go" button on whatever he had planned.

"In that case, you'll be pleased to hear I put many hours of careful thought into it."

My fingers flew over the keys, switching the security system into red mode and sending out an alert to the necessary Blackwood employees that we were under attack and they should go to the nearest place of safety.

"That's so sweet of you. Nobody here even remembered my birthday until my assistant reminded them this morning. It's so special that you thought of me all the way from your cave, or your evil lair, or whatever you call it."

"I prefer the term estate."

"Estate. Or hacienda?" I took a stab in the dark. Was he from South America?

"Hacienda will do, I suppose."

"Wow! You must be loaded."

"I've done very well for myself, yes."

"I'm not surprised. Look at your qualities—creative, tenacious, charming. Oh, and modest. Don't forget modest."

I had two more backup control rooms booting up and coming online. Nothing on the trace yet. The Richmond office messaged back to say they were commencing lockdown procedures and would await further instructions.

"Do I detect a hint of sarcasm?"

"Me, sarcastic? Never."

"Oh, I think you are. I also think you're stalling. Goodbye, Ms. Black."

Shit, shit, shit.

The phone clicked as he hung up, followed almost immediately by the guardhouse exploding in a ball of flames. I heard the boom, and the screen showing the interior of the main room dissolved into fuzz. Another camera in the grounds filmed the blazing remains lighting up the night sky.

Damn, the man was obsessed with his fucking grenades, wasn't he? Anger gave my adrenaline a kick-start and heat flooded through my veins. I only hoped Seth and Mick saw my message in time and got into the bunker below the building before it blew up.

By now, everyone in the movie theatre would be on their way to safety, so I hit the button to bring down a steel shutter in the doorway to the control room. The walls were already reinforced. That room was full of complicated and expensive equipment, so I wanted to keep it intact if I could. It would be a pain to replace, although ultimately it was all disposable. Everything was except our lives.

Six steps took me to the wall, where I stared into an iris scanner disguised as an intercom. A panel slid back, revealing a narrow staircase going up and down. I went down.

The beauty of designing a house from scratch is that a person is only limited by their imagination, modern construction materials, and how much money they're willing to spend. Thanks to an innovative architect, a bunch of confidentiality clauses, and a truckload of cash, Black and I had incorporated some interesting features, none of which appeared on the plans we'd filed.

With a house as big as mine, it was easy to miss little bits of lost space. Maybe a gap between two walls just wide enough for an extra staircase, or a room a tad smaller than the outside dimensions would suggest. Thanks to a hastily constructed wall, we'd hidden from the planning inspectors the fact that the basement extended far beyond the house, and the tunnel boring machines we'd employed moved in and out under cover of darkness.

Oh yes, I loved birthday surprises.

Chapter 3

LUKE DIDN'T REALLY get American football. Why did everything take so long? He wasn't that keen on English football either, or soccer as everyone here called it, but at least they got on with it. The Yanks spent more time standing around than actually playing.

And there we go... Stopped again.

The cheerleaders were all right, even if they weren't a patch on Mack, but after a while, Luke got sick of watching them shake their pompoms. A quick glance around the room showed everyone else was into the game, judging by the enthusiastic way they shouted at the screen every time one of the man-mountains moved. Or maybe the lack of enjoyment was a British thing? Like him, Emmy came from England, and Luke had caught her looking bored earlier too.

But where was she now? Her seat was empty, but he hadn't noticed her leave. That probably answered his question—she couldn't have found the game that fascinating if she wasn't watching it anymore.

Still, there were worse places he could be. The dull entertainment and the relative weirdness of being at his ex's birthday celebration were far outweighed by the fact that Mack was curled up beside him and the company of the new friends he'd made over the past few weeks.

He hadn't been sure about coming to America with Mack so soon, but he was pleased he'd taken the plunge. It already felt like home. He was staying with Mack in her apartment at the moment, but last weekend, they'd discussed buying a place together. Not right away, but soon.

As Luke mused over how much his life was changing, and for the better, Mack's phone vibrated against his thigh. She leaned back and fished it out of her trouser pocket.

"Message?" he asked.

She nodded absently, still watching the game, but as soon as she'd read it, she sat up straight and looked around the room. Luke realised everyone else was peering at their phones too. What was going on? And why didn't he get a message?

Luke leaned across to look at Mack's screen as the room fell silent. Only the football commentator kept talking, although Luke couldn't fathom what was so exciting to the man.

Code: Red. Attack imminent. Go to place of safety and await further instructions. EB.

EB. Was that Emerson Black? She had to be kidding, right?

Nate turned off the TV. "What the fuck is she playing at? And where the hell is she? She was here five minutes ago."

"I don't know," Dan said, "But she's not often wrong, so I say we do as the message says first and discuss it afterwards."

Everyone murmured their agreement as Nate walked to the far wall. His body shielded exactly what he did, but a few seconds later, a panel in the wall slid back to reveal a hidden corridor behind.

"What the hell is that?" Luke whispered to Mack.

"*That* is what happens when a pair of paranoid billionaires with an obsession for security build a house together," she answered, pulling him towards the opening.

Everyone piled through, and the wall closed silently behind them. Only Evan looked vaguely surprised at the developments. So the others all knew about the secret passage? Why was Luke always last to find out about everything? The partygoers filed along the dimly lit tunnel, past several doorways, and Luke's feeling of unease grew with every step he took on the rough concrete floor.

Ahead, Nate pushed open a door to reveal a replica of the control room on the floor above. Monitors blinked into life as the systems woke up and came online.

Luke stood in one corner as the others milled around and talked quietly amongst themselves. They seemed calm, but an undercurrent of urgency lurked under the surface.

"Hey..." he tried, but nobody looked in his direction. Even Bradley was totally focused on the cupboard he was fishing around in.

Mack and Nate sat side by side, and as their fingers skimmed over the keyboards, the bank of screens popped up images from cameras covering the grounds. North, south, east, west. Then Blackwood's Richmond headquarters appeared, lit up in the darkness, followed by other Blackwood locations from around the world.

Luke was just about to try another question when gasps broke the near silence. One screen dissolved into static while another showed flames leaping into the night sky. What the hell...? That looked like an explosion. Surely this had to be some sort of joke?

"Well, fuck me. The bitch was right," Dan muttered.

As soon as the words left her mouth, Emmy barrelled into the room via a staircase on the far side.

"What the hell...?" Nate echoed Luke's thoughts.

"Black's killer. He's come anyway. I bloody hope Seth and Mick got down below before that went up."

She motioned to the monitor showing the guardhouse, now a shell of its former self with the fire still blazing. Wisps of smoke drifted across the picture, giving the scene an eerie feel. Sweat trickled down Luke's back as he began to realise the seriousness of the situation. He hadn't signed up for this.

"Do you know what else we've got?" Nate asked Emmy.

"They're in the woods. Switch to thermal imaging."

Mack hit the button to change the mode, and the cameras surrounding the house showed an ominous picture. A number of glowing forms crept slowly towards the house. Even with their blurred outlines, it was obvious they carried weapons.

"Mack, start tagging and tracking them."

Mack clicked away, assigning each intruder a number. Luke hadn't seen this side of Mack before. To him, this was the girl who cried at the end of sad movies and puked if she saw a nasty photo. But now she worked quickly and confidently, no hint of drama. At her command, the software working the cameras that covered the whole house, all the outbuildings, and parts of the grounds would now follow each person as they moved.

According to Mack's calculations, there were fourteen bad guys roaming the estate.

Luke counted the people in the room. Discounting Jed, who still walked with a limp, and Bradley, who Luke couldn't imagine holding a gun let alone firing one, there were eleven including himself. But he didn't know how to shoot either. In fact, he'd always been kind of averse to the idea until he met Emmy, but right now, he was having a rethink. If he survived the battle building up outside, he'd take lessons, but for tonight they had ten. Ten people who might be useful.

He gave a nervous cough. "Is this room secure enough to keep those people out until the police arrive?"

Emmy laughed. "The police? Are you having a laugh? They'd make a complete balls-up of everything then bury us under paperwork. We'll deal with it ourselves, and they can help clean up afterwards."

Luke looked at her carefully, searching for signs she was kidding, but her expression remained determined. Was she serious? Sure, Blackwood worked in place of the police on some jobs, his sister's kidnapping being a case in point, but this looked like a war was about to start.

"But there are more of them than us, and they've got machine guns."

"And what do you think we have? Water pistols?"

Luke tried again. "Shouldn't you play it safe?"

Emmy smiled, only there was no mirth in it, and the glint in her eyes scared him. "I prefer to play it dangerous."

What the hell had he got himself into?

Emmy turned her back on him and asked more

questions. "How's Riverley Hall looking? And the guesthouse? Anything at the office?"

Nate called up more locations on the monitors. "They all look clear."

"Get the office on the phone."

It was odd to see Emmy taking charge and ordering everyone around. Usually, she seemed quiet and almost deferential around Nate. Nobody else batted an eyelid though, which led Luke to believe she'd been in similar situations before. He didn't know whether to be more or less worried by that.

"Do you want them to send reinforcements?" Nate asked.

"Fuck no. If I was Black's killer—let's call him Blanco for today's purposes—that's the first thing I'd expect. Lock everyone down then have a team sneak out the back. I bet you a hundred bucks there'll be a group of Blanco's foot soldiers waiting somewhere around the exit to the driveway."

Nate called headquarters and communicated the instruction, nodding as he hung up. "Done."

Next, Emmy picked up the phone herself and dialled Blackwood in London. "I want Ryan to go to Tia Halston-Cain immediately. Get him to take her somewhere safe, and he doesn't leave her side until this is over. Everyone else stays in lockdown."

A lump rose in Luke's throat. "Do you think Tia's in danger?"

His sister had already been through hell a few months back when she got abducted. He dreaded the thought of her being flung into another nightmare, one of the sort he was living through right now.

"Just a precaution, but I'm not taking any chances."

Luke's heart thumped against his ribcage. Bad enough that he was stuck in this horror movie without his sister getting pulled into it as well. He sure hoped Emmy knew what she was doing.

"What's going on outside?" she asked.

"They're stacking up at the doors," Nate said. "Looks like they're about to come in."

"Right, there's ten of us excluding Luke, Bradley, and Jed..." she started.

Jed opened his mouth, but Emmy interrupted whatever he was about to say. "Don't give me that, Jed. You've got a broken bloody leg, so you're not going anywhere near this one. You can't creep quietly in a cast, and I didn't drag your ass out of Syria just for you to get shot at home." Jed closed his mouth, but he didn't look happy. "So, as I was saying, there's ten of us. Mack, you're staying here. Luke and Jed can help you. Carmen, you're on the roof at Black's. The rest of us split. Evan and Logan, you head for the guesthouse. Jack, you and Alex come from Black's. Me, Nick, Nate, and Dan will head upstairs, and the team down here can direct us where to go."

Thank goodness Mack would be staying in the relative safety of the basement. The last thing Luke wanted was for her to go out and get shot at.

"What's Black's?" he whispered to her. "I thought that was Emmy's nightclub?"

"It's also her other house. There's a tunnel leading over there and another that goes to the guesthouse, which means we can move around without being seen. Emmy wants teams to come out of the other buildings and attack Blanco's men from behind. Carmen will be on the roof backing them up as a sniper. It's three hundred yards away, which is a walk in the park for Carmen."

Luke recalled seeing another large house close by, but he'd never paid much attention to it. The roof was just visible through the trees that bordered Emmy's lawn. That belonged to Emmy too? She had a serious problem with sharing.

Then again, did the strange setup really surprise him? He'd already worked out that she was certifiable.

Briefing over, the teams filed out, followed by a few last words from Emmy.

"Guys, if you could avoid shooting people in the back, that'd be helpful. The cops get upset about it, and I'm sick of dealing with their questions. Oh, and if we can get one or two alive that would be good." Her eyes and her voice both hardened. "I've got some questions I'd like to ask."

CHAPTER 4

THE NINE OF us who would be going up top exited the control room and headed through to the armoury. I pulled on a black turtleneck over my "bad girl" T-shirt as I walked. There was no sense in sticking out like a hooker in a convent if I had to go outside.

Now to pick up my toys.

Bradley handed me my custom-made thigh holster, and I strapped it on, selecting a Glock 9mm for the right-hand side and a silenced .22 for the left. Extra magazines clipped onto the back of the belt, then I added a knife to each side. Those slotted in neatly next to the guns.

Blanco's team may have been more heavily armed than us, but I didn't plan on getting into a "my gun's bigger than your gun" pissing match with them. There was simply no point in weighing myself down with half a ton of lead when one bullet to the head would do the job. Two if I wanted to be really sure. In situations like this, I preferred to keep the manoeuvrability.

"*Now* you look like the Black Widow," Bradley said, the queen of inappropriate comments. "I'm not sure about those boots, though."

"I don't need fancy boots to shoot people."

"Just try not to get blood everywhere, okay?"

I checked the laces on my rubber-soled combat

boots one last time then clipped on a headset for communications. We tended to run with open channels most of the time rather than messing around with push-to-talk buttons, and Mack's specially modified software automatically reduced the volume of anything noisy like gunshots.

All our earpieces were custom moulded, so they fitted closely with little sound escaping. As I turned my radio on, Mack's running commentary came through loud and clear, and I learned Blanco's men had breached through the back and sides of my home. Apparently, they'd tried to blast through the front door as well but got defeated by the reinforced steel. Score one for Team Blackwood.

Carmen, Jack, and Alex took off through the tunnel for Riverley Hall. I should probably mention that as well as being my personal trainer, Alex used to be a major in Spetsnaz GRU, a series of special forces units controlled by Russian military intelligence. I'd worked with him on a few jobs over the years, and he scared the shit out of me. In terms of unarmed combat, he was the best I'd ever seen, although I was in two minds over whether I wanted him to use those particular skills today. Like Bradley said, blood was a bitch to clean up.

Black's basement housed a second, smaller control room so Jack, Alex, and Carmen could take another look at what was going on before they went upstairs. Once they'd confirmed it was clear, a hidden staircase would take Carmen all the way to the roof.

I'd considered the possibility Team Blanco might also have a sniper, but it seemed unlikely. The only position with a good line of sight and enough elevation was Black's roof, and the pressure sensors said nobody was up there yet. There was no point in reminding Carmen to be careful—I'd only be insulting her intelligence if I did. She'd been doing this for enough years and with enough success to know how to operate safely.

In the gloom on the monitors, Team Blanco prowled through the house, and I forced myself to tuck away my anger at the violation of my home and replace it with the cold detachment I was famous for. Squinting at the screen, I noted they were wearing headsets too.

"Luke, could you try and listen into whatever frequency they're using? It'll probably be secure, but Mack's got software that'll help."

"Sure thing, I'm on it."

At least Luke hadn't flipped out. I'd been worried he might—I mean, having pizza and a ball game interrupted by a fourteen-man assault team had to be unsettling for anyone—but he seemed remarkably calm, all things considered.

I watched for a bit longer, learning more about our enemy with every passing second. The pair who killed Black had been freelance, hired in for the job, but seeing these men glide around the house, I could tell they weren't just a team of mercenaries thrown together at the last minute. No, they were far more polished, moving in pairs, each man interacting with his teammate in a way that indicated they'd done this many times before.

This wasn't going to be easy.

Then again, nothing in my life had ever been easy.

And far from shying away from the difficulties, I'd learned to embrace them, using each pile of shit that flew my way to grow stronger. For me, the outcome tonight was never in any doubt. No matter what Team Blanco slung at us, Team Blackwood would throw it back tenfold, plus we had the advantage of being on home turf.

Team Blanco cleared the ground floor and split, with four men heading to the basement and eight upstairs. The remaining two stayed in the kitchen, no doubt ready to assist wherever they were needed. Their initial body language showed confidence, no doubt bolstered by our lack of retaliation, but that soon turned to confusion when they couldn't find us. Anywhere.

Luke managed to patch into their radio channel. Their communications were brief and, interestingly, in Spanish. The fact they'd chosen that dialect in such a pressured situation indicated it was their first language. But no matter. All of our team, with the exception of Luke, spoke fluent *Español*. Even Bradley, although he was more likely to ask *si esos zapatos vienen en púrpura* at Madrid Fashion Week.

"*Hay alguna señal de ellos?*" one of them asked. Any sign of them?

There was a burst of static, then, "*Nada.*"

"We are sure they are here?"

"We saw them go in. They couldn't all have left, not when we've been watching the house for the entire day."

I suppressed a shudder. Knowing they'd been so close while I relaxed with my friends gave me the creeps. Time to upgrade the security system, at least, if there was anything left to upgrade. The current one covered the house, the outbuildings, and the driveway but not the woods. Last time we'd tried motion sensors in the trees, we spent most of our nights chasing deer, but we couldn't keep relying on my intuition.

I winced as an intruder caught sight of his reflection in a polished kitchen cabinet and shot a grenade at it. Seconds later, the sprinklers came on downstairs, making a hell of a mess.

As I watched a river running through my lounge, I tried to stay positive. If the assholes had been outside all day, they wouldn't be fresh. And now some of them were dripping wet as well.

Another of the men spoke up from the basement. "There is fresh food down here and it is still warm. They cannot have gone far."

"Then they must be hiding. We'll have to go through the house again. And remember, the boss said they will have weapons."

It was time. Carmen confirmed she was in position on the roof, covering the east side with her infrared scope and rifle. Alex and Jack were hiding to the north, watching the back, and Evan and Logan had snuck out of the guesthouse to take the front and west sides. Those four were ready to pick off anyone leaving the house or come inside if we needed them.

My team took one of the hidden staircases, with Nate and Dan going to the second floor and Nick and me taking the first. Jed kept us informed while Mack did the same for Nate and Dan.

Adrenaline was fuelling me nicely by the time I reached the top of the stairs. My resolve was rock solid, and despite the disaster befalling my house, I had a smile on my face. I know I shouldn't have enjoyed moments like this, but let's be honest, I fucking did.

I glanced sideways at Nick, and his lips quirked

upwards at the corners too. We were one pair of sick puppies.

It was hard relying on someone else to be my eyes, but I'd known Jed long enough to trust his judgment, and in any case, I had little choice. CCTV covered the whole house, but normally the internal cameras were turned off when the place was occupied. I mean, who wanted their bedroom antics recorded?

Nate had originally planned to install a simpler system, but Black insisted on gold standard. "Just in case the house ever gets invaded, Diamond," he'd told me at the time. Some might have called it paranoia, but I called it foresight.

The staircase Nick and I took led to a narrow passage that came up between the study and the sprawling master suite Black and I had once shared.

"One's in Black's bathroom, the other's in your dressing room, Emmy," Jed told us. "He's looking in your underwear drawer."

"Seriously?"

"Yeah. Pervert. It's not as if you're gonna be hiding in there, is it? The other one's in Black's bedroom now."

I slid the panel in front of me open a few inches. It moved silently on hidden tracks, and the large, abstract painting on my bedroom wall shifted a little to the left. When I peered through the gap, I got a good view of the doorways to both Black's bedroom and my dressing room, but crucially, I wasn't in line of sight for anyone exiting either of them. *Come on, assholes.* I slowed my breathing and sighted in my silenced .22 on the nearer of the two, the bedroom doorway. The moment a black-clad figure appeared, I took him out with a double tap to the head.

One down.

Even a silenced pistol makes a noise, and his colleague rushed out of the dressing room.

Two down.

I wanted to say first blood to me, but I still didn't know the fate of Seth and Mick in the guardhouse which was another reason to get this situation resolved as soon as possible. Five seconds later, I'd melted back behind the painting.

On the radio, I heard the zip of a bullet as Nick took out a guy in the study. Now we just needed to deal with his teammate, who'd stayed outside in the corridor, and preferably before he found the body. There was a third exit to the small vestibule I stood in, which led in the right direction.

"Is my exit to the hallway clear?" I asked Jed.

"Confirmed clear. Your target's around the corner to your left, facing away from you."

"I'm going for it."

"Good luck."

Luck? I didn't need luck. Not when I had two guns and a fuck-ton of anger fuelling me.

I slid back another panel, this one fronted by a nearly life-size oil-on-canvas of my horse, Stan, painted by an old friend half a decade ago. Half a lifetime, it seemed like. Time had slowed since Black died.

There were no lights on in this corridor, but shards of moonlight came through the windows and a faint glow glimmered from the master suite. Five steps, ten, and I rounded the corner in a crouch. And there he was —asshole number four, walking away from me.

Heeding my own advice not to shoot anyone in the back, I whistled softly, and he spun around. Dark hair, a goatee, and a faint expression of surprise right before I put a bullet between his eyes. I followed up with a second, just to be sure, and he crumpled to the carpet with a soft *thud*. Four down, and I couldn't help smiling.

Heartless?

Of course I was heartless. I'd given my heart to Black, and when he died, he took it with him.

But I didn't have time to dwell on sentimentalities because I had a dead body at my feet, right where one of his buddies would undoubtedly trip over it. I started to drag it into the linen closet, only for Jed to interrupt.

"Emmy, incoming. Middle staircase from the second floor."

I didn't have time to go back the way I'd come, but I didn't want to go forwards either because I'd be boxed in. And worse, the only room that lay ahead was Bradley's bedroom. Most people slept as far away from me as possible, but Bradley had insisted on having that one because it had the best view of the sunset.

Shit. *Think, Emmy, think!*

That particular hallway was quite narrow, so I braced my shoulders on one wall and my legs on the other then climbed upwards, wedging myself near the ceiling. Awkward, but it worked.

A few seconds later, my opponent came into view, dashing towards his dead buddy. Medical attention was a waste of time since the bastard's brain had a couple of new lead accessories, but in the darkness, he didn't know that. Instead, he stooped to check for a pulse, cursing under his breath when he didn't find one.

The newcomer straightened, and I saw the moment he realised he was a sitting duck. His back stiffened, his gun came up, and he looked both ways. Trying to get out or searching for me? Well, he wouldn't manage either successfully because he didn't look up and he chose to go forwards.

I dropped to the floor behind him and followed, catching him as he came out of Bradley's en-suite.

Another one down.

It should have been a moment to celebrate, but I groaned instead. Fuck. There was blood on the carpet, splatters and a pool spreading out from under the guy's head. The metallic tang assaulted my nostrils.

Hell, I'd never hear the end of that. No way would Bradley ever sleep in this room again. In my head, I could hear him muttering about death cooties and the guy wasn't even cold yet.

Why did this shit keep happening to me?

Nate announced over our secure channel that he'd tagged the last one upstairs, coming out of my housekeeper's sewing room. She loved making quilts, and apparently the light was good in there. Now? There was only darkness.

Eight down, six left. Six walking dead, roaming my first floor and basement.

"They're starting to panic," Jed told me. "They can't get a response from the others, and they don't know what to make of it."

Excellent. I slipped back in behind Stan's portrait and met up with Nick, Nate, and Dan to go downstairs for the Battle of Little Riverley: Part Two.

But as we descended inside the walls, we missed one of the remaining *pendejos* coming to look for his *amigos*. He must have stumbled across a body or two, and he must also have been a less experienced member of the team, because he hurtled back to the ground floor, yelling in rapid Spanish.

The others whispered furiously over the radio for him to shut up, and he seemed to come to his senses and did so. I sighed. The lion was out of the wardrobe now, and I stowed my .22. With the need to remain secret no longer an issue, I might as well have the stopping power of the Glock.

Given that four men had checked the two visible rooms of the basement—the movie theatre and a large games room—and found nothing, I figured they wouldn't expect anyone to come from down there. So I did exactly that.

Water trickled down the basement stairs as I snuck up to the ground floor. The sprinklers had stopped the fire from taking hold, but the smell of smoke still grated at my throat. One of Blanco's men came out of the lounge, and when I shot him with the Glock, half of his skull disintegrated thanks to Carmen's hand-loaded ammo.

"That was for my kitchen, you fucker."

Not to mention my husband.

I hustled back to the basement, ready and waiting for my next victim, but when Team Blanco found the headless dude, they'd had enough.

"Fall back," came the cry over the radio, and the five remaining soldiers tripped over themselves to get out.

"Heading for you, Dime," Mack told Carmen.

Nate had given her that nickname years ago because when she picked up a rifle, she could hit a coin from a thousand yards every time.

"What, all of them?" she asked.

"Yup."

No way, surely? But yes, the pressure had got to them and they stupidly left through the same door, walking right into Carmen's sights. She waited for the last man to get outside before letting loose.

One sharp crack followed another, then a third and a fourth, before a muttered "Dammit" came over the radio.

"How many did you get?"

"Three. The others ran around the east side."

"Now they're going north," Jed said. "Heading towards Alex and Jack."

That left two of them against eight of us. I liked those odds. So much so that I decided to delegate their capture.

"Okay, you guys take the final two. I'm going to the guardhouse with Nick. How's it looking?"

"Fire's out, but no signs of life."

Shit. "Carmen, we're coming out your way."

Nick was right behind me, one hand on his gun and the other on the small of my back. That light touch told me he didn't think this was going to end well either. So much death, and for what? Drugs? The ongoing vendetta of a man who hid in the shadows?

Well, I had news. I lived in fucking darkness now, and I was coming for him.

CHAPTER 5

NICK AND I went out the side door and ran to the tree line, careful to avoid stepping in the mess left by Carmen. She'd gone for the men's torsos, and the custom loads from her favourite Accuracy International sniper rifle had punched through flesh and bone, leaving my terrace looking like a scene from the zombie apocalypse.

That gore would be a nightmare to scrub off the flagstones.

Sticking to the shadows, Nick and I made our way down the driveway. My adrenaline spiked as I thought of what we might find, and cold dread spread through my veins despite my earlier exertions.

Up ahead, the guardhouse was still smoking. Dark, acrid plumes rose into the darkness, and as we got closer, I smelled the unmistakable stench of burning flesh and had a sudden flashback to Black in the taxi. I stopped and heaved, and it was only sheer fucking willpower that stopped me from losing my dinner into the bushes. And that made me even angrier with myself. I'd seen enough horrors that I should have been well past the point of wanting to throw up.

Puking was for amateurs.

Circling the guardhouse, guns drawn, the only sound we heard was a faint hissing as the sprinklers in what was left of the ceiling did their job, the automatic shut off long since destroyed. I swept a torch around the inside. A mess of twisted metal gleamed back at me, tangled amongst broken furniture and sparking electronics. Streams of sooty water trickled along the floor and down the steps, the River Styx reduced to miniature.

In Roman mythology, the Styx separated us from the underworld. Rather than pay Charon, the ferryman, to carry me across, I stepped into the waters of hate, allowing them to seep through my heels and into my soul.

If it was my last act on this earth, Blanco would pay for what he'd done tonight.

I radioed Mack. "Can you release the lock on the bunker from there? The entire control panel's gone."

The bunker could also be opened from inside, but I had no idea whether anyone had made it to safety, and if they had, whether they'd be in a fit state to work the catch. But the lock was electronic, on its own protected circuit, so hopefully Mack could help.

"I should be able to. Hang on." Half a minute passed. "It says it's unlocked."

"Great. Can you shut off the electrics down here completely now? There's water everywhere and some of the panels are throwing off sparks."

"Two seconds... Done."

"Want me to go first?" Nick asked from over my left shoulder.

I turned and gave him a look. "I do my own fucking dirty work, Nick. When have I ever asked anyone else to go first? I'm still perfectly capable."

He backed away, hands in the air in apology.

"Sorry, Ems, I didn't mean it like that. I just thought... Never mind..."

His words trailed off as I stepped gingerly over the threshold, tiptoeing through the debris. The guardhouse had been the old gatekeeper's lodge, a two-bedroom cottage belonging to the derelict mansion that once occupied my house's footprint. I'd gutted it, combining the lounge and one of the bedrooms into the main office, with a picture window and door facing onto the driveway. At the back, I'd left the tiny kitchen, bathroom, and second bedroom so the guards had somewhere comfortable to use on their breaks.

And at Black's behest, the old cellar got turned into a bunker fitted out with emergency supplies and an air filtration system. Back when the plans were drawn up, I'd doubted it would ever be used. Today, I hoped it had.

Nick and I edged towards the hatch in the corner of the main room, the ceiling making ominous creaking noises above us. Jagged shards of plaster hung amongst the remains of the light fittings and sprinkler system. All it needed was for that lot to fall down and this disaster of a day would be complete.

My sense of smell dulled as I poked through the rubble, and I knew that just like after Black's death, the hideous aroma would stay with me for days. But I couldn't stop, not when I'd been the one to stir up this hornets' nest. I stepped over a broken chair and continued with the search.

Half buried under a collapsed table, I found... Well, I didn't know who it was. He was so badly burned, it was difficult to tell. His limbs were drawn up in the pugilistic position typical of fire victims, his hands clutching desperately at nothing. *Breathe, Emmy. Just breathe.* I gritted my teeth, motioned at Nick to step around the side of the body, and carried on. We were still missing one man.

Nick helped me to heave a battered filing cabinet off the hatch, then he bent and lifted it back. Inky blackness gaped up at us. I shone my torch into the hole, and the light revealed a crumpled form lying motionless on its side at the bottom of the ladder. Hell, this didn't look good. Nick lit the way as I shinned down. Whoever it was wasn't moving, and before I got halfway, I could make out the blackened, blistered skin stretched over his torso.

"Is he breathing?" Nick called.

"Hang on."

I knelt next to the body and put my cheek under his nostrils. A faint trickle of air whispered over me, accompanied by a groan.

"Yes, he is, but shallow. He needs medical attention yesterday."

Now I was closer, I recognised Seth, which meant it was Mick whose life had been stolen.

Son of a bitch.

Sometimes, I wondered what my purpose in life was, but that night I knew. I was the angel of death who would send Blanco to hell, and I'd have a smile on my face while I did it.

But that plan had to wait. Instead, I got on the radio. "Mack, we need an ambulance. What's the situation at the house?"

"Still ongoing. The fire's out, and I've shut the sprinklers off."

"Get the ambulance on its way and tell them to

hang back until we confirm it's safe. Same with the police, because undoubtedly they're going to turn up at some point."

"Calling them now."

"Is there anyone free who could run down here with a first aid kit, an extraction pack, and a spinal board?"

"Evan's on his way. How are they?"

"Mick's dead, and Seth's going to be if he doesn't get to a hospital fast. We could do with some extra manpower too."

"Shit." She paused to compose herself. "Mick was a good guy. There's one left alive up here, and Alex is dealing with him. I'll send who I can."

I blocked whatever Alex might be doing from my mind and returned to the problem in front of me. Alex was well capable of looking after himself.

From their positions, it looked as if Seth and Mick had been trying to get into the bunker when the blast happened. When Seth got halfway in, the grenade came and he got blown the seven feet to the bottom of the ladder as the hatch flipped shut behind him. Unfortunately, Mick hadn't been so lucky, if you could call Seth's state lucky.

"Hurry up, Evan," I whispered as Seth groaned again.

There wasn't much I could do until help arrived except talk to him, hoping my voice registered. Hearing was always the last sense to go when a person slipped into unconsciousness. Maybe my words would make it through?

Nick stayed up top, checking the rest of the building. "Ceiling's not looking good."

Tell me something I don't know.

Evan must have sprinted because the first aid kit arrived in my hands sooner than I expected. Our first aid kits weren't the type of thing you'd buy in the local pharmacy. We kept half a hospital on hand, good for everything up to minor surgery.

I may not have been a doctor, but along with Nick and everyone else on Blackwood's core team, I'd undergone extensive training in how to deal with trauma. Sad to say, I'd had a reasonable amount of practical experience over the years too. While we waited for the professionals to arrive, we gave Seth oxygen, fluids, and pain relief then manoeuvred him onto the spinal board.

"How's he doing?" a voice asked from over my shoulder. Nate had arrived with Logan in tow.

"Not good. We need to get him outside."

With four of us helping, we made short work of lifting Seth out of the bunker, through the guardhouse, and into the cool night air. I was checking his pulse again when Mack radioed through.

"I've given the emergency services the all-clear. Two minutes for the ambulance."

Right, time to sort out the story with Nate, because the police wouldn't be far behind.

"We don't know who these guys were, okay? Throw in some speculation. It could be something to do with Black's murder, maybe something at work, or just a home invasion. The sniper must have been one of theirs, getting confused."

"That works," he agreed. "No sense in dragging Carmen into it. Also, when I shot motherfucker *número uno* upstairs, I did it with his buddy's gun then put it back in the hands of the dead guy, so I guess there was a lot of confusion going on."

"I'll call a few people, get some different agencies involved. They can fight among themselves."

"Good plan. I don't want to get tied up for days answering questions. I take it we're allowed to look for Mr. Blanco now, after this?"

Too damn fucking right we were. I paused and looked Nate in the eye. He had a secret love of Shakespeare, so I thought it appropriate to quote Hamlet.

"The readiness is all."

He gave me a nod. "You've made the right decision."

"Nobody comes into my fucking house like that. I mean, did you see the state of the kitchen?"

"You're gonna need it remodelled again. The kitchen woman's gonna have a heart attack. Oh, and speaking of heart attacks, Alex had one left alive, but the asshole must've had a dodgy ticker because when Alex started twisting his arm, he just keeled over, retched a bit, then died."

"Shit. I wanted the chance to speak with him. And by speak, I mean burn his skin off with a blowtorch, an inch at a time. Dammit. It's drugs that caused all this, though. That much I'm sure of."

"How do you know?"

"Blanco called me again, just before the attack. That's why I sent the alert to everyone. He told me I'd ignored his last warning, and all I've been working on this week is that bad coke thing. Plus it was an old case of Black's, so it fits."

"Yeah, it does." Nate turned his head as sirens sounded close by. "I'll get everybody working that angle as soon as we get free of the police. By the way, they caught a pair outside Blackwood. Hired in, not from the same team as that lot." He jerked his thumb back towards the house. "The night shift guys questioned them before the cops picked them up. They were just a couple of kids from a local gang, said some dude paid them five thousand bucks to spray a car with bullets at a certain time, only no car came because you stopped that."

"Mick's blood's still on my hands. And Seth's too if that ambulance doesn't get here soon. Where the hell is it?"

As if on cue, the ambulance rolled slowly through the gateway.

"Don't hurry yourselves, will you?" I muttered under my breath.

The medics jumped out and strode towards us. My team picked up Seth, strapped onto his board, and I grabbed the drip and oxygen bottle.

"What are you waiting for? Christmas?" I growled at the medics, who seemed more interested in the smoking remains of my home. "Just open the damn doors."

They scurried to the back of the ambulance, and we carried Seth inside, securing him to the stretcher. The pair of them took over for an assessment, although there wasn't a lot they could do that we hadn't already done.

"Is anyone coming to the hospital with this man?" the taller of them asked.

"Yeah, me."

Nick decided he was joining us and climbed in the back too. As the ambulance sped into the night, I

gripped his hand, my dark thoughts brightened only by
the fire inside me.

CHAPTER 6

AT TIMES, I was tempted to hop into the front of the ambulance and drive myself, it went so bloody slowly. At least when we drew up outside the hospital the doors opened instantly, and a trauma team descended on poor Seth and whisked him away. Another overzealous doctor tried to lead me into the emergency room.

"Hey, get off me!" I snapped, yanking my arm away from him.

"I need to check you out. You're bleeding."

"It's not my blood."

"Are you sure?"

"I think I'd know if I'd been injured."

Or would I? Hmmm. A plan started to form in my mind. It seemed to be working at somewhere close to full capacity now, which meant I had all sorts of devious ideas popping up.

Making an effort to sound really blonde, I turned back to the doctor.

"On second thoughts, I feel a bit dizzy. A checkup mightn't be a bad idea."

I swayed for effect, and he helped me to an uncomfortable plastic seat.

"Sit there, ma'am. I'll come right back with a wheelchair."

As soon as he'd disappeared inside, Nick put his hands on his hips. "What the hell? You're not dizzy. You don't even know what dizzy feels like."

"Yes, I do. The first time Black took me up in a stunt plane, he did six barrel rolls followed by a loop-the-loop, and I got dizzy then. Just trust me. I know exactly what I'm doing." At least, I hoped I did. "Can you get hold of Damon Belcourt at the DEA and ask him to meet me here?"

Nick rolled his eyes. "I'll call him. Anything else?"

"Yeah. You can pick out a nice black outfit to wear to my funeral. And stop rolling your eyes."

Before Nick could come up with a smart-arse answer, the doctor reappeared and wheeled me into the hospital. He parked me in a cubicle, checked my vital signs, then peered down at me.

"How many fingers am I holding up?"

Three. "Er... Two?"

"What day is it?"

"April."

"What state are you in?"

I looked at my blood-spattered clothes. "Not a very good one."

"I meant which American state?"

"Oh. Kansas?"

He scribbled notes on my chart. "I'll get the nurse to come in."

Satan's assistant duly arrived, poking and prodding hard enough to bruise. I may not have been in pain when I arrived, but she soon rectified that. By the time she'd finished, I had a new career as a human pincushion and Belcourt was hovering beyond the curtain in his cheap grey suit. Super.

"Stay in bed," the nurse ordered. "I don't want you fainting. I'll be back once I've checked on another patient."

Time for a little chat with my new favourite agent.

Over a cup of really bad coffee, I outlined the events of the night, leaving out some small parts, like the secrets hidden under my house, but laying out my theory about the attack being linked to the drugs case and possibly Black's death.

Belcourt rolled his eyes. "You never do things by halves, do you? This is too big for me to deal with on my own. I need to call my boss."

"Well, get on with it, then."

I listened while he gave his superior an abbreviated version of what I'd just said. After a short pause, he hung up. "Crane's on his way over."

Great, we only needed a couple more people and then we could have a party.

Before Agent Crane arrived, Seth's wife did. I needed to speak to her, and I couldn't say it was something I looked forward to. Seth was a real family man, and he'd been married to Carla for just over four years. A shotgun wedding, he always joked, although he doted on his wife and son and never stopped talking about them. I'd met Carla a few times when she brought Justin over to swim at Riverley, and she'd been blessed with such a sunny disposition I hadn't liked her at first. How could anyone be that nice? But I soon came to understand that was just the way she was.

Not today, though. Today was overcast with rain showers in Carla's world. She clutched Justin's hand as they sat side by side in the corridor, her face streaked with tears. Justin was dressed in a superhero outfit, complete with cape.

"Hi, Carla."

Her lip quivered as she looked up at me. "Emmy, what happened?"

I glanced at Justin. How much should I say in front of him? "There was an accident at the guardhouse. An explosion." I crouched down. "Hi, Justin."

He stayed silent, glaring at me with a sulky expression.

"He only answers to 'Batman' at the moment. Or Bruce if he's not wearing his cape," Carla explained.

"Hi, Batman."

"Hi. Where's my dad?"

"Your dad's with the doctors, and they're helping him to get better." Fuck, I hoped that was true.

"Can I see him soon?"

"The doctors need a little bit more time. They have some special machines they need to use. So your job is to stay here and make sure no bad guys get past. Can you do that?"

He looked at me like I was stupid. "Of course I can. I'm Batman."

I ruffled his hair before turning back to Carla.

"How bad is it?" she asked.

"It's not good." I couldn't lie. "The top half of him was caught in the flames, and he's got some nasty burns. He was unconscious when we found him, but he was breathing on his own."

"That's a good sign, isn't it?"

"Yes. And he's a fighter. If anyone can get through this, Seth can."

"Do you know what caused the explosion?"

"Yes." How much did I tell her? "It looks as if a

missile was fired into the guardhouse."

Carla clapped a hand over her mouth. "Who would want to hurt Seth like that?"

"It wasn't about Seth. It was about me. They attacked the house too."

"Did anyone else get hurt? Did the police catch them?"

"Mick didn't make it. He was in the guardhouse with Seth. And yes, they've been caught."

A tear ran down her cheek. "Poor Mick! He's such a..." She caught herself and sniffled. "He *was* such a sweet man. Only last weekend, he came over to our house for a barbecue. I don't think he has any family."

"I don't think so either, but we'll check. If there are any relatives, we'll find them."

Mick was an army veteran, an only child, and an orphan. He'd grown up in care before he adopted Blackwood as his family. A bit like me, really. There were going to be a lot of upset people in the office tomorrow because he'd been popular with everyone.

In the background, Belcourt came into view with Crane, whose high forehead and chubby cheeks made him look far too young to hold the level of responsibility he did. When he caught sight of me, he raised an eyebrow.

I focused back on Carla. "I've got to go. The sharks are circling." I nodded at the pair of DEA agents. "Make sure the hospital knows that Seth's to have the best of everything. If the treatment's not covered by his insurance, I'll foot the bill. And if you need anything, just call one of us."

She clutched at my hand. "What if he doesn't make it?"

Her trembles transferred to me, and I tried to give her a reassuring smile. I'm not sure if I pulled it off, because I wasn't convinced Seth would survive either.

"I'm scared too, but we have to stay positive."

I was trying to make Carla feel better, but I'd lied. I wasn't scared. A mixture of apprehension and anger simmered away inside me, not fear.

Anger because whoever Blanco was, he'd walked into my life and tried to destroy it piece by piece. First my husband, now my home and my friends.

Yes, I knew I'd stepped on his toes by inadvertently investigating his business, but I'd barely found anything, and his reaction was overkill. That was where the apprehension came in. If his response to me busting a few low-level drug dealers was to send a squad of mercenaries to make my birthday bash go with a bang, what would he do when I went after him personally?

I gently extricated myself from Carla's grip and snuck back to my cubicle. Crane took the high-backed chair next to the bed while Belcourt hovered at the foot, waiting. I kicked back on the lumpy mattress and went through the story a second time for Crane's benefit.

"Officially," he told me when I finished, "I can't be seen to condone any actions that might break the law."

"But unofficially?"

"Unofficially, if Blackwood can take out the network supplying the bad coke, we'd owe you one. Senator Trent's calling me ten times a day, wanting minute-by-minute progress reports. I can't get on with anything else. It's driving me crazy. Crazy!" He ran a hand through hair he didn't have. "Last weekend, I had to miss my son's sixth birthday party because of a drugs bust, and my wife's not speaking to me because of it. Just tell Belcourt what you need, and we'll do our best to assist."

"Okay, so first favour. You can help me convince people I'm dead. It'll be a whole lot easier for me to find this fucker if he doesn't think I'm looking for him."

Crane and Belcourt both rolled their eyes. What was it with that tonight? "Fine, but it's going to take more than us to do that."

"I know. Leave it to me."

I called an acquaintance at the FBI. Mack had kept her word, and they already had agents on the scene.

"Agent Stone. Long time, no speak."

He groaned, long and loud. "What do you want?"

"I love you too. I'm at the hospital. Do me a favour and get your ass over here."

"Why do I get the feeling I'm not going to like this?"

"I have no idea. Don't we always have fun together?"

"No."

"I'm in the ER. Hurry up."

He arrived twenty minutes later, looking like he'd rather be anywhere else. Well, that made two of us.

"So, tell me again," he said. "Why should the FBI be taking over this case?"

I ran through possible options in my head. "Because if you identify the dead dudes in my house, I bet at least one of them had weapons he shouldn't have been carrying. Oh, and maybe, just maybe, because they were trying to murder us all."

Plus I'd rather have the FBI than the local cops, because the local cops didn't like me very much since they thought I'd killed Black. That had the potential to make everything a little awkward.

"So you want me to wade in with my size twelves and fix up your mess?"

"Yeah, pretty much." I gave him a snarky smile. "A bit like when you lost that informant last year and the whole paedophile case you and eight other agents had spent seven months working on was about to get flushed down the toilet, and I waded in with my dainty size fives and fixed up your mess."

He rolled his eyes at me. Seriously, why all the eye rolling? But he owed me a favour, and he knew it. He looked at Belcourt and Crane, who both shrugged, then turned back to me.

"Okay, you need to lie down and put a sheet over your head. Which one of us gets to wheel the gurney?"

The final part of the jigsaw was Dr. Beech. Dr. Beech worked in the ER, but he also spent many hours tirelessly fundraising for the hospital. In the last decade, he'd organised fairs, hosted dinners, and wheedled cash out of everyone who crossed his path, culminating in the opening of a new paediatric wing. The Blackwood Children's Centre. He was only too eager to go along with our little charade, and I think he was secretly thrilled to be assisting with a real, live FBI investigation, which was how Agent Stone sold it to him.

By the time his shift ended, Dr. Beech was the happy recipient of an IOU for a new incubator to go in the neonatal intensive care unit, and I was the proud owner of my very first death certificate. Dr. Beech was so chuffed with the night's events he even offered to do a quick interview with the waiting press, and flanked by Agents Stone and Belcourt, announced my sad demise from unexpected internal bleeding to the reporters gathered outside the front door.

While my cohorts played the media, I snuck out to the car park. When I called Dan to pick Nick and me up, I'd assumed she'd bring one of the company's Explorers, but she turned up in Nate's Porsche 911. The three of us stood in front of it, staring down at the impossibly small trunk at the front of the car.

"How the hell am I supposed to fit in there?" I asked. "What do you think I am? A bloody contortionist?"

Dan shrugged. "Everything else was blocked in. The cops turned up, then the fire brigade, the FBI, several ambulances, a carload of people from the DEA, some of Jed's buddies from the CIA, and even a couple of guys from the NSA as well. I don't think they wanted to be left out. It's like a fucking circus."

"Well, make sure they don't poke around in my house."

"Don't worry. Your legal team's there too, snarling at anyone who comes close. Oliver's been guarding the front door like Cerberus. The acronyms are hanging around outside, arguing over who's got the biggest dick."

Good. As long as they were chasing their own tails, they wouldn't be bothering us. Not that I was particularly worried. We'd defended ourselves against an armed gang who'd tried to kill us all, and that was clear-cut. But in the meantime, I didn't want to get stuck in endless rounds of questioning over who shot at who first. I'd arranged to meet with Stone tomorrow—well, later today—to give a full statement, and he'd agreed to deal with the locals for me.

That gave me time to get Blackwood's own investigation started. I hoped that having lost his entire team last night, Blanco needed some time to regroup, which would give us a clear run at him for the next week or so. I didn't want to waste a second of it.

With that in mind, I made sure Nick took the driver's seat then limbered up and squashed myself into the tiny space in the front of the Porsche.

Revenge, sweet revenge, here we come.

CHAPTER 7

AN UNDERGROUND GARAGE lay beneath the old stable yard at Riverley Hall, and it was into there that Nick drove the Porsche. As soon as he popped the trunk lid up, I unfolded myself, grateful to be standing up again as I cursed the ridiculously stiff suspension on Nate's car. I tried to rub some feeling back into my arms and legs while Dan got out of the passenger seat.

"You okay?" Nick asked.

"I'll live."

A short tunnel led from the garage to Black's basement, and we took that. It wasn't a good idea to show my face above ground tonight seeing as the people hanging around hopefully thought I was dead by now. Although "Ghost sighting at local mansion" could have made an interesting headline.

I considered going up to Black's house for the evening, but my heart lurched when I took a step in that direction. Too many reminders of him still lurked upstairs. I needed to keep my emotions firmly in check right then, so I headed for the longer tunnel leading to my own basement instead. When I reached the control room, Mack, Luke, and Bradley were frantically typing and clicking away while Alex calmly cleaned his gun. Seemed they'd been down there the whole time, which made sense. There was no point in giving the cops more people to get their claws into.

Had they found anything? I stepped closer, reading over their shoulders. Mack and Luke were researching the Colombian drug scene while Bradley looked at new dining tables.

"What happened in the dining room?"

"You don't want to know," he said.

"It was just a few bullet holes," Alex tried to reassure me.

Oh, that's okay then. As long as it was only a few. If Alex had been involved, then Bradley was right; I probably didn't want to know.

"Bradley, you understand you can't redecorate the house yet? The bodies are still warm."

"That doesn't stop me from planning." He pointed at the bank of monitors, where half of the screens still showed grim pictures. "The place is a disaster."

"The place is a crime scene. It'll be weeks before you're allowed back inside."

"Which is about how long the Italian marble for your new kitchen will take to arrive. What do you think of Makassar Ebony for the units?"

"We're in the middle of a murder investigation here. Do you think you could at least hold off on the renovations until we neutralise the guy who destroyed my house?"

"But—"

"What if the motherfucker comes back and has another go? All your hard work would be wasted."

"I suppose you've got a point."

"How about you find me a coffee instead? Two sugars. Thanks."

"Fine." He huffed, but at least he went to hunt for

caffeine.

As Bradley stomped off into the tunnels, Nate appeared, having escaped the clutches of the hordes upstairs. I watched them on the monitors, hanging around like vultures.

"Some of the cops tried to come in, so I turned the sprinklers on again," Mack told me.

"Good thinking." Downstairs was already ruined. Adding more water wouldn't make much difference.

Nate stood next to me. "You're looking remarkably good for a dead woman."

"It's amazing what a bit of make-up can do. So, what's going on?"

"Alex got a name for Blanco out of one of them before he died," Mack said.

Finally, a breakthrough! About bloody time, but the fact that it took the death of one of my men and the injury of another left me raw inside.

"Great. Who?"

"We've done some research, and it fits with your theory that drugs are behind the whole thing."

"Who is it?"

Mack pushed back her chair and turned to face me. "He's a Colombian drug lord. I've been pulling up everything I can on him, and he seems meaner than a wet panther. He's been at the top of the pile for years, and one reason he stays there is because he does nasty things to anyone who tries to cross him. The man's crazy by all accounts, not to mention bloodthirsty. He's got two sons who work with him, and they're just as bad."

Luke clicked his mouse and read from the screen. "Last year, he was suspected of beheading six members of a rival cartel and impaling them on sticks outside their leader's compound."

"What's he called?" I clenched my fists. *Tell me, who do I need to kill?*

"It's believed he now controls a larger portion of the drug trade coming out of Colombia than anyone else, and his foot soldiers are totally loyal," Mack continued. "That's not surprising. It says here that when one of his henchmen betrayed him six years ago, he made the guy eat his own balls to show he no longer had any."

"His fucking name, Mack?"

"Oh, yeah, sorry. It's Eduardo Garcia."

Despite what Nick had said earlier, I really did feel dizzy at that moment. No way. It couldn't be Eduardo.

In front of me, Mack continued to list his wrongdoings, but I tuned it out, turning her revelation over in my mind and reminding myself to breathe. On paper, yes, it all fitted. Eduardo Garcia was indeed one of Colombia's primo drug lords, with a taste for violence and a small army at his beck and call. He certainly had the money and the connections to have arranged Black's assassination and the little visit we'd had earlier in the night.

But I still didn't believe it was him. Because what—or rather who—the others in the room didn't know, was Eduardo Garcia. But I did.

"Alex, how exactly did you get this name?"

Alex looked up from his gun and leaned back in his seat. "I warmed the *mudak* up by abusing a few pressure points, then when he started sweating, we held him down spread-eagled across the dining table."

Bradley interrupted, his expression a mix of excitement and disgust. "He shot between the scumbag's legs, and told him if he didn't confess who sent him that instant, the next shot would go one inch higher."

"And then he said it was Eduardo?"

Alex shrugged. "No, I had to shoot his testicles off first. Then he told me."

Bloody hell, no wonder Bradley was looking for a new table.

"So at that point, if I were him, I'd have assumed I was going to die," I mused out loud. "Everyone else on my side was already dead, so there was nobody to help me. I'd have spilled the name of someone I didn't like very much and hoped the people who took out my team would also wipe out my enemy. Victory even in death."

"I suppose that could have happened," Alex admitted grudgingly.

"In that case, could we look for alternatives to Eduardo Garcia, please." It came out as a command rather than a question, and all heads turned to look at me.

Mack spoke first. "What makes you so sure it's not him? It could easily be Garcia, looking at this data. It's not like any of us have ever met the guy, is it?"

Her questions were perfectly legitimate. In her position, I'd have asked them too. The trouble was, how should I answer her?

"Or have you met him?" Nate guessed the truth first. Dammit, he'd known me too long, and he realised I was holding something back.

Shit. How should I put this? I decided to try for vague.

"Our paths have crossed over the years. Often enough to say there are others we should put ahead of him when it comes to narrowing down our list of suspects."

I should have known that wouldn't wash with Nate. He gave me his grumpy, squinty look.

"Precisely how well do you know him?"

"Well enough to believe he wouldn't have done this to me. I mean to us. So can we please look at who else it might have been? Starting with his rivals?"

"Well enough? Emmy, he's a fucking drug lord."

"So? I'm not exactly squeaky clean myself."

"That aside, we can't discount our prime suspect just because you say you don't think he did it. We have to check into it a little more than that."

"Fine. I'll look into it. Leave it with me."

"What precisely are you planning to do?"

"I'll talk to him."

"What, you're gonna call him up? What are you going to say? 'Hi, Mr. Garcia, I was wondering if you murdered my husband? And whether the fourteen men who came to kill me the other night were anything to do with you?' If so, you're even more out of your mind than I thought."

"No, of course I'm not just going to call him up. That would be rude. I'll go and visit him."

In my head, I was already packing.

"You're insane. What, you plan to waltz up and knock on his front door?"

"Don't be ridiculous." Eduardo didn't have a knocker. If you got as far as his front door without being shot first, his butler opened it automatically.

"What, then?"

I could hardly explain I had a system for meeting Eduardo. That when he knew I was there to see him, he'd send somebody to collect me.

"I'll find a way," I hedged.

"You're not going," Nate told me.

"Yes, I am."

"No, you're not. You're not going to fly to Colombia to have a chat with a violent, borderline psychopathic monster who's suspected of trying to kill us all. What if it *was* him? He'll probably shoot you on sight."

"All right, all right. I won't go." I hated being forced to lie to my friends. "But can we at least consider the alternatives? And for fuck's sake, let's not go wading into Garcia's business and upsetting him."

"That sounds remarkably sensible." Nate seemed surprised I'd caved so easily, and I couldn't blame him. After all, I wasn't well known for taking the sensible approach. "Mack, Luke—can you look into other prominent drug dealers as well? There must be a couple of dozen with the cash and resources for this."

A chorus of agreement followed before Luke and Mack carried on working at their screens, fingers hammering in a staccato rhythm, no doubt fuelled by adrenaline from the night's events and the prospect of a resolution to the horror stalking us.

I didn't share their enthusiasm. The idea of Eduardo being mixed up in this filled me with dread. Rather than sitting with them, I retreated to a quiet corner and wrapped myself up in a blanket, trying to get some rest but without much success. Instead of sleeping, I planned what I'd say to Eduardo, turning jumbled words over in my mind. Of course, I still planned to visit him, no matter what I'd said to Nate. It was perhaps the only way to get this mess cleared up.

And I was certain it wasn't Eduardo. Well, almost.

Ninety-nine percent, maybe. That other one percent? Well, if I was wrong, I'd be joining Black sooner than I anticipated, wouldn't I?

The theory that Eduardo was behind this bothered me for one main reason: he had no motive to kill me. The opposite, in fact. This was the man who'd once told me if he'd ever had a second daughter, he'd have wanted me to be her. The man who never forgot my birthday. The man who insisted his chef perfected the best recipe for macaroni and cheese because he knew it was my favourite. The man whose two sons treated me like a sister, threatening to take the head off any person who so much as looked at me funny.

The threat was quite literal, in Sebastien and Marco's cases. They'd had enough practice at it.

We were working under the assumption that the motive for the killings was our investigation into the bad coke flooding New York and the surrounding areas, which also didn't fit with Eduardo. While the two of us had never got into the specifics of his family business, we'd had several "what if" discussions over the years, some of which I suspected weren't so hypothetical. From those, I'd gleaned most of his trade hit the West Coast and the Southern states. A little probably made its way east, but it didn't make up a major part of his revenue.

Eduardo also prided himself on supplying a good quality product. I couldn't recall discussing particular chemicals with him, but we'd talked about the cutting of drugs and Eduardo categorically told me he'd never do it before shipment. So if Black was right, and the levamisole got added before the coke arrived stateside, then that spoke against Eduardo's involvement too.

My overriding hope was that by naming Eduardo, the arsehole from last night had given us a big clue. Because surely whoever his real puppet master was, he had to be someone with a grudge against Mr. Garcia, didn't he? That left me with one big question—would Eduardo be able to shed light on his identity?

I itched to get going, to travel to Colombia and speak to him. Patience wasn't something that came naturally to me. I planned to slip out the following evening, and having to squander a whole day before I could take what was, for me, the most logical next step in the investigation irritated me to no end. I smacked my head against the wall in frustration, but that achieved nothing more than a headache.

Time was precious, and every day I wasted was a day I'd never get back.

Tick, tick, tick. While the seconds marched by, I needed to catch up on sleep, give a statement to the FBI, and sling a few things in my suitcase.

It promised to be a long twenty-four hours.

CHAPTER 8

I STOOD IN my bedroom at Riverley Hall, taking a mental inventory. I'd had to venture upstairs, no matter how depressing the memories might be. What did I need for my trip to Colombia? On the bed, a small suitcase lay open with the essentials piled inside.

Normally when I went abroad, I was going somewhere I owned a house or an apartment, but I had neither in Colombia. I kept a few things at Eduardo's, clothes mainly, but he'd bought a lot of the outfits for me and they weren't to my taste. Dresses, tops, skirts, cover-ups for lying out by the pool, all very conservative. I wore everything anyway, because it pleased him, but I still needed to take my own clothes for when I wasn't at his place.

A passport lay beside the suitcase. Tonight I'd become Maria Delgado, one of two identities I used to travel to Columbia. Maria worked as an interior designer. I'd just put on the wig that matched her passport photo, and along with her papers, I'd take fabric swatches, wallpaper samples, and a sketchbook with drawings of room concepts. If anyone cared to check, I even had a website, although if they called the number listed, Sloane, my office assistant in Virginia, would inform them I wasn't currently taking on new clients.

It was a solid identity, just as long as nobody asked me to actually sketch anything, because I couldn't draw for toffee. It was Bradley who'd filled up the pad with pictures for me, and they certainly looked the part.

An envelope slipped into the back of the sketchbook held a collection of photos—one of everyone associated with the case. Fourteen dead gunmen, although missing bits of face made some of them a bit fuzzy, plus the pack we'd used after Black's murder containing photos of the guys from the van. Obviously, the driver got burned beyond recognition, but Mack had found a shot of him from a surveillance camera in the hotel parking lot and enhanced it as best she could.

As I threw extra clothes into my luggage, I clung to the hope that Eduardo or someone on his staff might recognise one of them.

When I'd checked forty-five minutes ago, right before sorting out my hair, everyone had gone to bed except Luke, who was determined to finish hacking into something or other before he went to sleep.

I didn't really care what.

Don't get me wrong, the information Mack, Luke, and the others found with their computer searches could be invaluable. But it had its limits, and I always believed that by talking to people face-to-face, by watching their body language and feeling the vibes they gave off, I could glean information not found in electronic format. Hence the need to catch a plane.

My phone chose that moment to ping with a text message.

Ryan: Still at Albany House. Tia's okay and behaving herself.

I bet she was.

Emmy: The bedrooms are out of bounds. All of them. This is not a hands-on job.

Ryan: How about the couch?

Emmy: I mean it.

Packing complete, I put in a pair of brown contact lenses. On a scale of one to Ashlyn Hale, my alter ego who'd dated Luke, I rated myself a seven for mediocrity. Finally, I fastened the necklace I'd received for my birthday around my neck and slipped the note that came with it into my wallet.

I'd be travelling commercial, so the only weapon I carried was a knife stuffed in the front of my bra. When the metal detector went off, I'd claim it was the underwire that caused it, as usual. I'd yet to find an airport security guard confident enough to give me a really good grope.

The clock struck midnight as I stole down the stairs and took the tunnel to the garage, keys to one of the Ford Explorers clutched in my hand. All was going swimmingly until I opened the driver's door, at which point Nate stepped out the shadows and climbed into the passenger side.

Oh, arseholes.

"Where the hell do you think you're going?" he asked.

"Would you believe I fancied a pizza?"

"And the pizza place will only serve brunettes?"

"Okay, you got me. Fine. I'm going to Colombia."

No point in lying, not to Nate. That was the downside of knowing someone for as long as I'd known him—trying to fib right to his face was pointless. He saw straight through it.

"I knew you would be."

"So where are *you* going?" I eyed up the holdall sitting on his lap.

"I'm coming with you."

"You've got to be kidding," I said, but the determination in his voice told me he wasn't.

"If you go, I go."

"No way. It could ruin everything. I've always gone to see Eduardo alone. I don't know if he'd even come for me if I was with somebody else."

"What do you mean, come for you?"

I sighed and spilled. "The way it works is that I check into a particular hotel, and when he knows I'm there, he sends somebody to pick me up."

Nate paused for a few seconds as he tried to rein in his exasperation, then offered a compromise.

"How about we travel separately? I'll keep an eye on you from a distance, but I'm not letting you go alone."

"It's not your choice."

"Before he died, Black and I made a promise to each other. If anything happened to either of us, he'd look after Carmen, and I'd look after you. As well as that, I care about you, believe it or not. I may not always agree with the way you do things, but I can't deny you get results, which is why I haven't locked you up and thrown away the key."

"Touching." And it really was, even if my reply came out snarky.

"Emmy, I'm coming along whether you like it or not."

I knew from experience that if Nate decided to do something, I wouldn't be able to change his mind, and if the situation had been reversed, Black would definitely have been on the plane with Carmen.

Secretly, I was also pleased at the prospect of having backup, especially from Nate, who'd spent a lot more time in South America than me and had the skin colour of a local.

"Fine. Whatever." Great, now I sounded like Bradley when his wilder decorating ideas got vetoed. "Just make sure you don't balls things up for me."

I should have told Nate not to talk as well, because on the way to the airport, he started with the interrogation.

"So, tell me, why are you so positive that Garcia won't execute you on sight? You've been hazy on that so far."

"Because if he had a problem with something Blackwood was doing, he'd talk to me about it, not shoot my husband."

"You can't be sure of that."

"Maybe not with one hundred percent certainty, but close to it."

"Why? All the information we found on Garcia suggests he should have been committed years ago. He's renowned for being violent and unpredictable."

"So people say, but he's not always like that. And he's as sane as you or I." Okay, perhaps that was a bad example. "Eduardo recognises that in order to maintain his position at the top of the tree, people have to fear him. He cultivates the image of being unstable, and yes, that involves doing some fucked-up stuff, but he's actually very smart. Calculating. And he's never given me the slightest indication that he wishes me harm."

"People change. When did you last see him?"

"Thirteen months ago."

"Speak to him?"

"The same," I admitted.

"So before Black's death, right? How do you know he hasn't taken offence to something one of you did in the meantime? You were trying to take out a network of cocaine dealers, after all."

"Firstly, it wasn't his coke; therefore they weren't his dealers. Which means that far from being upset, he'd be pleased. Secondly, I may not have seen him or spoken to him, but he did send me a birthday gift and a note yesterday. A note that basically said he hoped Black's killer came to a nasty end. And even if he was an olive short of a pizza, which he isn't, he's hardly likely to have a diamond necklace delivered to me in the morning and then follow it up with a death squad later on the same day."

I fished the note out of my bag and passed it over to Nate, and he flicked on the interior light to read it. "I don't see anything in there that says he hopes the killer's dead. And what's more, you don't even know for definite that this came from Garcia."

"Yes, I do. It's not the first time he's sent me a birthday present, and I recognise his writing. And he says he hopes I get closure like he did. He got his closure with death."

Nate's sideways glance told me more questions were coming. "I'm intrigued—how do you know so much about Garcia? Or know him at all, for that matter? He's not the type of person who's easy to cross paths with."

"I did a job for him once."

Nate groaned. "I take it this was one of your 'special' jobs that didn't go through Blackwood?"

"It mostly did. Only one part stayed off the books."

"Drugs related?"

"No, not at all." After recent events, I figured Nate had a right to know. "It was eleven years ago. Do you remember Robert Frost?"

"The congressman's son? The one who turned out to be a serial killer?"

"The one and only. His fourth victim was a college girl called Camilla McKinley. Happy go lucky, nineteen years old, her whole life ahead of her. Top of her class in biochemistry. They found her naked body in a disused storeroom at Virginia Tech three weeks after she died."

"I remember that. The cops fucked it up, didn't they? Lost some of the evidence."

"And that's when we got hired to investigate."

"Didn't you point the finger at Frost, but he hung himself before you got a chance to pass our files over to the police?"

"That's what it said in the report I filed, yes."

"I get the impression there's a 'but' coming?"

"I used a teeny bit of poetic licence in what I wrote. My report said Camilla's stepfather hired me, but the client was actually her real father. I knew him as Edward Graydon."

"I'm getting a bad feeling about this."

"I didn't find out until later that Edward Graydon was Eduardo Garcia."

"How much later?"

"When I met him to present my findings. I spent a month pretending to be a college student, but it didn't take long to finger Frost as the culprit. He may have been rich and handsome, but there was something cold about him. He gave me the creeps, and that's not easy to do. When we went on a date, he left me in the car while he paid for gas, and I found a pair of gloves, a knife and a length of rope in his glove compartment. Most guys that age would have a condom and some breath mints."

"That's hardly conclusive, though."

"Most guys wouldn't have six perfectly preserved pairs of women's breasts in their freezer either, which was what I found when I poked around his house. That was enough for me."

"Fair enough. I'll give you that one."

"So after that, I flew to Colombia to tell Edward what I'd found, and that was when I met Eduardo. Even back then, he travelled abroad as little as possible. He believed because Frost was the son of a congressman, and because that congressman was well known for being a devious prick, there was a good chance sonny-boy wouldn't get everything he deserved. And I agreed with him. It wouldn't be the first time someone rich or famous got away with murder—just look at that ex-football player."

Another groan. "I think I know where this is going. I take it Frost had a little assistance with his suicide?"

"Someone as arrogant and self-centred as he was would never have contemplated killing himself."

"Did Black know you killed Frost?"

"He had the feet end when we chucked him over the balcony."

"I might have fucking guessed. And you've kept in touch with Garcia since then?"

"Yes."

"Care to elaborate?"

"We have dinner every so often. Shoot the breeze."

"You're officially nuts, you know that, right?" Nate shook his head in disbelief. "Why didn't you tell me?"

"Around the time the Frost thing kicked off, your cousin had just died from an overdose. After you spent half an hour ranting about the dangers of drugs, I thought it was best to keep quiet."

"My cousin was a prick. I got pissed because I had to deal with the paperwork. Anyhow, that was a decade ago. You've been seeing Garcia all this time?"

"Yeah, but it's not the kind of thing you bring up in casual conversation, is it?"

"Only you could think it was perfectly normal to drop around for dinner with the leader of a Colombian drugs cartel."

"He's still just a person like anyone else. Well, maybe not quite, but he's not the monster everyone makes him out to be."

"I'll have to reserve judgment on that for now. So, what's your plan?"

"Check into the Coralia Club Hotel and wait."

"That's it? That's your whole plan?"

"Yes, but don't worry. It's a really nice hotel. The staff have always looked after me well. Mind you, Eduardo would put them six feet under if they didn't— he owns it."

With Nate sighing like an out-of-shape asthmatic, I pulled into short-term parking at Dulles International Airport. We split up once we were inside the terminal, queueing separately to buy tickets. Then, after half an hour of avoiding each other in the departure lounge and a much-needed gin and tonic for me, we took off for the sunny climes of South America.

CHAPTER 9

A COMPLIMENTARY GLASS of champagne and as many canapés as I could eat made the five-hour flight to El Dorado International Airport in Bogotá go quickly. Nate took a seat across the aisle from me, two rows in front, but he passed on the free booze in favour of sleep. I couldn't. While the miles flew by, I thought about what to say to Eduardo.

For all my confidence over his innocence, I really didn't know him that well. After our initial meeting, our contact had been limited to me flying out to Colombia once or twice a year, and never for more than a few days at a time.

The first time I went to Cali on business after the Frost episode, seeing Eduardo had been the furthest thing from my mind. As I recall, I'd gone there to search for a missing teenager who'd run off with a man of dubious character who also happened to be her maths teacher. We'd tracked her to Colombia, and her parents thought the troubled girl might respond better to my approach than a show put on by the Colombian police.

It was only my third trip to the city, and as I'd liked the hotel where I met with Eduardo, I decided to stay there again. The Coralia Club was a well-appointed five-star on the outskirts of town, but the area was still busy enough to enjoy the nightlife. Inside was an oasis of calm with its lush tropical gardens and a large, oval-shaped pool.

On my second night there, I'd sat back in the hotel's Ristorante Solsticio, an elegant, old-world style lounge with excellent food and discreet yet efficient service. I only had my phone for company while I stared at the menu, trying to decide between the fish and the chicken. Maybe I could order both and eat half of each? Would that look greedy? I'd considered getting room service, but my table by the window had a view over the busy street outside, and my inherent nosiness won out.

Before I could make a decision, I felt a presence behind me.

"Would you mind giving me a m—"

Oh, it wasn't the waiter. A heavyset man with a perfectly trimmed goatee glowered down at me, dressed in a black suit and not even trying to hide the fact he had a gun under the jacket.

After a brief moment in which I started calculating whether I could get the pistol out of my thigh holster faster than Danny Trejo's uglier brother could draw from his shoulder rig, he spoke in a way that could only be interpreted as a command.

"Mr. Garcia has requested your company this evening."

Well, I had my gun, and I hadn't ordered dinner yet, so I figured what the hell, I might as well go. That and I didn't particularly want to cause a scene in a very nice restaurant where I might well want to eat again sometime.

"Why not?" I pushed my chair back.

The big dude ushered me into a waiting limousine

which swiftly drove south for an hour or so. Neither he nor the driver spoke during the trip, and I was left to stare out of the window, watching the roads get smaller and the scenery get greener.

Eventually, we drew up at an ornate pair of gates, set into a wall topped with razor wire that stretched into the distance as far as I could see. The gates slowly swung open, and we continued up the driveway, past a pair of gun-toting security guards who gazed at us with bored expressions.

The instant the car came to a halt, a servant rushed over and opened my door. I stepped out into the muggy evening and he ushered me towards the house, a sprawling peach-coloured affair whose three storeys wrapped around a central courtyard. Little touches, like the gold-plated doorknobs and manicured topiary, screamed *look at me, I'm rich.*

I was just wondering what on earth possessed someone to have a life-sized statue of an elephant covered in gold leaf smack bang in the middle of their hallway when Eduardo stepped out of a side room.

"Emerson, I'm so glad you agreed to come." He took my hand in his, bringing it to his lips and kissing it.

"I wasn't aware there was a choice."

"For you, there is always a choice. But I am glad you decided not to exercise that choice in my hotel dining room."

"I'll admit, I thought this could be an interesting experience. Nice elephant, by the way." A tiny bit of sarcasm might have crept into my voice.

"It's an atrocity, is it not? But my fourth wife loves elephants, and she is good to me in many other ways, so I indulge her."

That was one big indulgence. She must have been *very* good in other ways. Ways I really didn't want to think about, what with Eduardo being old enough to be my father and all that. His Interpol file was hazy on his age, but I put him at around fifty, perhaps a little older. He clearly looked after himself and stayed in good shape, although too much time in the sun had given him a network of wrinkles on his face. His hands too. Hands were always a giveaway.

He wasn't a big man, standing at five feet nine, give or take an inch, but he exuded a power that made everyone snap to attention when he entered a room. Like a fine wine, Eduardo had aged well. I'd done some research after my last trip and seen pictures of him in his youth, but the salt and pepper hair he sported now gave him a distinguished appearance that meant he was never short of female admirers. That day, he'd worn a pale pink linen suit. Another of his wife's choices? I wasn't sure about the colour, but I figured as the slightly eccentric billionaire boss of the second biggest drug cartel in Colombia, he could wear anything he wanted.

And now Eduardo led the way through to the dining room. "I heard you were staying by yourself. A beautiful woman should never dine alone, so I thought you might like to humour an old man by keeping him company."

"It'd be my pleasure." Even if he had practically kidnapped me to get me there.

Eduardo's chef served up a feast of culinary delights —a light salad of quail eggs and asparagus to start followed by pigeon for the main course. And his desserts were to die for. I suspected they needed to be if he didn't want to.

"Would you like anything else?" Eduardo asked.

"I'd better not. Your chef's a genius."

"Alejandro trained in Paris. I found him in a restaurant in Bogotà and made him a better offer."

"I'd end up the size of your elephant if I ate this food every day."

Eduardo smiled. "Life is short; I understand this better than anyone, so I might as well enjoy the best things while I can."

The old guy made surprisingly good company, and I found myself being unusually honest with him. In our respective lines of work, there were few people we could discuss things openly with, but there we were, with him knowing what I did and me knowing what he did.

We never made any promises explicitly, but neither of us worried about the other passing on our stories to the outside world. The reason was simple—if he talked, he knew I'd kill him, and if I talked, I knew he would kill me. It may have seemed a strange basis for what was to turn into a lasting friendship but hey, it worked.

And that night, we conversed until the early hours over a couple of excellent bottles of wine. Eduardo taught me some interesting things about smuggling, and I made him laugh by describing my exploits shutting down a paedophile ring.

"...so I turned up at the police station with three of them handcuffed naked in the trunk. The cops didn't know which bits to grab to haul them out of there."

"You should just chop their bits off, angel. Problem solved."

"I tried that once, but the paperwork was

unbearable."

Eventually, it got too late for me to contemplate going back to the hotel, so I stayed the night in a bedroom filled with so much gold it looked like an Indian wedding had thrown up all over it. The next morning, after I'd drawn back the gold curtains to admire the view, taken a bath in the gold-plated bathtub, and brushed my teeth with a golden toothbrush, I kidded Eduardo that I preferred silver.

Before the car dropped me back to the hotel, he told me it was one of the most enjoyable evenings he'd had in a long time.

"Would you like to do this again sometime?" he asked.

"Of course. You're good company, for an old dude anyway."

He leaned down and kissed me on the cheek. "In that case, I will see you on your next visit."

We needed to be careful—it wouldn't look good at home if the news I was consorting with a well-known drug kingpin got out. Likewise, if people in Colombia saw Eduardo with me, my connections to the DEA could have put his operation in jeopardy.

With that in mind, we'd agreed on a system. In future, I'd check into his hotel under an alias, and he would send someone to pick me up when it was safe.

Simple, but the system worked. I'd been doing exactly that for the last ten years.

CHAPTER 10

AS I SIPPED one final gin and tonic on the plane, I ran through my story. I didn't want to accuse Eduardo of anything, but at the same time, I needed to push him enough to get a genuine reaction when I told him one of the attackers gave my team his name. That was how I'd know whether he was mixed up in this.

The aircraft landed with a gentle bump, shaking me from my thoughts, and after disembarking, I went to find a connecting flight to Cali. The city lay three hundred miles from Bogotà, so flying there was faster than driving. An hour later, I clambered onto a small plane with Nate and seven other passengers for the final leg of the journey.

By the time we'd landed at the snappily named Alfonso Bonilla Aragón International Airport in Palmira, I'd shed several layers of clothing as the temperature climbed into the low thirties. In the terminal, I bought a bottle of water then strolled outside to find a cab, leaving Nate to do his own thing. As I rode to the hotel in a battered Toyota, the city was coming alive with the hustle and bustle of daily life.

The air-conditioned lobby of the Coralia Club provided a welcome respite from the heat. Luxurious, quiet, classy. They'd changed the decor since I was last there, and a pair of newlyweds posed for photos next to a cluster of palm trees in one corner.

"Maria Delgado. I don't have a reservation, but—"

"One second, ma'am."

The instant I gave my name, the manager came and took over my booking, sending the receptionist who'd greeted me to fetch a cold drink as he offered me a seat. He tapped away at the computer before shaking his head.

"I must apologise. We only have the second largest suite available. The largest is occupied by a couple on their honeymoon."

"It's fine. I don't need a suite at all. A regular room will be perfectly adequate."

"No, no, you will have the suite, please, Ms. Delgado."

As I left the lobby with a porter carrying my small bag and the manager marching in front of me with the room key, I saw Nate coming in the front door out of the corner of my eye. At least he'd arrived okay.

I'd been in my room ten minutes when the phone rang. What did my uninvited companion want?

"You got here, then," I said.

"Emmy, I only had to find a hotel. It really wasn't difficult. Give me a little credit."

"Sorry. I mean thanks for coming."

"That's better. What room are you in?"

"The Palm Suite."

"A suite? Don't you think that's overkill for the amount of time we're going to be here? I just asked for a basic double."

"So did I. There's a standing instruction to put me in the best room available whatever I say."

I could almost see his eyes roll.

"I spoke to Nick. He needed to know where we were before people started getting worried. Needless to say, he's not happy. With either of us."

"I'll tell him it was all my fault when I next talk to him, that I made you go. He'll believe that."

"No, he won't. Because I told him I trusted you, and I thought this was the best way forward."

He did? It was rare for Nate to stick up for me like that. He hadn't been my biggest fan when we'd first met, and we'd had a number of differences of opinion over the years.

"Thanks for having so much faith in me."

"You've earned it. So, what do we do now? Call Eduardo?"

"I don't have to. The hotel manager will have phoned him the second he got back downstairs."

"You mean it's just a case of waiting? There's nothing else we can do?"

"Nope. I'm going to the gym."

I did an hour on the treadmill, running until the nervous energy inside me settled before moving onto weights. Nate came in after half an hour, and we studiously ignored each other until I left. With little else to do, I spent the afternoon sitting by the pool, reading through the case notes on my tablet and turning over every so often so I didn't burn.

Relaxing in the sun felt odd with all the shit going on back home. Wrong. But fifty bucks said the authorities monitored this hotel because of who owned it, and who knew how many ears were listening?

Come on, Eduardo.

Just before six, there was a knock at my door, and I opened it to find one of Eduardo's men standing there.

Usually, I'd just follow him to the car, but this time, he motioned me back inside and closed the door behind us.

Silently, he handed me a mobile phone, and I held it up to my ear.

"Hello?"

"Emerson?"

"Well, yes. Who else would it be?"

"I got word that you'd died in a home invasion. I need to make sure it's really you before inviting you to my estate."

"Fair enough. I can understand you might have a few questions, so shoot. Not literally," I hastened to add, eyeing the bulge under his pet gorilla's jacket.

Eduardo's proof-of-life questions were like those asked in a kidnapping—things that would only be known by us or our closest acquaintances.

"What is the other name you use when you come to visit me?"

"Lauren Bailey." No hesitation on my part.

"And what was the problem you helped me with many years ago?"

"Frost."

"Good answers. Can you pass me back to Javier?"

I passed the phone over, and after listening to further instructions from his boss, Javier led me down to the waiting limousine. I was used to this now, so I settled in for the ride.

After a small delay due to an accident ahead of us, we arrived at Eduardo's. I knew my way around after all this time, so I walked ahead of Javier into the entrance hall. The golden elephant was long gone, as was Eduardo's fourth wife. I didn't know what happened to her. I didn't *want* to know. Eduardo was on his sixth now, and this one had an obsession with fresh flowers. The almost overwhelming smell of roses permeated the room, and I stifled a sneeze.

One night when we'd drunk too much aguardiente, he'd confessed the only woman he'd ever truly loved was Camilla's mother, but he thought she was too good for the type of life he led. Once he completed his education, he'd left her and Camilla behind in the United States and returned to Colombia, where his father required him to take over the family business.

"This wasn't a life for her," he said. "I thought America would be safer for them both." Years later, his voice still caught when he spoke about her, and it was evident how much he cared. Now, he tended to marry shallow women who he quickly tired of and traded in for a new model.

Would wife number six be any different? Only time would tell.

A few seconds after I arrived, the man himself walked out of a side room and embraced me in a tight hug.

"My sweet angel, I thought you were gone," he said, his voice thick with emotion.

I'd always been 'angel' to Eduardo. I'd never asked why. Was it because I helped him with Frost? Or because of my normally blonde hair?

"Someone tried to kill me. They didn't succeed, needless to say. That's what I want to talk to you about. I need your help."

"Anything for you, angel. We will have dinner, and you can tell me everything. It was short notice, but Alejandro is making something nice."

We ate outside on a softly lit terrace, classical music playing quietly in the background. Once the food was laid out, Eduardo's staff melted away, leaving just the two of us.

"What happened, child?"

I started from the beginning with Black's death, glossing slightly over my little break—or rather breakdown—in England and finishing off with the events of two nights before.

"What makes you believe I can help?" he asked.

I laid out my theory about the attacks being connected to the drugs trade, and then it came to the moment of truth. "Before the last member of the team died the other night, he gave one of my colleagues the name of the man who sent them."

"Under duress?"

"Yes."

"And what was the name?"

"Yours."

I watched closely as shock and disbelief crossed Eduardo's face. "Angel, I assure you it was not me. I would never do anything to hurt you, and I would never have hurt your husband either. I know how much he meant to you, and you know how much you mean to me."

"I didn't think it could be true, but I had to see your reaction. You understand that?" And based on the way he grasped my hand, my instincts were right.

"Yes, child, I understand. You would not be doing your job if you didn't ask. So, how can I help you to find this person? By trying to frame me, he has invited my retaliation as well."

That was kind of what I'd been hoping he'd say. "I

think the bastard gave your name with the expectation that I would seek revenge against you. He couldn't have known we're friends. So my theory is his boss is somebody who wants you out of the picture, which means he's most likely a rival of yours in the cocaine trade."

"And you were investigating tainted coke coming into the East Coast?"

"Yes, contaminated with levamisole."

"There was a theory that adding levamisole would help keep drugs fresh during transportation, but it didn't work very well, so most people have stopped using it. It was not something I ever did, though. Call me old-fashioned, but I like to stick with my tried and tested methods."

Just as I thought.

"Sometimes the old ways are the best ways. Do you know who the big players are on that side of the US?"

"There are a number of them. I can provide you with a list, but we will need to find a way to narrow it down."

"I brought photos of all the dead mercenaries. I'm hoping you might recognise some of them."

"Certainly I will take a look. Actually, wait a minute. Let us find Sebastien and Marco first. They get out and about more than me, and they may also have seen these men."

As well as Eduardo, I'd got to know his two sons over the years, half-brothers by his first and second wives. At twenty-eight, Seb was the eldest by three years. Both chips off the old block, they'd followed in their father's footsteps in every way, and we'd had some fun times together over the past decade.

Seb in particular shared my wilder traits. I smiled to myself as I recalled the game of dare we'd played one night that led to us almost drowning. It happened the day one of Eduardo's rivals had been particularly rude to him at a charity soccer match. They'd been supporting opposing teams, words were exchanged, and Eduardo was still seething about it all the way through dinner.

After a few beers, Seb and I decided it would be an excellent idea to break into the other guy's house and decorate his lounge in the colours of Eduardo's team. Spray cans in hand, we'd evaded a team of armed guards and snuck through the hallways until we reached our target. Pristine walls stretched in front of us, but when I said I couldn't draw, I meant I couldn't draw.

"What the hell is that supposed to be?" Seb asked after my initial effort.

"A football player."

"Why does he have a chicken's head?"

"That's his nose."

"No, it is a beak. And where is his mouth?"

Okay, he had me there. Seb came over to help, and we were laughing about the buckteeth he gave the player when a maid walked in.

With the sound of her screams echoing behind us, we jumped out the window hand in hand, and the resulting chase wasn't something I'd want to include on my professional résumé. We'd ended up at the bottom of the dude's boating lake, holding onto each other and our breath as torches swept overhead. My lungs had been ready to burst by the time we made it to the surface, and worse, my top had gone see-through.

Gentleman that he was, Seb gave me his T-shirt, and I'd got to enjoy the glorious sight of his muscled torso all the way home.

Sigh. I missed those days.

Both boys still lived at home—it was safer and easier for the family to live in one compound, and there was plenty of space. Eduardo dispatched a servant to find them, and in the meantime, another member of staff served dessert.

The boys arrived as I swallowed my last mouthful of crème brûlée. Seb greeted me with a grin and a tight hug, looking fit and tanned as usual.

"It's been a while, Emmy," he whispered as his lips brushed my ear. "Too long."

"You're right."

Marco, who'd always been kind of shy around the ladies, gave me a little wave.

Greetings over, we went inside to the lounge where the lighting was better. I took the sketchbook from my bag and passed the pack of photos over to Eduardo.

"Sorry about the quality of some of those. We did our best."

"It cannot be helped, angel. These things happen when you shoot someone in the head."

His pragmatism was refreshing.

Eduardo started flipping through them, slowly, his expression giving nothing away. Would he recognise anyone? I caught myself digging my fingernails into my palms and forced myself to relax. *Hands in your lap, Emmy.*

He got to the end of the pile then passed them on to Seb.

"Anything?" I noticed Eduardo had paused for

longer on one of the pictures.

"Maybe. I want Sebastien to have a look before I speak my thoughts."

Seb flicked through, stopping on one particular photo as well. The same one? He showed it to his father and murmured something I couldn't make out.

"Yes, I think so too," Eduardo said. "I have only ever seen him with a beard though, and the hair is different."

My pulse sped up as he passed that picture to Marco, who also nodded his confirmation. I leaned forward, heart thumping against my ribcage. Which of the men had they recognised?

"You've got something?"

Seb nodded and slid the photo over. "That one is Carlos."

CHAPTER 11

I LOOKED DOWN at the photo Seb passed me and stifled a groan. A picture of Black had been left in the pack by accident. I vaguely recalled the team including it when they canvassed the hotel staff for witnesses, just in case the morbid needed to see who had died. His handsome face stared out at me from the shiny paper, and my soul ached with sadness.

It was him the Garcias had recognised. Charles. The English version of the Spanish Carlos. I knew Black had never met any of the family, but Eduardo had his sources just like I had mine. Although Black and I tried to keep pictures of ourselves out of the public domain, they must have seen a photo of him sometime.

"No, that's Charles. He never called himself Carlos. Do any of the others look familiar?"

Seb's brow furrowed in confusion. "No, no, he was always Carlos. I have never heard him called anything else. You recognise him? Why are you asking us, then?"

"Of course I recognise him. We were married for almost twelve years."

Eduardo's face, normally relaxed and friendly, clouded over.

"You were married to Carlos Ramos?" he thundered, leaping to his feet.

Huh?

He slammed his cane down on the wooden floor and advanced towards me. Okay, now I understood where he got his reputation from. He looked a little angry.

"What are you talking about? I was married to Charles Black. You know that."

I stood up and faced him toe-to-toe, hands on hips. He may have been acting psychotic, but two could play at that game.

"Well, that's Carlos Ramos," he yelled, pointing at the photo. Spit flew onto my face, and I resisted the urge to wipe my cheek.

"No, it bloody isn't. It's Charles Black."

"It is Carlos Ramos, Emmy," Seb told me, speaking more gently than his father. "The lack of beard confused me at first, but all three of us can see the likeness."

I answered him without looking. I wasn't about to break eye contact with Eduardo. "No, it definitely isn't."

"Yes, it is," Marco said. "We must have a surveillance photo of Carlos somewhere we can show you. I'll try to find it. That will prove that we're right."

Silence reigned for the five minutes it took him to get back. Eduardo sat on the sofa, glowering, muttering something about me "consorting with the enemy." I remained standing and stared out the window, not seeing much but my own reflection because of the darkness outside.

The eyes looking back at me showed my confusion. What the fuck was going on?

Marco came back with two photos, which he put on the table next to the one of Black. I peered at them closely.

The first was taken from a distance with a long lens, the subject standing at an angle. The tiny figure didn't show any detail, but the stance was pure Black. Upright, confident, hands clasped behind his back.

The second had been shot from much closer with Carlos slightly off-centre. There was a bit of blurring, but I had to admit they were right. The man bore more than a passing resemblance to my husband. If this wasn't Black, it was his doppelgänger.

"I met him once," Marco said. "A couple of years ago, at a party, and he looks even more similar in person. They have the same eyes."

I sat down. Well, my legs gave way and I plopped onto the sofa.

"How can this be? That's Black, but it isn't. He's never had long hair like that."

"Maybe he wore a wig?"

"I guess. But why? Why would he have another identity he didn't tell me about? We didn't have any secrets between us. We told each other everything."

"I don't know, angel. Not yet."

Eduardo must have realised how shocked I was by the latest revelations, and he'd stopped looking at me with murder in his eyes. Instead, he took my hand, trying to comfort me.

"Who is Carlos Ramos, anyway?"

"He's the eldest son of Hector Ramos. Hector Ramos is a rival of mine, and yes, he does supply the East Coast of the United States. He is also, how do you say, mad as a box of frogs?"

"Black's father was American. He died when Black was sixteen."

"Hector Ramos is still very much alive,

unfortunately, and he is not a nice man. While I find it necessary to commit violent acts out of necessity, Hector Ramos does so because he enjoys it. He is ruthless."

Great, a psycho. Well, I always said I liked a challenge. "So where does he live?"

"Further south than us, in the Amazonian region. As far as I know, his sons live with him as mine do with me."

In a heavily fortified compound? This got better and better. "Sons? How many?"

"Carlos has a younger brother called Diego. I've rarely known Carlos to travel, although I've heard Diego makes regular trips abroad."

"Well, Carlos can't be Black. Black hasn't even been to Colombia for years. The last time he came here was when I was...twenty-one." In terms of my pretend age, anyway. "Three days into the trip, he got arrested and accused of shooting some street kid. The police claimed they had an eyewitness who saw him leaving the scene, which was bullshit. He only came here to advise a client on a security system. The bastards locked him up for almost a week before he managed to escape, and once he got out of Colombia, he swore he'd never come back. That's why Nate and I deal with all our business over here." Then I thought of something else. "Wait, when he told me about it, he said they kept yelling 'Give in, Carlos, we've got a witness this time' at him. It annoyed him to no end because they couldn't even get his name right."

"I've seen him here more recently than eleven years ago, Emmy," Seb said.

"When was that photo taken? And where?" I

pointed at the clearer of the two surveillance shots.

Marco turned it over and read the faint pencil scrawl on the back. "April 22nd, three years ago. In Cali."

I got out my phone, opened Black's calendar, and flicked back in time. Sloane was meticulous about keeping our diaries up to date. "Okay, three years ago, on April 22nd, Black was...on a yacht. Off the coast of Somalia, with me, and I'd damn well have noticed if he'd skipped off to Colombia for a few days."

We'd been hunting pirates with me as the bait. We caught seven, plus I got a suntan and a fat cheque from the shipping company who hired us.

Marco voiced the question we were all thinking. "So, what the hell is going on?"

I had no answers. None at all. Just when I thought I'd relocated my brain after its absence in England, it took off again. "I just don't know. There must be two of them. One person couldn't be on two different continents at the same time."

"Maybe it's coincidence," Seb suggested. "They say everyone's got a double out there, don't they?"

My gut told me otherwise. "No way. This is connected to the drug trade somehow. I'm sure of it."

"Brothers, perhaps?"

"Black was an only child."

"Are you sure?"

"A secret brother? No way. He'd have told me." And even if he hadn't, I'd have found out for myself, nosy little bitch that I was. Stray paperwork, a whispered conversation... But I'd seen nothing.

"What if he didn't know?" Seb asked.

"I suppose it's possible, but how would that work?

Either Black's parents must have adopted him, or they gave up Carlos. He never had an inkling of either."

Eduardo had simmered down from earlier, and now he gripped my upper arms as he looked into my eyes. "I don't know either, angel, but we will find out."

I truly believed he'd do his best. But would it be enough? My life had been tilted on its axis once again, and I didn't know where to begin with unravelling this mystery.

"It feels like my whole life's falling to bits at the moment."

"We will fit the pieces together again. I promise you."

Eduardo gathered me up in his arms, holding me tight. My eyes prickled as he kissed my hair, telling me everything would be all right. Fucking hell, an assassin being comforted by a drug lord—how surreal had my world become?

A long minute passed before Eduardo let me go. "Let us rest. We will start our search for the truth in the morning."

"There's a friend who came with me, and he's staying at the Coralia. He's known Black longer than me."

"I will send a car for him tomorrow. Now, we sleep."

CHAPTER 12

SLEEP? THAT WAS all very well for Eduardo to say. I barely slept a wink that night. After a lengthy phone call to Nate where I updated him on the situation and found him as incredulous as me, I spent hours in my silver room tossing and turning.

Yes, silver.

After my flippant comment to Eduardo many years ago, he proudly showed me the room he'd redecorated just for me on my next visit. Everything was silver. Silver sheets, silver tiles in the bathroom, matt silver wardrobe with glossy silver accents. He'd even found a silver television. The room had been made-over several times since, usually when he had a change of wife, but the overwhelming theme was still fucking silver. I'd tried so hard to pretend I loved it.

I was still blinking from the glare coming off the furnishings when Nate arrived in the morning. A uniformed butler led him out onto the terrace where I was sitting with Eduardo, soaking up the first of the morning's rays. Nate eyed up the older man with suspicion, but Eduardo acted oblivious, greeting him with a handshake like they were old friends then offering him some pastries.

"They're Emmy's favourites. My chef makes them especially for her."

Nate perched on a dainty wrought iron chair and picked up one of the tiny morsels, clutching it between thumb and forefinger as if he wasn't quite sure whether it was safe to eat.

"It won't poison you," I told him, popping another one into my mouth.

He chewed his pastry slowly before a smile spread over his face.

"You're right; these are good." He helped himself to a couple more.

"So, about the whole Black/Carlos thing. Any ideas?"

"I've been racking my brain. I'm certain Black didn't know he had a brother, if that's what Carlos is, and looking at the photo of Carlos, I agree he's Black's double. But I didn't meet Black until three months after his parents died in that car crash, so I never saw the relationship between them first-hand. It was still pretty raw for him. If anyone brought up the accident, he shut down. Even years later, he never wanted to talk about them, not really. Did he ever say much to you?"

I shook my head. "Not about the accident. Occasionally he mentioned his life growing up. His mother doted on him, but he found it a bit stifling sometimes. His dad was pushy, I think, but fair. He was determined his son would make something of himself, not just sit around like a spoiled rich kid."

"Yeah, Black said he never dished out money."

"He made Black work for everything, but that left him with a lot of respect for his dad. That's why he followed in his footsteps into special forces."

"That's more or less what I got too."

I sighed. "So how do we find out more? His only

living relative is Miriam, and I'd rather pull out my own toenails with pliers than ask her for information. I doubt she knows much anyway—I got the impression from Black that his father hated her as much as everyone else does."

Nate stared off into space for a minute, pondering. "When he first joined the Navy, Black used to speak to one man. An old colleague of his father's. I think he was the one who pulled strings for Black to get into the Navy in the first place, even though he was technically too young. He might be worth tracking down."

"What's his name?" I asked.

"Arthur Stapleton."

"Black used to go and see him from time to time, and I tagged along occasionally. Arthur's old now, and I'm not sure his mind's what it once was."

"You game for a visit?"

"Sure." It wasn't like I had any better ideas.

"Where is he? Do you know?"

"In a retirement home in Maryland. He wanted to be near his daughter. Sloane will have the exact address —Black used to have her send gifts on the holidays."

"We'll see what these guys come up with today, and if things aren't moving, we'll go back and talk to Arthur."

Eduardo sent out anyone available to dig up whatever they could on Hector Ramos and his sons, Nate started digging through Blackwood's contacts, and I asked Mack to look at things from her end as well. By mid-morning, information started coming in.

Hector Ramos's name cropped up a number of times in DEA reports, which confirmed Eduardo's opinion that he wasn't a nice man. His rise up the ranks had been relatively recent. Until he murdered his boss seven years ago and took over his operation, he'd been floating on the periphery.

We'd found little mention of Carlos, but Hector's other son, Diego, appeared to be even more of a shit than his father. According to the Colombian authorities, Diego had been single-handedly responsible for the murder of over a hundred people, including a handful in the States. At the bottom of the list of his known acquaintances were the names of the men who'd killed Black.

We had to be on the right track, didn't we?

I became more certain of Hector Ramos's guilt when Luke sent over a police report from the previous year. The cops suspected two of his henchmen had blown up a rival's car with an RPG on the outskirts of Cali. Sound familiar?

Mack dredged up more photos of Carlos, and bloody hell, he looked like Black. He had a beard in every picture so I couldn't see the shape of his jaw, but the top half of his face was identical. My mind started wandering. What if Black got killed in a case of mistaken identity? Anyone seeing one without the other could be confused.

Then a crazy seed of hope sprouted in my chest. What if *I'd* been mistaken? What if Carlos had been in the car and not Black?

That stupid notion lasted about half an hour, until Marco returned in the early afternoon bursting with news.

"I talked with an office assistant who works for Ramos's lawyer. He told me everything I wanted to know for a couple of grams."

Good to hear the barter system was alive and snorting in Cali. "And?"

"The lawyer visits the estate every month to meet with Carlos. Always Carlos. The lawyer never speaks to anyone else because there's some sort of written agreement that says he's not allowed to. Carlos deals with the finance and legal sides of his family's business and insists that all meetings are held at his home."

"When was the most recent meeting?"

"Last Wednesday, out at the compound, as usual."

The last ember of hope in me fizzled out when Marco threw that bucket of water, and I struggled to keep my face neutral as he continued. I was not about to cry in front of him.

"My guy overheard the lawyer say Carlos is sharp as a tack. He's made some good investments over the years. A lot of the money is locked away, but Carlos has been releasing cash each month for a while now. The year before last, it was the other way around. He invested for the long term back then."

"Things change in the murky world of finance." Luckily my own portfolio was well balanced. "At least we know Carlos has been around recently."

"Yes, it seems that way. I will speak to more people this evening."

I felt bad for not doing more to help, but I was out of my depth here in Colombia. Kind of numb too. Just when I thought the pain of Black's death was starting to fade, a new revelation popped up and punched me in the face.

And as the sun began to set, Sebastien brought information as well.

"I tracked down a chemist who used to work for

Ramos."

"Used to? He got out alive?"

"Only because he has terminal cancer. He's on his death bed now, which is probably the only reason he agreed to speak to me."

I felt a flicker of guilt for disturbing a dying man, but I tamped it down. Needs must.

"What did he say about the levamisole?"

"Hector was very fond of it. Insisted it went in everything. The man worked for Ramos for almost a decade, poor *malparido*." Seb shook his head in disbelief. "He said Hector was closer to Diego. Treated him like the son he was, whereas Hector rarely saw Carlos and when he did, he ordered Carlos around like any other employee."

"Interesting family dynamic."

"Isn't it? Why would he favour one son over the other?"

That was a question neither of us could answer. Seb hoped to have more news over the coming days, but he didn't want to arouse suspicions with his questions, so progress wasn't going to be as fast as we'd like.

A fact I bemoaned to Nate in my room that evening.

"I just wish there was more we could do."

"Itchy trigger finger?"

"Something like that."

"Softly, softly, catchee monkey, Ems." He took a sip of the fancy drink Eduardo's butler had made him. "I'll admit, Eduardo isn't the threat I thought he'd be."

"I hate to say I told you so, but I did."

I couldn't help grinning, because who doesn't like being right? Nate only glared at me. Ouch.

"How about you stay here and work with the

Garcias, and I'll coordinate things in the US? I can stop off in Maryland on the way home to visit Arthur and see if he's able to shed any light on Black's childhood."

"You know I'm going to kill Ramos, right?"

"I wouldn't expect anything less of you." Nate slung an arm around my shoulders and squeezed. "And if it wasn't you, it would be me."

So I stayed in Colombia. After all, I was dead, and what better way to enjoy the afterlife than with good food and sunshine? It had the added advantage that if Ramos began to suspect I wasn't as lifeless as I made out, Eduardo's hacienda was the last place he'd imagine me hanging out.

When we told Eduardo of our plans, he just nodded. "You realise if we continue down this path, we will be starting a war?"

"No, Eduardo, we won't be starting a war. Ramos already started the war when he came out of nowhere and killed my husband. We'll be finishing a war."

"Good answer, my angel."

CHAPTER 13

AT LAST, WE were getting to the bottom of this whole mess. I was convinced of it. But the turmoil in my head? That still had a way to go. After overcoming my shock at finding Black's double, I tried to work out why the Ramos family wanted my husband dead in the first place.

"They probably thought Black was trying to put them out of business," Seb said as he watched me pacing from his position on a floral-print chaise longue, stretched out with his arms folded behind his head.

"But he'd barely got anywhere. I saw his notes."

"If they found out his reputation, they'd have been worried that would change."

"I guess." I dropped the rounds out of the revolver I'd borrowed from Eduardo, spun the chamber, and reloaded them. "Do you reckon they knew what he looked like? That he was Carlos's double?"

"If they did, perhaps they got worried he might muscle in on them. You know, imitate Carlos and get inside information or something."

"Black running a drugs empire?" I scoffed. "Like that would ever happen. No offence."

"Then they could have feared the opposite. Maybe they thought Black would take Carlos out to protect his own reputation?"

"That's crazy. They should have tried negotiating."

"Men like the Ramos family don't negotiate."

Didn't I know it? The whole situation made me feel sick. I cursed them under my breath for forcing me into this position.

"When we see them, perhaps we can ask why they did it," Seb suggested.

"I'm planning to."

I didn't have the network in South America that Eduardo did, so I was reliant on his team doing my legwork. At least by being in Colombia, I could speak freely with the Garcias, something that wasn't so easy from the United States due to Eduardo's paranoia that big brother constantly monitored everyone's phone calls.

Which, to be fair, he most likely did. The NSA was the only part of the government that actually listened to its citizens.

Snippets of information came in, and I set up an old-fashioned corkboard in one of Eduardo's many living rooms, pinning record cards on it in groups to try and arrange my thoughts. Nick got over his initial anger at me, probably because he was dead wrong about Eduardo even if he wouldn't openly admit it like Nate did, and we stayed in almost constant contact. He had an electronic version of my board in one of the operations rooms at Blackwood and added information to that from all the sources we could unearth.

Eduardo took care of me in his own special way. He realised how miserable I was and tried to cheer me up. And Eduardo's way of doing that involved spending money, stacks of it. His wives usually responded well to that approach, I gathered, and he didn't see why I should be any different.

His current wife, Floriana, was a tiny, quiet woman with surgically enhanced tits and impossibly white teeth, and he'd obviously sent her out shopping on my behalf. When I returned to my room that evening, I could barely get through the door from the amount of bags on the floor, and I counted no less than eighteen bunches of flowers spread all over the place.

Over dinner, which Alejandro turned into a work of art, Eduardo presented me with a tiara. A bloody tiara! What the hell was I supposed to do with that? If I ever happened to re-marry into royalty it might come in handy, but it wouldn't be much use while I scraped around in the jungle, would it? Unless I used it to dazzle the bad guys into submission.

Still, it was very sweet of him, and I appreciated the gesture. I felt a pang of jealousy for Camilla, completely irrational given that she wasn't even alive anymore. Why did I feel that way? Because her father cared so much he'd put her needs first, far above his own, even though she never knew him.

We had that much in common—my father wasn't part of my life either, although I doubted his motives were as noble as Eduardo's. My mother always claimed she didn't know who he was, but I'd never quite believed her. When I was a little girl, I used to fantasise that my daddy would come sweeping in to save me from whatever dingy squat we happened to be living in at the time and take me to live in a proper house. A home where I ate a hot meal every evening and he helped me with my schoolwork then read me a story before I went to sleep.

One day, I'd stupidly told my mother I hoped he'd

come back so we could be a real family. Big mistake. Huge. I choked on her cigarette smoke as she blew it in my face, and she laughed before she slayed me with her words. "You really are a stupid little cow, aren't you?"

Although I didn't get my fairy tale, I did get Eduardo, and also Jimmy, the ex-boxer who'd looked after me between the ages of fourteen and sixteen. So I hadn't done too badly, after all.

And now? Now I had a tiara.

The next day, Nate called mid-morning. Maryland was an hour ahead of Cali, and he'd just got out from visiting Arthur.

"The old guy's away with the fairies most of the time. He called me Caroline twice. But he seemed to have moments of lucidity, and if it's true, what he had to say was interesting."

"Go on."

"It seemed like he'd been waiting to get this off his chest for years. Either that or all the medication he's on loosened his tongue. Once he'd started talking, he wouldn't stop."

"Hurry up and tell me, would you?"

"Apparently the circumstances of Black's birth were a little unusual."

"In what way?"

"Well, John and Audrey Black were stationed in Colombia for a year before baby Black's arrival. John was a diplomat, but we all know enough about Black's father to understand there would have been more to his role than that."

"Colombia? Black never mentioned that."

"He probably didn't know. Anyhow, John asked for a six-month sabbatical rather suddenly, an unusual request according to Arthur, but John had enough clout for it to be granted. When he and Audrey sailed out of Cartagena on their yacht, they told Arthur they were heading back to Florida via the British Virgin Islands and the Bahamas. Five months later when they turned up in Naples, Charles was with them."

"Holy shit. So it's possible Black could have come from Colombia, and they smuggled him onto the boat with them?"

"John claimed Audrey didn't realise she was pregnant when they left Cartagena, and that she gave birth three months into the voyage. When Arthur first saw Charles, he was supposed to be two months old. But Arthur had kids himself, and he swore the baby was older than that."

"Which would fit with Black having been born in Colombia."

"Yes. Arthur said he didn't question it too much because of how happy John and Audrey were. They'd been trying for a baby for years, and Audrey miscarried at least four times. Arthur said the stress of it almost tore them apart."

"So, what? They stole a baby?"

"Stole it, bought it, came to some sort of arrangement with a surrogate. That's what Arthur reckoned, especially as Black got older. He shared his father's build and his mother's colouring, but he didn't look like either of them. Arthur kept his mouth shut because John and Audrey were his friends, and he could see Charles had a comfortable life. But now they're all dead, I think he was just glad to tell someone about it."

"If it's true, it answers some questions. Maybe he and Carlos Ramos really were twins, and for whatever reason, the Blacks took one baby and left the other. That would make Hector Ramos his dad." I shuddered. "What a horrible thought."

"Yeah, it defies belief someone who's spent his life fighting for good could have such a bastard for a father."

"And also that a father could kill his own son."

Nate shrugged. "The whole family's whacked though. There's probably something in the water down there."

"Or they believe in taste-testing their own products."

"That too."

I left Nate to travel back to Virginia and went to update Eduardo on the latest developments. He was as shocked as me at the news Hector Ramos might be Black's father.

"How could the man kill his child? His flesh and blood? That is like me shooting Sebastien or Marco."

"Well, clearly he's wired up wrong."

"I would rather put the gun in my own mouth."

Seb walked in, snacking on an empanada. "What did I miss?"

I told the story for the second time, but even as Seb shook his head, incredulous, he had a proposition for me.

"I have just heard Diego will be a guest at a party tonight. It's a fundraiser for a new drugs rehabilitation centre in the city. Would you like to go? I thought you might be interested to see him in person."

I tried not to laugh, but I couldn't stop one snort escaping. "Hang on. You're saying that you and Diego Ramos, representatives of two of the largest drug operations in the country, will be raising money to get people off drugs? For a moment there, I thought I misheard you."

"Hey, don't be so judgmental. Your politicians do exactly the same. They attend dinners and parties to raise money for victims of war, and then the next day they send more soldiers to create more wars. Besides, it is like your 'keeping up with the Joneses.' If one cartel attends, we all have to."

"I still think it's crackers."

"Tell me about it." Eduardo nodded his agreement. "I went to one of those dinners once, and I was seated opposite the head of the Medellin cartel. I had to be nice to him and his wife all evening. Then the next day we were involved in a shoot-out, twenty men on each side. I hit him in the arm." He sighed. "Those were the days."

"All right, I'll go. We can't get too close, though. He might recognise me."

"I doubt it," Seb said. "He thinks you're dead, and even if he didn't, the last place he'd expect to see you is on my arm."

I knew it was all too easy to miss things if you weren't looking for them. Seb was probably right.

Seb made the arrangements for the evening, and Floriana brought ten different dresses, all silver, all expensive.

"So you can choose your favourite," she said.

I discounted anything tight and picked out a halterneck gown with a strappy back and a full skirt so I had somewhere to hide my gun. Priorities. Floriana did my hair and make-up too, heavier than I'd normally wear and I nearly choked on the hairspray, but it looked all right. And what do you know? There *was* a use for that tiara.

I'd been to fundraising dinners the world over, and the one in Colombia wasn't any different. I plastered on a smile and balanced on my stilettos while Seb whispered "doctor," "lawyer," "drug dealer," "drug dealer," "politician," "drug dealer" as we worked our way through the crowd. The bambuco band playing away in the corner looked as bored as I felt, but at least they were getting paid to be there. A waiter swept past, holding aloft a tray of champagne, and I stared longingly at it before taking another sip of my orange juice. Vitamin C made a poor substitute for alcohol on an evening like this.

Half an hour after we walked in, Seb nudged me and cut his eyes towards the door. "Diego."

Ramos junior stood shorter than I'd imagined, about five feet seven, and sported a bit of a potbelly. The living Barbie doll at his side would have towered over him even if she wasn't wearing five-inch heels. Someone needed to give him a box to stand on.

He headed clockwise around the room while Seb and I went the other direction, and eventually, our paths crossed. The little toad shook hands with Seb then looked me up and down, his gaze lingering on my chest. Good. While he stared at my tits, he wasn't paying attention to my face.

Seb introduced me out of politeness. "This is Maria."

Diego stepped forward to kiss my cheek, and I leaned back slightly, holding out my hand instead. My fingernails jabbed him in the chest. Oops. He looked surprised but shook, his hand clammy.

"Diego Garcia," he told my cleavage. "Delighted to meet you, Maria."

"The pleasure's all mine, Diego," I replied in Spanish after I'd managed to un-grit my teeth.

Unfortunately, Seb had made me leave my gun in the car and when I denied having any other weapons, he'd patted me down and pocketed the knife I'd hidden in my bra. Arsehole. Even so, I considered strangling the man in front of me with my bare hands—the right angle, a little leverage, and I could snap his neck like a chicken. Actually, not quite like a chicken. I'd feel remorse over the bird. Diego, not so much.

He kept talking, his serpent-like tongue darting out to moisten his little sausage lips. I was tempted to cut it out, or better still, make him wear it as a Colombian necktie. It was important to preserve local traditions, was it not? Perhaps Eduardo could give me some tips.

"This is Lucia," he said, introducing the bored-looking blonde.

Oh, right, this was the part where I was supposed to be nice. I managed a grimace that might have passed for a smile and shook backwards-Barbie's proffered hand.

Seb took over the conversation and went through the full repertoire of bullshit—business, the weather, tourism, the usual. Finally, he got to the good bit. "Your brother didn't come tonight, then?"

I held my breath, waiting for the answer. Where was that fucker?

"No, Carlos stayed behind. He had things to do."

Maybe a bombing, shooting, last-minute execution, something like that. Still, at least Diego had confirmed his whereabouts.

"And give my best to your father. Is he busy too?"

"He's also at home." Diego patted his stomach. "Food poisoning. He ate some bad shellfish a couple of days ago."

Aw, my heart bled for him. I hoped he shat himself to death.

Lucia interrupted to ask where I got my shoes, and by the time I'd lied and told her I got them shipped in from Paris just for the occasion, Diego was turning away to talk to the next couple. Dammit.

We hung around for another hour or so, watching Diego until he left. Seb managed to win a deep-sea fishing trip for two in the charity auction before we went back home ourselves.

"Do you like fishing?" I asked as we drove off.

"I don't even like fish."

"Why the hell did you bid for a fishing trip, then?"

"I felt I should put something back into the community."

In addition to an endless supply of coke, obviously. How selfless. Don't get me wrong, I liked Seb, but the whole thing was so two-faced it left me cold.

I wanted to reply "How very noble of you," but I bit back the sarcasm. "At least we know where Carlos and Hector are."

"Yes, and the old *cabron* is ill, even better. What did you think of Diego?"

"Arrogant. Short." Dead.

Seb laughed. "You've summed him up perfectly."

As soon as we got back to Eduardo's estate, I kicked my heels off gratefully before slipping out of my dress and between my silver sheets to get some sleep. I needed a clear head the next day.

Why?

Because tomorrow I'd start planning in earnest how to make Colombia a Ramos-free zone.

CHAPTER 14

ALEJANDRO SERVED BREAKFAST early on the terrace, and as I nibbled a slice of melon, I watched in fascination as a hummingbird buzzed around the fragrant vines that trailed over Eduardo's pergola. A servant tried to present me with another plate of pastries, but I waved them away.

"You don't like those?" Eduardo asked.

"They're delicious, but I'm getting fat."

"I don't need to find a new chef, then?"

"No! The one you've got is great." *Please, don't shoot him.* I hastily changed the subject. "Do you know where Ramos lives?"

"His compound is much like mine, except it's not so easy to get to."

"Not so easy to get to" turned out to be an understatement. The Ramos family home was buried deep in the jungle, around a hundred and twenty miles as the crow, or rather the helicopter, flew from casa Garcia.

Eduardo described the location to the best of his knowledge, and Agent Belcourt and the DEA added their two cents worth. They knew what we were planning, and while the agency couldn't openly condone it, Belcourt promised they'd buy us all beers if we pulled it off. Then Jed cajoled his buddies at the CIA into making a satellite pass for me, which provided Mack with a detailed set of high-resolution photographs.

They were well worth the Superbowl tickets they cost me.

For the next few days, I spent the mornings training and the afternoons planning. Training consisted of gym sessions, running around the trails on Eduardo's estate, martial arts drills, shooting, and throwing. Throwing was a skill that shouldn't be neglected. When I hurled a knife at my enemy or tossed a gun to a colleague, I needed to know it would reach its target.

Seb, Marco, and their core team started joining in with my training sessions. They got frustrated at first because they got outperformed by a girl, but it did make them up their game. In truth, they weren't bad, but they'd got lax because they didn't push themselves regularly like I did. Alex yelling via a satellite link did us all good. The following week, as we got closer to action, I picked my team for the assault on the Ramos compound.

Some choices were straightforward.

Nick and Dan were obvious. Both were in excellent physical condition, Nick had extensive combat history, and Dan had street smarts. Not to mention we'd spent so many years working together we could read each other's thoughts. Plus I wanted Logan and Evan. I knew how Logan worked and trusted him, and Evan's stint in the army gave him plenty of experience with jungle-based operations.

Other choices were harder. I agonised over Nate, Mack, and Carmen. We needed an electronics specialist on site, which meant Nate or Mack. Ideally, I'd have

Nate, as he had far more field experience than Mack. But we also needed a sniper, and Carmen was the best. My problem was Josh, Nate and Carmen's son. If this job went wrong, as so many things in my life had tended to do lately, I didn't want to leave him an orphan. Which left me with Mack and Carmen.

Jed was another question mark. He'd only just got the cast off his leg, but since the attack on the house, he'd split his days between the gym and the shooting range. Alex said he'd worked hard on the weights, but his cardio had been limited. The doctor may have given him a clean bill of health, but was that enough? Would I rather have Jed at eighty-five percent or someone else fitter who might not have Jed's training and ability?

In total, I needed twelve people from Blackwood plus a sniper. Seb and Marco were bringing another half dozen men with them, which took our numbers up to twenty-one. We'd worked on the assumption Ramos would have a similar setup to Eduardo regarding staffing, and Eduardo had at least sixty people on his estate at all times once you added in the domestic staff and the guards. The servants might not be trained soldiers, but they were still capable of picking up a gun and shooting somebody if the need arose.

I'd quit drinking by that point, so Seb and I sat down with glasses of mango juice to deliberate over our final team.

"I've got my six," Seb said. "Are you any closer to a decision?"

"Eight definites, including me." I'd added Alex to my list too. "And I think I'm just about there on the extras." I ticked them off on my fingers. "Jack, Malachi, and Gage are all ex-army, and Isaiah's a trained medic as well as being a sneaky bastard."

"That leaves one."

"Jed. It's got to be Jed."

From the satellite photos, we saw the Ramos estate covered an area of about twenty acres, a large clearing blasted out of the rainforest. In addition to the main house, there were numerous outbuildings, and the whole place was surrounded by the dense undergrowth typical of the region.

Access was via an unpaved road that twisted its way through the forest from the nearest settlement fifteen miles away. As well as that, a small grass airstrip ran along one side of the property, and Seb's sources said Diego was a keen pilot.

Nate set up a video link so I could brief everyone stateside. I felt a bit under-equipped sitting in Eduardo's chintzy lounge while they were surrounded by state-of-the-art technology, but needs must. At least Eduardo had found me some decent guns by then. We ran through the outline of my plan, the team selection, and each person's role. In a couple of days, the guys from Blackwood would fly over to Colombia to join me, and I'd made a list of equipment for them to bring.

"Where are we landing the jet?" Nick asked.

"Eduardo's arranged for us to borrow the private airstrip he uses."

"Is that going to cause us a problem with our luggage?"

Eduardo spoke up from his place at my side. "The staff will turn a blind eye as long as we've paid the landing fee."

"Are you sure?"

"*Hermano*, nobody's worried about anything being

smuggled *into* Colombia."

So the preliminaries were sorted, right?

Wrong.

The day after the briefing, Nate called while I was in the gym. "Carmen and I had a discussion last night."

For "discussion" I heard "argument."

"And?"

"I'm coming instead of Mack. I've got more experience at this type of operation in that type of terrain."

A minor setback but not an entirely unexpected one. Nobody could shoot like Carmen, but if I had Nate, he'd be able to fight dirty at the compound as well as just sorting out the electronics.

"I'll find another sniper to replace Carmen. You know it was a decision I agonised over in the first place. What do you think of Slater?"

"Well, here's the thing. Carmen's also coming. She refuses to stay behind and, quote, let me have all the fun."

"What about Josh?"

"Bradley's going to look after him while we're away. I understand your thinking but, Emmy, neither of us plans on dying."

"Is there anything I can do to change your mind?"

"No."

"In that case, I hold no responsibility when Josh comes back from Bradley wearing a pair of pink skinny jeans and a faux-hawk."

Despite my worries, I was secretly happy to have

both of them coming. I loosened up inside a little knowing that Nate would be next to me when we went into the compound. Out of everyone at Blackwood, I'd known him the longest, and I trusted him to get the job done.

The team showed up two days later, and we spent the next fortnight researching, planning, rehearsing, and training. Or in more normal language, cursing, sweating, suffering, and aching

Midway through the first week, Nate and I took a trip out to the Ramos compound, trekking through the dense rainforest from the next valley. Just going a couple of miles took most of the day.

"I hate the fucking jungle," I muttered as I clambered over a slippery log.

Ahead of me, Nate hacked at a clump of tough, leathery vines with a machete. "We're on the same page."

It wasn't like in the movies where the hero and heroine skipped down a mossy path while birds chattered happily in the trees. Here, it was an impenetrable wall of green. Everything had to be either skirted around, climbed over, or chopped through, which in thirty-degree heat and high humidity wasn't fun, let me tell you.

Add in assorted wild animals to watch out for and nasty flying things that bit any piece of exposed skin they could get their jaws into, and you get the picture. After slipping off an algae-covered rock into a pool of fetid water, I found myself wondering what the hell I was doing there. And, fuck it, I'd just trodden in monkey shit.

Why didn't I just retire? I could sit at a country club sipping drinks with the occasional game of tennis thrown in for fun, instead of crawling through rotting vegetation on my way to dance with death while getting dive-bombed by a squadron of angry mosquitos.

Because I owed it to Black. That was why.

I slapped another of the little bloodsuckers away and got on with it.

At least perimeter security at the compound wasn't up to much, just a flimsy chain-link fence and a few pairs of armed guards on patrol. I threw a handful of dirt at the fence and waited. Nothing. No alarms went off, no troops came running.

"Much easier than Syria," I muttered, recalling the trip I'd made out there not so long ago.

We hunkered down in a tangle of bushes and waited. And waited. And waited. Nate glanced at his watch as the guards sauntered past again.

"It's been an hour since the last pair," he said.

They didn't even look alert. The two of them smoked and laughed, guns slung over their backs rather than at the ready, clearly not expecting anybody to be stupid enough to come through the jungle.

After the guards had been past once more, confirming our suspicions they were on an hourly schedule, we snuck around to the entrance. Security there was better. A metal barrier spanned the drive, five feet high, manned by a team of four guards who sheltered from the early afternoon sun in a brick hut. The good news was they looked bored out of their minds, more interested in watching television than checking for an imminent attack.

"Doesn't seem like they're expecting us, does it?" I whispered to Nate.

"No. I'm not sure whether to be pleased or concerned."

"It's about time we got a break."

Altogether, we counted ten guards patrolling, which with the four game show fans, made fourteen.

"Two shifts or three?" Nate mused.

"I'd go with three. Eduardo reckons that's standard."

"So there's another twenty-eight foot soldiers somewhere."

"Plus more in the house, I'm betting." I did a bit of adding up. "I reckon forty-five to fifty men."

"Probably about right." Nate jerked his head forward. "And don't forget the ladies."

I trained my binoculars on a dour-faced woman collecting washing from a line and folding it into a basket. A nervous-looking girl scurried up to her carrying a tray of food. She said a few words, frowned, then moved on. From her facial features, I guessed she was Japanese, and although her baggy dress came to her feet, there was no hiding her swollen belly.

"Who would want to have a baby in a place like this?" I muttered.

"Wonder what she's doing here? Everyone else looks native."

I stiffened as Diego walked out of the main building. The two-storey stucco-covered villa looked alien in the jungle setting with ornamental stone dragons either side of the front door and a trio of large-breasted ladies forming the centrepiece of an ornamental fountain. Who thought that was classy? And no, you don't want to know where the water was coming from.

Diego looked at ease in a pair of board shorts and flip-flops, a far cry from the suit I'd seen him in at the party. I couldn't see a weapon on him, but to wear that outfit, he must have been doused in mosquito repellent. Or maybe they just found him as repulsive as I did? He scratched his balls as he wandered across the courtyard to chat with a guard on the other side. Delightful.

I'd hoped to see Carlos, but there was no sign of him. Curiosity ate away at me. Would he look as much like Black in person as he did in the photos? Would he walk like him? Talk like him? I hadn't told Nate of my plans to have a little chat with Carlos when we stormed the place. Before I killed him, that was.

We didn't see Hector, either, and after a day of skulking around, we figured he was either holed up in the main building or somewhere off-site. I'd taken hundreds of photos, and Nate had put together a rough map of the compound, adding little details that the satellite photos couldn't give us like the guards' patrol routes and the most frequently used doors.

As dusk fell, we backtracked out the way we came, and the trek back was slightly easier as we were more familiar with the terrain. The RIB we'd motored down the river in was still exactly where we'd left it in the next valley over, moored to a sturdy tree and hidden under camouflage netting.

"I was thinking we'd come in the same way for the actual operation," I said.

"Makes sense. We know we can do it now."

"Then we spread out around the compound and

come at them from all angles. I want to hit the place hard and fast, take out as many men as possible before they realise what's happening."

"And leaving? You're sticking with the choppers?"

"I don't think there's a better option."

Eduardo had offered a pair of ex-military Hueys to pick us up at a pre-appointed time and fly us straight back to his place. It wouldn't matter about the noise at that point, and I wanted to get clear of the area fast.

I also had to plan for the worst. If anyone got hurt, speed would be of the essence. A trek through the jungle or a bumpy road trip would lessen a casualty's chance of survival if their injury was serious. Helicopters were definitely the way to go.

Once we got back to Eduardo's place, Nate and I updated everybody on what we'd found. As pictures of the Ramos's jungle lair and the main players popped up on the projector Eduardo found for us, the operation became real.

"I'll send a couple of men to watch the road in and out," Seb said. "That way we can see who comes and goes."

"That's the biggest unknown." And my biggest fear, put into words. "I want to get all three of the Ramos clan. Hector, Diego, Carlos. I don't think I need to explain how much difficulty we'll be in if any of them escape."

And people in that line of business would always have an escape plan. If they went to ground, it could be weeks, months even, before we found them.

"They may try to fly out when we attack," Nate said. "Our first priority is to disable anything in the hanger."

"Agreed."

We'd taken a look inside a few of the buildings while we were there. The one next to the airstrip contained a single-engine prop-plane, but more concerning were the two empty spaces next to it. I guessed there was another plane or two around, or maybe a helicopter. Possibly a boat too, since the river was nearby. Drug money bought a lot of toys.

We spent most of the night formulating our plan, and the resolve hardened on my team's faces as we assigned tasks and hashed out the details. We *would* win this thing, no matter what.

CHAPTER 15

THE BIG MOMENT finally arrived.

For the past few days, Team Blackwood had run, jumped, shot, and fought with Seb's men. With Eduardo's blessing, we'd taken over his guesthouse and practised clearing it, room by room, until we could anticipate each other's reactions. Finally, after one last drill, I felt we were ready.

The atmosphere hummed with tension as we checked our gear and loaded it onto the helicopters, but there were no raised voices, no short tempers. My guys were professionals.

The two boats were already stowed in pods underneath for transport to the drop-off point. We'd inflate them on-site and carry them into the water. I went over the schedule one more time with the pilots then made them repeat it back to me to check they were clear on what they needed to do.

Yesterday evening, we'd eaten our last meal as a team. No matter what happened, it would be our final night together at Eduardo's, and as I watched the guys bonding over non-alcoholic drinks, I knew those ties would carry over to the battlefield. As the evening wore on, a nervous energy permeated the air. I'd known that same feeling a hundred times over, except this mission meant more to me than any other.

This time, I wanted revenge, plain and simple.

I woke an hour earlier than I needed to, but I didn't stand a chance of getting back to sleep. Instead, I kept myself busy by checking my kit again, even though I'd already unpacked and re-packed it half a dozen times.

Camouflage-clad men showed up at the appointed time, lounging around on the dainty gilt furniture in Eduardo's family room while we waited to depart. The man himself strode past every so often, tapping his cane, making sure his men were doing everything as instructed.

The launch site for the boats lay a hundred and thirty miles away, and from there, we'd have a ten-mile ride before the trek to the compound. While we wreaked havoc, the helicopters would wait at an abandoned airstrip five miles from our pick-up point. Evan and Nick had scouted it out with a couple of Eduardo's men, and it was the safest place we could find.

Flying conservatively, the tanks on the helicopters gave us a range of three hundred miles—with the flight out, the shuttle to the airfield, and the flight back, there wouldn't be any spare fuel for them to spend time circling. Our timing on this operation had to be perfect. *Everything* had to be perfect. Diego, Carlos, and Hector's deaths depended on it.

"Ready to go?" Nate asked.

"In a minute."

Before leaving, I stopped to speak to Eduardo. He'd come through in my darkest hour and done more than I could ever have asked. I took his hands in mine.

"I need to thank you for everything you've done for us."

"Angel, I've known you for ten years now, and you brought a light I thought had been extinguished forever into the life of an old man. Anything that is in my power to give you is yours."

I wasn't going to cry, dammit. I resisted the sniffle that threatened to escape. "Eduardo, I don't know what to say, other than I'll try to help you in any way I can as well."

"You already are, angel, by removing Ramos from the scene. I cannot claim my motives are entirely selfless."

I hugged him, and he leaned back to look at my neck. Fair enough—it wasn't every day I accessorised for combat with diamonds.

"You're wearing my gift?"

"I know it seems silly, but it makes me think of you, and of Black, and reminds me why I'm about to put myself through this fresh hell instead of taking a nice holiday to Bora Bora."

"It also symbolises that you will get through this, and you *will* come back. I'll see you tomorrow."

With that, Eduardo turned and walked away, leaving me to board the helicopter to hell.

The journey to the drop point went smoothly, and we motored down the murky but calm waters without any problems. The crocodiles sunning themselves on the bank paid us no heed, and nothing leaked. Good start. We tied the boats up at our landing point, transferred all our gear onto dry land, then camouflaged the hulls. Oddly, the lack of issues concerned me. According to Murphy's Law, something would always go wrong, and I preferred to get the inevitable over with at the beginning of a job rather than later on.

Just as I'd had that thought, Felipe, one of Seb's men, fell into the river. I breathed a sigh of relief, then felt bad about that, then relaxed when Seb fished him out before he got nibbled by any piranhas.

Our schlep through the jungle was a little easier than the previous week because Nate and I had already cut through some of the undergrowth. Easier but not faster, since we needed to travel quietly. Moving twenty-one people through dense foliage in silence wasn't straightforward, especially when they were carrying enough equipment to stage a coup in a small country.

As we neared the compound, the time came to split up into five teams of four. Carmen would be on her own, doing what she did best.

"Stay safe, hotshot," Nate whispered, giving her a kiss goodbye.

"You too."

As their fingertips parted, she melted into the greenery beside us, and after a few seconds, she'd disappeared from sight.

Our plan called for her to climb a nearby hill to give her an elevated position. We'd selected the location to give her line-of-sight over most of the compound while still having excellent cover. Not that she was easy to spot. When she'd tried out her ghillie suit the day before yesterday, I'd almost tripped over her.

Next, we split into our sub-teams. A week ago when Nate asked who I wanted with me, I hadn't hesitated in my answer. Dan and I had been finishing each other's sentences for a decade, and Nick had proven countless times over the years that he'd got my back. Jed made up the fourth corner of our group, and I was glad to have the son of a bitch on my side. His leg seemed to be holding up, or at least if he was in pain, he refused to admit it.

Slowly, slowly, we got closer to our target, the only sound around us the incessant buzz of mosquitos and the occasional cry of something louder. Bradley, ever the helpful one, had taken great delight in telling me about the spectacled bears and jaguars that lived in the area.

"And the golden poison frogs, don't forget those," he'd said, looking up from his iPad. "They're quite rare, though."

"Enough, Bradley."

Although the frogs were cute—I had an old friend who used to keep a couple as pets.

Once we got within fifty metres of the compound, we found a hidden hollow between two trees and hunkered down for the night under ponchos. We'd attack as dawn broke. Why dawn? Firstly, because we'd have enough light to see by, and secondly, it meant the people inside the compound would be sleepy and at their most vulnerable.

One by one, the other four teams confirmed they were in position, and while we'd been fighting through the jungle, the pilots had radioed to say they'd landed safely. The last person to call through was Carmen.

"Good to go," she said.

"How's the view?"

"Could be better. One of the guards took a leak, and let me tell you, Mickey Mouse boxer shorts are not a good look on any man."

"With you there."

Nate had designed an excellent communications system, which allowed us to talk with Mack and Luke as clearly as if they were standing next to us. They'd be keeping an eye on things electronically throughout the operation, monitoring internet and phone traffic and checking on our eye in the sky from the safety of the control room at Riverley Hall.

"Everything was quiet on the latest satellite pass," Mack told us. "No noticeable activity on the road in."

Apparently, I was now providing the staff in the CIA communications department with corporate hospitality at the Superbowl as well as just seats.

As daylight faded into dusk, we took it in turns to rest, with one pair getting some shut-eye while the other two watched the shadows.

"I'm taking the opposite shift to you," Nick told me. "At least if I'm awake while you're asleep, I stand a fighting chance."

I got where he was coming from, but for all Nick's worries, I had no trouble sleeping soundly in the middle of the jungle. Even with water dripping onto me and the noises of wild animals in close proximity, my subconscious understood I needed to recharge so I could function in the required manner. It was a question of some deeply buried survival instinct kicking in.

I took the final watch with Jed, and we huddled together to keep warm, sharing our ponchos. *Tick, tick, tick.* I itched to get started, because the sooner we did our thing, the sooner the Ramos family would be shaking hands with Lucifer and complaining about the temperature.

Seb's men, the ones watching the movements in

and out of the compound, had reported Diego's return early yesterday afternoon while we were floating down the river. They'd got a good look at him as he slowed his Ferrari to a snail's pace to navigate the potholes. Hector had ploughed through in a Land Rover the day before that, smoking a suspicious-looking cigarette with his comb-over flapping in the breeze that came through the open window. Those photos had arrived by email before we left, so at least I knew who I had to kill.

Neither of them had driven back out, so unless they'd gone by air, they were still inside.

The big unknown was Carlos. In all our surveillance, all our digging, we hadn't seen any sign of him. Where was he? Eduardo's sources agreed he was reclusive, but the lack of confirmation left me twitchy. The only person we'd been able to find who'd seen him in recent months was his lawyer. And Diego, of course. Thanks to him, we knew his brother was home on the night of the fundraiser. I just hoped Carlos hadn't got a sudden urge to take a skiing holiday or something equally irritating.

But as I sat on the spongy floor of the rainforest, listening to the chatter of the monkeys above, I vowed he'd die no matter what. If I didn't get the bastard today, I'd hunt him to the ends of the earth until I pushed him right off it.

When the moon punched out and the first shards of sunlight filtered through the jungle canopy overhead, we assembled our equipment.

"Very Lara Croft," Jed whispered, patting me on the

arse.

Hey, so I liked my thigh holsters. They were comfortable, okay?

"Fancy going treasure hunting when this is over?"

This time, his hand lingered on my backside. "I already know where the treasure is."

"Manslut."

Okay, time for a radio check. Each team was designated a colour to keep things anonymous in case anybody managed to cut in on our communications.

"Team Black, ready," I whispered, trying to smooth out the catch in my voice.

Nate's voice came from his position to the north, his tone businesslike. "Team Red, ready."

He was mirrored by Seb in the south. "Team Green, ready."

"Team Blue, ready." Jack's guys in the west were good to go. They'd be checking the aircraft hangar first.

Marco's grey team checked in, then the pilots waiting five miles out confirmed, "Orange, ready."

Finally, Carmen let us know she was with us. "Pink, ready." Of course she was pink. Carmen was always pink.

Like wraiths circling the underworld, we crept forward, stopping just short of the tree line. Our first task was to take out the roving patrols, silently if possible. According to the schedule they stupidly kept to, they were due any minute now.

Right on time, a pair of them strolled past. Their guns were safely in their holsters as they chattered away in Spanish, comparing the quality of the output on two pay-per-view adult channels. They didn't notice when Nick and I fell into step behind them.

"No, those ones, they are too artificial," the shorter of the two guards said. "The ones on 308, yes they are smaller, but also more bouncy."

He put his hands to his chest to emphasise his point just as I snapped his neck. I winced at the pop as he crumpled to the ground.

Beside me, Nick had done the same with his target. We grabbed their arms, and Dan and Jed gave us a hand with the feet as we hid them in the undergrowth. The creatures that inhabited it would be spoiled for choice tonight. I planned to provide them with a veritable buffet.

So far, so good.

"Red, clear. Does anyone know how to get bloodstains out of nylon?" came Nate's dulcet tones.

"Blue, clear. Proceeding to the first objective."

It was at that moment Mr. Murphy made his second appearance, and I heard the unmistakable *pew-pew-pew* of an automatic weapon from the south.

Oh, shit.

It didn't last long, but the damage had been done. As Seb announced, "Green, clear," my team was already on its way to the villa.

We moved from cover to cover, zig-zagging stealthily across the compound. Twenty seconds passed, then Nick and I shrank back behind a storage tank as the front door burst open and four men shot out, waving guns.

In the way we'd practised, Nick and I took two each, then Dan and Jed ran forward and we stacked up outside the door. We'd rehearsed this so many times it was instinctive—we had a building at Blackwood built especially for the purpose. The first person would go through the door and break left, the second person broke right, the third went left, the fourth right. We hugged the walls, forcing our targets into the centre of the room so we didn't take each other out with friendly fire. We kept moving. If we stopped moving, we were dead. We trained until our movements flowed like water down the Amazon, a deadly dance, choreographed to perfection.

And now it was time for our main performance.

CHAPTER 16

INSIDE, THE HOUSE seemed bigger than it did from the outside. I barely took in the decor as we swept through each room, but it was obvious even from a glance where the Ramos family spent a good chunk of their income. The place made Eduardo's villa look tasteful.

We met little resistance as we prowled through the bottom floor. All the fun was going on outside, where the high-velocity rounds from Carmen's rifle broke through the crackle of small arms fire.

A muttered, "Bitch" came over the radio.

"What's up?" I asked Nate. His team had cleared the gatehouse and come in through the other end of the villa.

"That old woman we saw threw a rolling pin at me."

I stifled a laugh and ducked into a doorway as a dude in pyjamas ran past, carrying an AK-47. He pitched forward as I put a bullet through the back of his head, coming to rest spread-eagled across a Queen Anne-style armchair upholstered in blue leather. I got more relaxed about my "don't shoot anyone from behind" rule when I was on holiday.

Nick paused next to me and jerked his head towards the stairs. I nodded my agreement. As we got halfway to them, a muffled *boom* shook the house, originating from the opposite end. Nick glanced at me, and Nate quickly came on the radio to confirm his team was okay. I shrugged and carried on walking.

"Keep going. We haven't come this far to give up now."

It was the right decision.

We found Hector Ramos in his bedroom, crouched in front of a safe, stuffing paperwork into a duffel bag.

His eyes widened as he saw us, and he reached for the gun on the floor next to him. *Nice try, estúpido.* I shot it out of his hand before he got it halfway up. A couple of fingers went with it. The bullet kept going through his balcony window, and the acrid smell of smoke drifted in through the hole the shattered glass left behind.

Under normal circumstances, I'd have been professional and just killed the bastard, but this was too personal. I stalked over to him, leaving Nick to watch the door. Hector collapsed back on the bed, clutching his hand and muttering curses. What a drama queen.

I stopped out of arm's reach and looked down at him. "Why?"

A fleeting flash of recognition lit his eyes, but after calling me a *puta loca*, which I took as a compliment, he fell silent. So I shot him in the foot.

"I said, why? Why did you kill Charles Black?"

He let out a howl of agony before fixing his gaze on me. "I don't know what you're talking about."

Did he think I was stupid? His knee went next.

"All that time you thought I wouldn't bite back? Well, I was just sharpening my teeth."

He simply glared.

"And then you tried to kill me. Do you have a death wish?"

Oh, if looks could kill... But they couldn't, and he clenched his jaw in an attempt to control the pain.

"Why didn't you stay out of our business?" he asked. "I warned you enough times. You left us no choice."

"I didn't even know I was in your business, you idiot. Your threats were so vague, I had no idea what I could and couldn't do. Then you were dumb enough to send fourteen men to my home. Fourteen! You might as well have shot them yourself and saved the airfares. Put that together with killing my husband in front of me, and you know as well as I do I couldn't let that go. And my question is why?"

His face hardened, and I was about to shoot him in the other knee when he started laughing. "You'll never know." He laughed harder, as if it was the funniest thing he'd ever heard. "You'll. Never. Know."

Sod the knee. I shot him between the eyes, the brain spatter vastly improving the appearance of his ugly ass bedspread. Parrots were so last year.

Nick stared at me as I gathered up the papers that were so important to Ramos and stuffed them into my rucksack.

"Don't look at me like that. He deserved it." I had a quick poke around in the open safe. The rest was all cash and drugs, and I didn't care about either.

"Poor bastard didn't know what he was up against."

"I'm the black fucking widow, Nicky." I finished rummaging and straightened up. "Chop chop, no time to waste. We still have two Ramos brothers to find."

He shook his head and followed me out, informing

the rest of the team over the radio of Hector's not-so-sad demise.

We didn't see another soul in the house, at least until we reached the lounge. There, we found Dan slumped in an armchair with a pistol in her hand as Jed bandaged up her leg. Blood oozed through the dressing as he twisted the tourniquet tighter.

"What happened?"

He pointed at a dead guy sprawled across the floor, an assault rifle lying out of reach beyond him.

"That guy came out of nowhere and hit Dan before we could get him."

"How bad is it?"

"The bullet missed the bone and artery, but it's still bleeding like a bitch."

"Okay, look after her. We won't be too much longer."

Nick and I made a last check around the north end of the building. The south wing was nicely ablaze, and smoke rolled into the air, darkening the rising sun. Where were the two Ramos brothers? An eerie quiet had descended over the compound, the loudest sound the crackle of the building flames.

My radio burst into life and Alex's voice came into my ear, as steady as if he was out for an afternoon stroll.

"I asked one of these assholes where our remaining two targets were."

This was Alex. For "asked," read "tortured until he told me."

"And?"

"Diego flew off in his helicopter yesterday evening, destination unknown."

"There was no helicopter in the hanger," Jack put in.

Marvellous. "And Carlos?"

"*Mudak* claimed he hadn't seen Carlos for months."

What? Diego said Carlos was home just a few days ago. "That can't be right."

"I tried a second one. He bled out quicker, but the result was the same. Diego told him Carlos moved out."

What the fuck was going on? I wanted to kick something. With steel toecaps. All this time and effort, and we were missing two of the main men.

As the team exited, one at a time, staying low, I glanced at the far end of the building and saw the flames spreading, window by window. There was poetic justice in that, with Hector about to be cremated as Black had been.

I cursed as I took in the wreckage of the compound. There wasn't any more we could do there, and with the state of Dan's leg, I didn't want to hang around. Felipe, who seemed to be having most of the bad luck, had also been shot in the shoulder.

"I'm calling the choppers in," I told everyone. "We leave as soon as they arrive."

Team Blackwood had survived mostly intact. One Ramos was down, and we could regroup and come back at the remaining two. The trip hadn't been an entire disaster, but that still didn't stop me from feeling utterly pissed off.

While we waited, the uninjured swept through the buildings one last time, apart from the burning ones, obviously. We found nothing. If men had gone to ground, we'd never find them now. Our plan had called for the element of surprise, for us to hit them before they had time to think about hiding. Six steps into the jungle and they'd be invisible.

The *thwap-thwap-thwap* of approaching rotor blades sounded over the tree line, and I looked up to confirm it was our two Hueys approaching. Yep, right on time.

Nick and Jed picked up Dan and carried her to the nearest helicopter. She'd barely murmured, but her face contorted in pain. I took one final, lingering look around before I followed them, my eyes pausing on the doorway of the house. Hector's funeral pyre. His mausoleum. A monument to the dead.

Or was it? A shadow darted across in the haze.

Were my eyes playing tricks?

I kept watching, and nothing moved but the smoke, but my inner nemesis wouldn't let me take any chances. If there was someone left alive, I wanted to know who.

"I'm going back in."

"We don't have time for this," Nate told me, and of course I ignored him.

Radio chatter came across the airwaves as the first Huey closed its doors and took off with both of the injured on board, then Mack's voice sounded, loud and clear.

"Eduardo's got a doctor waiting for Dan and Felipe."

At least that was one problem solved. I preferred to avoid visiting the local hospital if it could be helped. The bribery system was more complicated over here, and I wasn't sure I'd find anyone as tame as Dr. Beech.

Now, about that shadow...

I'd got as far as the lounge when I sensed

movement behind me and whirled around, gun up. I'd been right; I wasn't alone.

The Asian woman Nate and I had seen on our first trip to the compound stood by a hideous painting of a donkey. When she saw the gun, she threw her hands up and sank to the floor, pleading with me in high-pitched Spanish not to shoot.

The sound of gunfire outside interrupted her, closely followed by Nick shouting in my ear to hurry the fuck up.

What was I supposed to do? Leave her there? She didn't seem to be a threat, and hell, she was pregnant. I took hold of her arm and started pulling her towards the door. In turn, she grabbed my wrist, dug her heels in, and tried to tug me back in the opposite direction, deeper into the house.

For fuck's sake.

The sound of shooting outside intensified, as did Nick's yelling, and I was tempted to let her burn.

"Look, lady, if you want to get out of this shithole, we're leaving now or our ride goes without us," I snapped at her in Spanish.

"Please," she begged. "You have to come with me."

"I don't think you understand. If we don't leave now, we're stuck here. And in case you haven't noticed, the building's on fire and there are men out there who want to kill us."

She burst into tears and jabbered in Spanish. I was considering whether to abandon her or knock her out and drag her along when my ears pricked up at the word, "Carlos."

"Carlos? Did you say Carlos?" Was she about to make me a happy woman?

Her head bobbed up and down. "Yes, Carlos. You come."

"Carlos is here?"

She nodded again.

I had a decision to make, and two seconds to make it in. The fact I was completely, undeniably, fucking nuts probably made that decision easier.

When she tugged again, I let her pull me along behind her. The radio crackled, and I spoke into the mike.

"Nick, get out of here."

"What?"

"I'm staying. Get out of here."

"Don't be stupid. Foot soldiers are shooting at us and we have to go. Get your ass in your damn seat!"

"I can't. You still have to pick up Pink, and if you don't do that now, I'll shoot you myself. Drop everyone off then come back for me. I'll meet you at last week's rendezvous point."

"You've lost your mind!"

"What's new?" I yelled back.

The rotor blades whined as the Huey took off, then the gunfire started up again. I needed to deal with that first.

"Hold on—I have to take care of a little problem outside," I told the woman. "Just stay here, okay?"

Without waiting for an answer, I ran to the door. A man crouched behind a wall, shooting at the helicopter with an AR-15. He clearly had no idea I was there because he'd left his back wide open. Two quick shots to the head took care of that issue.

Another guy started shooting, and I fired a quick burst back but missed as he ducked behind a vehicle.

Over by the hillside, the helicopter descended for Carmen, and I needed to hold him off long enough for her to climb on board. I was almost grateful when he popped his head up and aimed at me instead. Someone threw a ladder out, and Carmen scrambled up it. Seconds later, the Huey sped away.

Good. Now I could concentrate all my efforts on getting rid of the trigger-happy thug. Actually, make that thugs. A second gorilla popped out of a building across from the house, and I dived sideways. My radio went crunch. Fuck it. Was I ever going to be able to go on a mission without destroying every means I had of communicating with the outside world? It appeared not, on current form.

It took me ten minutes and two magazines to eliminate the pair, by which point the helicopter was long gone. Even if I had been able to call it back, it wouldn't have had enough fuel anyway.

Well, happy days. I might as well have another look for Carlos—I had time to kill, after all. I ran back to the villa. The woman hovered in the doorway, unsure what to do with herself as smoke billowed out around her. A splintering crash from inside made me hesitate—nothing about this was a good idea. Then I thought of Black, and I thought of Carlos, and I stepped into the gloom.

The woman took point and I followed her through the house, both of us doubled over in a crouch as the smoke drifted above us. I almost bumped into her as she stopped in an alcove. Her fingers trembled as she felt along a wooden panel, but she must have found a hidden latch because the wall swung open to reveal a set of concrete steps going downwards. A cellar. I guess

I wasn't the only one to have secrets in my house.

I hesitated at the top of the stairs, not knowing what to expect, but she urged me on.

"It's all right. It is only him down here."

Acrid smoke was swirling in the cellar already. There must have been another entrance from the south wing where the fire was worse. We didn't have much time. The woman led me along a narrow passage, dark and dank-smelling, slippery underfoot. Our steps echoed on the stone floor until we got to a dead end. A single metal door blocked the way, solid except for a panel of bars at the top and a narrow hatch in the middle, big enough to slide a tray through.

A prison cell.

She pointed at it. "Carlos."

Carlos was in there? What the hell?

It was black inside. I peered through the bars and smoke, and as my eyes adjusted to the gloom, I saw a man crouched at the back, holding a cloth over his face. When he felt my gaze, he straightened slightly and turned his head.

If I'd been surprised earlier, it was nothing compared to what I felt now as dark eyes stared at me from under a floppy fringe.

The woman had been telling the truth. It bloody well *was* Carlos.

Wasn't it?

CHAPTER 17

THE MAN WAS hazy through the smoke. Hair curled around his shoulders, a grimy layer of filth coated his skin, and a pair of tattered, too-big trousers hung around his waist. He lowered the cloth from his face as he walked towards me.

"Took your fucking time, Diamond."

My heart stuttered.

Was it Carlos? Or was it...

"Black?" I whispered, squinting through the gloom.

"Who else would it be?"

How was I supposed to answer him? Logic told me it was Carlos playing some kind of elaborate trick. But most would say I'd left logic behind in Virginia, perhaps even in London fourteen years ago. Had a miracle happened and Black was standing here before me?

Or was I dreaming? Was this my subconscious, taking cruelty to a new level? I pinched myself hard.

Well, that hurt.

How could this be happening?

Because if it *was* Black in front of me, then who died in the taxi in Richmond? It could only have been Carlos, surely? Someone got incinerated, and that someone had shared Black's DNA.

Unless there was a third brother. Fuck me, that

didn't bear thinking about.

I must have spent too long considering because he cleared his throat and interrupted me. "Will you stop zoning out and get the damn door open?"

The man looked like Black, and he sure sounded like Black. But I had to be positive before I un-caged him. It was Black himself who'd trained me to think first and act later. I needed a proof of life question, something only the two of us would know the answer to.

"What was I wearing when we met?"

Apart from Jimmy, nobody, not even our closest friends, knew I'd been a stripper when Black and I first crossed paths. I'd only admitted to stealing his wallet.

"Have you gone completely out of your mind?"

Probably. "Just answer the damn question, will you?"

I gripped the bars, my knuckles turning white as I waited for his reply.

"Fine." He bent over and retched, then straightened up. "A slutty schoolgirl outfit and running shoes."

My heart stopped then restarted again with a stronger beat, the one that had faltered when I watched a taxi blow up outside the Green Mountain hotel on the outskirts of Richmond.

And with that pounding came the realisation I'd left the love of my life to spend eight months festering in a Colombian hellhole.

"Emmy, what the fuck's wrong with you? Get me out of here."

And if I didn't rectify the situation, we were both going to die in it.

I snapped out of my stupor. "Do you know where

the key is?"

"No." He looked past me to the pregnant chick. "Jane, do you?"

Jane shook her head helplessly.

Not to worry. Black had taught me to be a good Girl Scout, so as usual, I was prepared.

I shrugged out of my slim rucksack and balanced it on one knee. Spare knife, bullets, paracord. The mangled remains of the satellite phone Nate had made me bring, which I'd somehow broken clean in two earlier. Now, where were the explosives?

Ah, there in the corner, a couple of small charges, just big enough to take out a door lock and equipped with Nate's special remote detonators.

I slipped one of them through the bars to Black. "You need to put it on from your side. It's shaped to blow outwards."

If I put it on myself, the force of the explosion would be directed right at him.

I grabbed Jane's wrist and pulled her along behind me as we got out the way of the blast. The uneven floor had seen better days, and when she stumbled going around a corner, I barely managed to keep her upright. Then there was an ear-splitting *bang*, and Black belted along the corridor towards us.

He grabbed Jane's other hand, and we half carried her towards the stairs. The smoke on the floor above had thickened into a dark blanket that invaded my lungs, and I could hardly see my hand in front of my face as I tried to get my bearings. But Jane knew the house better, and she led the two of us outside before collapsing onto the ground.

Black fell to his knees beside her, coughing, while I

gulped in clean air. The smoke stung my eyes. I didn't dare to rub them—my hands, along with the rest of me, were coated with a fine layer of soot. Black and Jane were the same.

I quickly came to my senses and pulled my gun out. With Black now holding Jane's hair out of the way while she threw up, one of us had to keep an eye out for trouble. The far end of the house collapsed as I took stock of the situation. I guess it could have been worse.

We were only stuck in the jungle fifteen miles from anywhere, surrounded by bodies and burning buildings. Fuck, I hated the smell of charred flesh. It reminded me of Black's... Hold on. He wasn't dead anymore. Right? I struggled to take that in. My eyes told me one thing, but...but...

I reached out and poked him.

He gave me a grumpy look. "What the hell are you playing at?"

"Just checking."

Jane's eyes darted from side to side as she took in the devastation. "What do we do now?" she asked, voice quaking.

I watched the tree line as I answered. Was anyone still there? "I saw a couple of trucks in a shed out the back. Let's start driving and go from there."

Jack's team had destroyed the plane, and no way could Jane get through the jungle to the boats we'd come in, which was unfortunately where I'd told Nick to meet me. The other option would be for us to split up, and I didn't like that idea. The only thing keeping Jane on her feet was Black, and if he'd been locked up all this time, he wouldn't be in the best shape either.

"Let me guess, you broke another phone?" At least

Black's sense of sarcasm was alive and kicking.

"I can't help it, okay? It just happens."

He shook his head in exasperation then picked his way barefoot over to the nearest corpse. I kept watch while he pulled the boots off the dead guy and wedged his own feet into them.

"Two sizes too small," he grumbled as he pulled the laces tight. "But better than cutting my feet to shreds."

We set off along the path cut through the trees. I say path, but it was more like a tunnel with the mossy green boughs meeting overhead. We'd almost reached the trucks when Jane veered off the track.

"Hey, you're going the wrong way," I called.

"I need to pick something up. It's important."

I raised an eyebrow at Black, and he shrugged. "We'd better go with her."

She elbowed through the damp foliage of a barely visible trail until we reached a tumbledown hut. The door hung off at an angle, but she pushed it open without hesitation and emerged a minute later clutching a small padded envelope to her chest.

"Any ideas?" I mouthed at Black.

His shake of the head said he didn't know any more than I did.

"We can go now," Jane informed me.

"Gee, thanks."

The makeshift garage contained two vehicles: a new-looking pickup and something that might once have been a truck in a previous life, but only its cracked tyres had stopped it from rusting into the ground. I found the key to the pickup tucked securely behind the sun visor. At least I wouldn't need to test my hot-wiring skills today.

Before we got in, Jane stopped and scanned the trees, squinting at the greenery.

"Come on. What are you waiting for?"

"Did you see a cat anywhere?"

What, another delay? "No, no cat."

"Can we look for him?"

"He can find mice or something. He'll survive."

"But he doesn't know how to live in the wild. He relies on me to give him food. He was supposed to be Diego's pet, but Diego's mean to him, so Kitty doesn't like him very much."

Kitty? Very original. Much as I loved animals, I didn't want to stay there any longer.

"Please?" Jane begged.

Black shrugged again. Wow, wasn't he Mr. Talkative today? I blew a thin stream of air between my lips, trying to hold on to my weakening patience, and even though I wanted to get the hell out of there, I guessed we both owed Jane for taking me to the cellar.

"What colour is Kitty?"

"He's big and black, and he has a red collar on."

"I'll have a quick look, but then we've got to go."

Black stayed with Jane while I made a fast circuit of the compound. Apart from the trees rustling in the wind and the burning buildings, I didn't see any movement. It was a lost cause. Kitty was either barbecued or hiding. When I returned to the vehicle shaking my head, Jane looked as if she was about to cry, but Black reached out and tenderly cupped her cheek.

"Animals are more resilient than we think."

He gave her the smile that always made my heart melt, and thankfully she climbed in without further protest.

I went to get in the driver's seat, but Black pointed me over to the passenger side.

"I'll drive, you shoot."

Fair enough. Shooting was a skill that quickly went rusty if you didn't practise, and if Black had got his hands on a gun during his time in Colombia, he wouldn't have been locked in a cell when I found him.

At the main gate, I hopped out and hauled the barrier open. Good thing it was manually operated because there wasn't a whole lot left of the guard hut after Nate's team had finished with it. It looked even worse than the one at Little Riverley.

"That was for you, Mick and Seth," I muttered to myself as I took my place at Black's side again.

The road, if it deserved to be called that, was covered in a six-inch layer of mud, which went some way towards disguising the potholes. Every time we hit one, the truck lurched and groaned together with its occupants. We could only crawl along. If we drove any faster, the truck would have left a trail of parts in its wake as they all shook loose. How had Diego ever made it through there in a sports car?

I watched in the rear-view mirror as Jane shifted uncomfortably behind me, hands cradling her swollen belly. How many months pregnant was she? She certainly looked like she was ready to pop. And who was the baby's father? One of Hector's guards, maybe? If so, Blackwood would be mighty unpopular because we'd killed all the ones we saw at the compound.

I looked at my watch as I worked out the next steps. It seemed like an age since the helicopter took off, but in reality, it had only left twenty-five minutes ago. Seb's watchers would have departed by now as well—we'd agreed they'd leave at dawn as we went in. I checked the fuel gauge. Half a tank. We'd be able to get to the hamlet fifteen miles away, and hopefully somebody there would have a phone that worked. Then we could call Mack, and she could divert the helicopter to pick us up.

I explained this to Black and he nodded his agreement, never taking his eyes off the road as he concentrated on steering around the worst of the ruts.

It was definitely one of the more unpleasant drives I'd been on. I'd have sold my soul to the devil to have a Huey back. Oh, wait, I did that years ago. Maybe he'd settle for a kidney instead?

The needle on the speedometer stayed firmly below twenty miles an hour as we trundled along. Nobody talked, and Black's knuckles turned white under the filth as he gripped the steering wheel. I switched between looking at the road ahead and checking our tail in case we'd missed somebody behind us.

Black had never been a chatterbox, but I thought he might have said a few words to me. I didn't even get a smile. Sadly, I wasn't surprised about that part. For all intents and purposes, I'd left him buried in a hole for the best part of a year, and he had every right to be furious.

What were his first words when he saw me? *Took your fucking time.*

And boy, had I. I'd flipped out for three months after I thought he'd died. Three fucking months! And all that time he'd been alive. I should have kept my head rather than being cowed by the likes of Hector Ramos.

Jane coughed behind me, and Black slowed the truck for a second.

"You okay?" he asked her.

"I think so."

"This'll all be over soon; I promise." He gave her a smile then snaked his hand through the gap between the seats and squeezed one of hers.

The rear-view mirror may have been dingy, but I didn't miss her blush when she gazed back at him.

Nor did I miss that he'd smiled at her, but not me. Well, clearly Jane had been there for him all the time I hadn't. When Nate and I first saw her on our recon, she'd been carrying a tray of food near the villa. Probably she'd been taking Black his meals. They must have built up quite a bond.

And me?

I'd been worse than useless.

Let's see, while Jane looked after Black, I'd managed to piss off to England and turn Luke's life upside down with my lies. After that, I'd nearly got myself killed in Syria and caused my friends no end of worry by disappearing for a week.

My pièce de résistance, though, had to be getting into Ramos's business and practically inviting him to my house to try and kill those same friends. And just for good measure, I'd got the place destroyed in the process. That was quite an impressive list of fuck-ups. *Way to go, Emmy.*

I sighed. All these years I'd been kidding myself I could make something of my life, but my mother had been right when she'd told me I was a total waste of space.

Stupid, stupid child.

Before I could berate myself further, my thoughts were interrupted by a horrible grating noise coming from the engine. The revs went crazy, and the truck slowed from its bumpy crawl to a complete stop. Fan-fucking-tastic.

Black and I looked at each other and rolled our eyes, kind of like we used to in the old days.

Why us?

CHAPTER 18

BLACK SWORE AND popped the bonnet, then climbed out of the cab with me following. As I peered down into the engine, I didn't need the years of knowledge imparted into me by Vinnie, the dude who taught me how to nick cars, to see the timing belt had snapped. That truck was going nowhere.

"Fuck and double fuck arse bollocks." I kicked the tyre, just for good measure.

"Well, that's one way of putting it."

Bloody great. Now we were stuck miles from anywhere with a truck that didn't go and a pregnant woman. When Mr. Murphy and Lady Luck duked it out to see who would get the spare seat in the back, it was obvious who'd won.

There was only one thing for it.

"I'll go back."

Black didn't answer.

"You know I have to. We can't ask Jane to walk far. It's seven miles to the Ramos place, eight to the nearest civilisation, and there's nothing else around."

"I could go," Black said, but his tone suggested he was offering more out of obligation than anything else.

"How much running have you done recently?"

"Not a lot." A beat of silence. "Okay, none."

So it had to be me, then. Seven miles, fifty minutes

in this terrain. There was that other rust-bucket of a truck back at the compound, clinging onto the last of its mechanical life, and I'd have to fetch it.

"You need to stay and take care of Jane," I told Black.

"Yeah, I guess you're right."

He gave her that smile again, and hurt crackled through me before I locked it away and pasted on a mask of my own.

Together, we pushed the broken pickup down the incline at the edge of the track and into the undergrowth. Luckily, despite being a prisoner for so long, Black had kept some of his strength, because the damn thing weighed a ton and the cloying mud didn't help. We shoved it until the bumper hit a tree, and although it wasn't completely hidden, nobody would spot it from a quick glance after we'd arranged a tangle of vines over the top.

Before I left, I shed my excess kit—there was no sense in being weighed down by Hector's paperwork. I gave Black my backup gun, keeping my favourite Walther P88 on my right thigh and a couple of spare magazines in the small of my back.

I was about to start running when Black called me over. "Diamond, do me a favour? Don't die."

Don't die? Did he have that little faith in me? "I wasn't planning on it."

On my trek back, I tried to put Black out of my head. And Jane. I didn't want to think of the relationship going on there. Or who the father of Jane's baby was. From the size of her, she had to be at least eight months pregnant, and how long had Black been gone? Almost nine. Yep, a toddler could have done the maths. I felt sick.

Black was my husband. *Mine.* Yes, I knew we'd never had that kind of relationship, but it would kill me if he'd fathered a baby with someone else. Still, I'd let him down so badly I didn't have the right to expect anything from him anymore.

Mind swirling, I tried to refocus my emotions. Alex had taught me that trick when I needed to fight him in training and my head wasn't in the right place. Instead of worrying about Black, I switched my attention to Diego. Where was he? I hated loose ends, and we needed to take him out before he got to us. I hoped Nate had been sensible enough to put Eduardo's people on high alert in case anyone realised the connection. Oh, who was I kidding? Of course Nate would have done that. He thought of everything. It was just me who kept screwing things up.

Once I settled into my stride, I made it back to the compound in forty-eight minutes. Not bad considering I was wearing boots and running through mud. Now I needed to get the other truck and return for Black and... Nope, still didn't want to think about it. Or rather, her.

Sweat dripped from every part of me as I jogged past the still-smoking guard hut and cut left to the trees, keeping my fingers crossed that Hector's men had been as lax with the keys in the second vehicle. I didn't want more delays while I coaxed the bloody thing into life. I was sick of this place—the sticky heat, the squadrons of bitey things, the arseholes with automatic weapons.

As I darted from one shadow to the next, I felt a prickle on the back of my neck. Another mosquito? No, something was up. I'd barely had time to process that thought when I heard the snick of a gun being cocked behind me.

Fuck. I stopped and turned around, raising my hands above my head as I did so.

Well, the good news was I'd found Diego.

The bad news was he had a pistol pointed straight at my head. Not only that, two caffeinated gorillas flanked him, and they both held guns as well. Big ones. Dammit, I hated being in this position.

Recognition flitted across his face. "You were with Sebastien Garcia the other week."

"Yes." Shit, now I'd managed to bring the Garcias into this for sure. Oh, what the hell, I might as well admit who I was to try and take some of the heat off them. "Emerson Black. And when I said it was a pleasure to meet you, I lied."

His eyes narrowed. "You killed my father, didn't you?"

"I don't know why you're so upset. You killed Carlos."

"That was an accident. It was supposed to be your husband, not my stupid fuck-up of a stepbrother."

Accident? Stepbrother? They weren't full siblings? This circus got crazier by the minute.

"You tried to kill me too," I said, stalling while I tried to work out what was going on.

"You took out fourteen of our best men, you bitch. Do you have any idea how hard it is to get good staff nowadays?"

"Well, they weren't that good, were they? They missed."

I couldn't help pointing that out, but it only pissed

him off more. Fire blazed in his eyes, and his finger shifted on the trigger.

"A mistake which I do not intend to repeat."

Great. I needed a plan. My pistol was still in my thigh holster, and by the time I reached for it, I wouldn't have a head anymore. I was contemplating my options when something large and black leapt out of the trees and launched itself at Diego. He got a shot off, but it went high over my left shoulder. I didn't hesitate. I drew my gun and fired into the men each side of him, then when the black thing rolled to the side, I double tapped Diego in the head.

What the hell just happened?

From the tangled mass on the ground wriggled what looked like a panther. It sat up and we stared at each other. Holy fuck, Bradley warned me there were big cats in the jungle, but I didn't think they came out and attacked people like that!

Would I be next? What if it wanted dessert?

I trained my gun on it, not breaking eye contact. The sleek black cat was a beautiful creature, and I didn't want to kill it if I could avoid doing so, plus it *had* just done me a massive favour. I took one step back, and it stayed still. I moved another foot, and it took a pace towards me.

Er, shit.

I glanced to my right, looking for something I could use as cover. There wasn't much, only trees and a few thorny bushes. Could panthers climb trees? I was pretty sure I'd seen a documentary a while back where they did exactly that.

And so our standoff progressed. The cat shifted slightly, and I glimpsed something around its neck.

What was it? I risked a step to the side. It was a red belt. A red bloody belt.

Jane's words came back to me: "He's big and black, and he has a red collar on."

This was her flipping pet? We definitely needed to work on her descriptive skills.

"Kitty?"

His ears pricked up, and he walked towards me. I stood dead still as he rubbed himself along my legs like a giant bloody house cat. Kind of cute, kind of scary. I tentatively reached down and scratched his head. He started purring, a deep rumbling noise that sounded remarkably similar to a distant aircraft taking off.

"Well, Kitty, I guess Jane was right. You didn't like Diego very much."

Jane said she'd been feeding him, right? He didn't seem so interested in feasting on Diego's still-twitching body, so maybe he wasn't all that hungry. We could leave that asshole for Kitty's wilder cousins.

With the big cat trailing after me, I walked further into the compound. Diego and his two buddies had to have got there somehow, and they didn't pass us on the road. And there it was—a shiny red Eurocopter, glinting in the sunshine. Hallelujah! The devil had finally come through for me.

I hustled over to my lifeline, staying alert for any more of Ramos's men. Kitty followed, his head swinging right and left, and I swear he was looking for bad guys too. I'd never been much of a cat person, but I was rapidly changing my mind.

When I opened the door to the helicopter, Kitty stopped and stared at me.

"What?" I asked him. "Do you want to come too?"

He leapt inside and sat in the co-pilot's seat, staring out of the window. Guess that answered my question. I climbed in after him and gingerly buckled the seat belt through his collar. Still purring, he expressed his gratitude by licking me, which felt like having my face sandpapered.

I shut the doors, strapped myself in, and warmed up the engine, the sound of the rotors sweet music to my ears. Once the turbine was good to go, I took off, following the road back to pick up Black.

To pick up Black and go home.

The trip was so much faster by helicopter, and I got to the dead truck in less than ten minutes. I had to fly a little further to find somewhere wide enough to land, then I hopped out and jogged back to find my passengers.

When Black saw me, he emerged from the undergrowth, holding Jane by the hand. A lump formed in my throat as he put his arm around her waist and guided her around the potholes, then helped her up into the back of the helicopter.

"Where did you find this?" Black asked, jerking a thumb at my new toy.

"I borrowed it from Diego. He won't be needing it back."

Jane's eyes went wide. "Did you kill him?"

"Yeah."

She nodded solemnly. "Good."

When Kitty realised who'd joined us, he tried to leap over the seat, almost strangling himself in the process. I unclipped him and he made another attempt, this time landing in Jane's lap.

"Kitty," she cried out gleefully. "You found Kitty.

Thank you so much."

They both looked so happy, Kitty energetically taking a layer of skin off her cheeks and Jane laughing as she let him do it. Ah hell, I might want to hate her, but I couldn't. She'd looked after my beloved husband when I was incapable, and her oversized moggy had just saved my life.

Black glanced at the feline lying across the back seat, shrugged, and climbed in next to me. There was a spare set of headphones on the console, and he settled them over his ears. Just like old times. A minute later we set off on our way once more, and as the helicopter rose over the rainforest canopy, I couldn't fucking wait to get out of that place.

CHAPTER 19

LUKE LISTENED THROUGH his headphones as the events at the Ramos compound unfolded. He couldn't help glancing sideways to check on Mack, although she remained remarkably unruffled under all the pressure.

"Nothing coming in from the local police," she said. "Base, the birds are five minutes out."

"Understood."

Yes, she'd stayed far calmer than Luke. His heart rate hadn't dropped under a hundred since the first shots were fired, although his chest swelled with pride at Mack's performance.

She'd wanted to go to Colombia, but he'd been secretly pleased when she got bumped from the team in favour of Nate. The wait when Tia went missing had been unbearable, and he'd dreaded having to go through something similar while Mack romped through the jungle. Of course he was worried about the others too, but he wasn't crazy in love with any of them.

The moment Emmy and her troops breached the Ramos compound had been both the most terrifying and compelling of his life, like being stuck in the middle of an action movie. He still couldn't believe the woman who shot Hector Ramos without a qualm was the same girl who'd lived in his house for two months. Who'd curled up with him on the sofa and watched slushy movies. He was damn glad they'd never got into a serious argument.

Now the team was on their way back, minus his ex. When she'd argued with Nick over getting in the helicopter, Luke had almost yelled at her to get on board himself. Almost. What he'd learned about Emmy over the past few months stopped him. She might have been moody, temperamental, and borderline insane, but she also had moments of brilliance and never did things without a purpose. Whatever the reason she'd stayed behind, it was probably a good one.

The radio beside him came to life.

"The doctor is set up in the blue bedroom on the second floor," a voice informed them.

Ah yes, the doctor. He pushed Emmy to the back of his mind, fears for the injured coming to the fore. Especially Dan with her gunshot wound. Luke had come to view her as a friend over the last few months, and then there was the look of fear that had come over Mack's face when she heard the news. She'd carried on checking the satellite feed, but all her colour drained clean away.

Eduardo had seemed nonplussed but immediately arranged for a medic who wouldn't ask any questions to be ready and waiting at his villa when the team arrived back, which would be any minute now.

Eduardo. Now he was one scary chap. His moods ranged from manic to ice-cold with a whole spectrum in between. Luke had read all sorts of things about him, and if there was a grain of truth in half of it, that man was seriously screwed in the head. How could Emmy be friends with him? Actually no, scratch that question. Nothing about Emmy surprised Luke anymore.

"Incoming," Mack said.

The sound of the rotors gradually faded as the pilots wound them back after landing, and the airwaves got busier.

"Nick, put me down. I can walk." That was Dan, and she sounded strong, thank goodness.

"You've just been shot in the leg."

"Yeah, but I can still hop."

"Shut up, this is faster."

Then Nate joined in. "Nick, hurry up. We have to get back for Emmy. You're sure she said to meet her back at the drop off point?"

"Positive. Hey, can someone get these birds refuelled?"

An inevitable argument followed about who was going back, until Nate pulled rank and nominated Nick, Logan, Seb, and Evan.

"It should be a straightforward pick-up, so four people will be enough. Too many cooks and all that."

"When has anything Emmy's said or done ever been straightforward?" Mack muttered from beside Luke.

"Are you sure she didn't say *why* she was staying?" Nate asked.

"No indication at all."

"Could someone have threatened her to say that?" one of the Colombians asked.

Alex's thick Russian accent came through. "That is an absurd suggestion. There is nothing Emmy does that Emmy does not want to do."

"Okay, okay, man. It was just an idea."

Luke imagined the guy shrinking away as the man-mountain that was Alex turned on him. Poor chap.

"I saw her after the helicopter took off," Carmen

said. "She was running across the courtyard, shooting at the man who was shooting at you. She was on her own then."

"Hell, what on earth possessed her to stay?" Nate voiced what everyone was thinking.

Radio silence.

Since nobody had an answer, they concentrated their efforts on getting the team prepared to go back and find out instead. As they loaded fresh magazines and re-stocked the first aid kit, the speculation began. Had Emmy spotted Diego? Did she get a lead on Carlos?

There was only one way to find out, and with Nick and Nate pushing things along, the team of four was ready to go in less than fifteen minutes.

If the pilot pushed the Huey to its top speed of a hundred and thirty-five miles an hour, the journey would take just shy of an hour. That was a long wait at the best of times, but with Emmy's life on the line, it became unbearable. Mack paced up and down the room, unable to sit still until Luke eventually pulled her onto his lap. He wrapped his arms around her waist, trying to keep her calm.

"Look, I haven't known Emmy for as long as you, but even in that short time, she's got herself out of more scrapes than most people have in a lifetime. She had, what, two people shooting at her? Compared to the Syria thing, that's a walk in the park."

"I know that logically. I do. But it's hard to stay calm when she's my friend and she's missing."

"Nick's on his way to pick her up. She asked him to meet her there. Whatever she was doing, she didn't plan on it taking long. And at least we know roughly where she is this time. Not like in Syria where she could have been anywhere in two countries and then turned up in a completely different one."

"I suppose. How long until Nick's team gets there?" Mack asked, even though she already knew the answer.

Luke replied anyway, looking at the clock on the screen. "Fifteen minutes."

As there wasn't much else he could do, he put the kettle on and made cups of tea, the British response to everything. He set them on the desk where they sat untouched while he and Mack waited for communication from the pick-up point.

When they finally heard Nick's voice come through their earpieces, it wasn't the news they'd hoped for.

"Well, we're here, but there's no sign of Emmy."

"She might not have got through the jungle yet," Nate said. "Is it safe to wait?"

"It's quiet as a grave around here." A pause. "Sorry, bad choice of words."

"For fuck's sake, Emmy, get your ass in gear," Nate ranted, even though she had no way of hearing him.

Mack resumed her attempts to wear a hole through the carpet as Luke watched the numbers on the clock tick past. Ten minutes, then twenty.

The tension was obviously getting to Nick too. "How do people feel about us going back to the Ramos compound and looking for her there?"

"What if she's already on her way to the pick-up point?" Nate asked, quite rightly.

"Yeah, I know, it's a stupid idea. But it's hard sitting here doing nothing when there's a chance she's bleeding to death a few miles away. What about loading up the other chopper and sending that over instead?"

"That's the next step. Although we're three men down now."

"Three?"

"Marco twisted his ankle jumping out the way of some bullets. Once the adrenaline wore off, he realised it was worse than he thought. The doc reckons it's only ligament damage, but it's the size of a watermelon."

"There are still ten people left."

Mack played devil's advocate from the next continent. "Nick, we still don't know where Diego or Carlos are. It's possible that someone recognised Seb or Marco at the compound and told them who it was that attacked the place. Worst case scenario is that they're on their way to Eduardo's right now, hell-bent on revenge."

"Okay, so why don't we put a couple of people in the second helicopter? They can come to the pick-up point and the four of us here can go on to the compound."

Luke didn't hear the answer because Eduardo's heavily accented voice interrupted.

"One of my team has just radioed in. There's a red helicopter coming in low on the south side of the estate. He wants to know if he should shoot at it?" The old man sounded hopeful.

"NO!" about six people shouted back.

"Not until we know who it is," Nate clarified.

"He will not be happy to hear that. My men here feel as if they have missed out on all the excitement today." Eduardo grudgingly passed on the instruction, though.

Nate assumed command. "Everyone inside. Carmen, get somewhere you can get a bead on it."

"Gotcha."

Carmen kept everyone updated as she dug herself in behind the stone balustrade bordering Eduardo's patio and started up a commentary. "I can see the helicopter coming over the tree line. Doesn't look as if it's in a hurry."

"She's got the best view, through her sniper's scope," Mack explained to Luke.

"Who's in it?" Nate asked. "Can you see?"

"Not yet. Give me a second."

Mack gripped Luke's hand. All they could do was wait.

Then Carmen's voice came back. "I think it's Emmy. It's someone with long hair, anyway, but she's filthy. Okay, it's coming closer." A short pause. "Yes, it's her. It's Emmy."

A collective sigh of relief rose from the contingent in Colombia, and Mack sagged back into Luke's arms.

"Thank goodness," he whispered to her. His cantankerous ex had survived once again.

"Nick, get back here," Nate ordered over the radio.

"With pleasure."

Carmen kept up her commentary. "She's landing down at the end of the garden."

Luke recalled from their research that Eduardo's garden was more of a park, at least two hundred metres long.

"She'd better have a damn good explanation for this," Nate growled. "And where in the devil's name did she get the helicopter?"

"Hang on. She's not alone. There's someone with her. Actually, no, I think it's two people. It's hard to see. There's glare on the windscreen. Oh."

"What?"

"It looks like... Well...a dog, I think, sitting in the back seat."

"Why the hell has she brought a dog? She already has a dog. Can you see who the other people are yet? They couldn't be holding her hostage, could they?"

"Nate! Don't be so ridiculous. Anyway, she's turned to the person beside her like she's talking. The rotors are slowing. They're getting out now. She's out. The person in the front with her is a man, quite tall. And it's a woman in the back. She looks pregnant, and they're all covered in dirt."

"Ah, we saw a pregnant woman the first time we visited the compound. Japanese-looking. That must be who Emmy went back for. But what about the man?"

"He's turning around. Uh, he's got long hair and a beard. His clothes look really tatty. No... It can't be..."

Carmen fell silent.

"Can't be what? Who?"

"Well, I'd say it's either Black or his evil twin." There was a pause. "And from the way he just high-fived Emmy, like Black always used to, I don't think it's the evil twin."

"Carmen, now isn't the time for joking."

"Nate, I'm damn well not joking. Get down here and see for yourself."

Luke heard the sound of running feet, muffled over the radio.

"Next time, we need to get a video feed as well as audio," Mack said.

"Next time?" Luke muttered faintly.

Mack ignored him. "Guys, what's happening? Is it really Black?"

"It sure looks that way," Nate said, incredulity in his

voice.

Luke shook his head in disbelief too. "Well, no wonder she stayed behind."

CHAPTER 20

BLACK WALKED AROUND the helicopter on his way to help Jane, pausing to give me a high-five in the way he always used to whenever we came back from a successful job. But why did he do it just then? Today hadn't exactly gone smoothly, had it? Habit, maybe.

He'd barely uttered a word on the way back. It wasn't that we used to talk all the time, because we didn't, but the silences between us had always been comfortable. Today, the words unspoken formed a gulf, one I had no idea how to cross.

What the hell should I say to him? Flying an unfamiliar helicopter, keeping low to avoid detection in a country where I wasn't supposed to be, meant thinking about it had been impossible. I'd needed every ounce of concentration not to crash and kill us all. Wouldn't that have been ironic? Black surviving more than eight months as a prisoner having goodness knows what done to him only to die in a rescue attempt.

Over at the house, tiny figures emerged onto the terrace, staring in our direction. I saw the moment when the team recognised Black. The stampede wasn't instantaneous, but then again, he didn't exactly look like his old self. When Bradley saw the length of his hair, he'd have a fit, and don't get me started on the beard.

I snuck another glance. Where the soot covering Black had rubbed away, his skin was as pale as the puffs of cloud hovering far above us. Had he spent any time above ground since he left? I looked for longer as he guided Jane onto the lawn. Muscles rippled through the grime, his six-pack sharply defined due to the amount of weight he'd lost. He was nowhere near as stacked as he used to be, but he didn't seem in bad shape, all things considered.

Nate reached us first, grabbing Black in a man-hug and thumping him on the back.

"Hey! Be careful," I warned. "Don't break him."

"I'm fine, Diamond." He lifted Nate clean off the ground as he hugged him in return. "Good to see you, buddy."

Everyone else crowded around, offering hugs, kisses, handshakes, and pats on the back. Dan hopped madly about before flinging her arms around his neck and hooking her good leg behind his waist.

"You're back!" she shrieked. "Now all we have to do is find Diego Ramos and we're golden."

I pulled my rucksack out of the helicopter and slung it over my shoulder. "We don't. I shot him."

Dammit, I should have put earplugs in, her screech was that loud. "Party! Champagne!"

"Not on duty, shrimp," Nick reminded her. "And it's not a good idea with the pills you've just taken."

"Yes, Dad."

I felt like a spare part. Not wanting to spoil the celebration, I backed out of the huddle of people and went to help Jane get her ridiculous pet out of the cabin. What were we supposed to do with him?

"Will Kitty be okay? I mean if we just let him out? Won't he run off? Should I try to find a leash or something?"

She reached a hand out and he rubbed against it. "I don't think so. He's quite timid. Diego and his men used to kick him around when he was small, and he'd come to me when he got scared. I used to hide him from them and make sure he ate."

She was right. Kitty jumped down onto the grass, shrank away from the noise, and slunk around to sit behind her. I scratched him on the head. He seemed to enjoy that.

"He likes you. I think you remind him of Lorena. She used to share a room with me, and she'd pet him that way."

My breath hitched. Had we left someone behind? Then I realised Jane had used the past tense.

"What happened to Lorena?"

"Diego killed her."

Boy, was I glad to have shot that bastard. Before today, I'd never felt joy at taking a life. A sense of accomplishment at completing a job, sometimes even relief, but never happiness. On that sunny day in Colombia, however, I made an exception.

Jane gazed over at Black, still stuck in the middle of the crowd. "They look pleased to see him. Are they all his family?"

You know that old saying about blood being thicker than water? Let me tell you, it's a load of bollocks. Your real family are the people who are there for you, day in day out, who'd put their lives on the line for you, related by blood or not.

"Yes, that's his family."

"He's lucky to have so many people who care about him."

"Yeah, he is. We both are. Do you have family? Because no offence, but you don't look like you're related to the Ramoses."

She cut her eyes to Black then shook her head. "I don't know."

Just then, my husband managed to extricate himself from the middle of the team, and he made his way swiftly over to Jane's side.

"Are you okay? Are you tired? Do you need to sit down?" Before she could answer, he turned to me. "What do pregnant women need?"

"How should I know? Do I have a child?"

His voice dropped to a whisper. "I'm sorry."

"Forget about it."

His eyes closed for a second, and I knew what he was remembering. Something I'd rather obliterate from my mind. Then he gathered himself together. "I shouldn't have said that. I just thought as you're a woman…"

"Okay, as a man, on a scale of one to ten, how painful is a vasectomy?"

"Point taken. A doctor. She should see a doctor."

"There's a doctor in the house," Nate said from behind Black. "Although Eduardo found him, and he's more of a trauma surgeon than a gynaecologist. Seems to be pretty good, though. Guess he gets a lot of practice around here."

"Why do we need a trauma surgeon? Exactly how much trauma have we had?"

"Dan and Felipe both got shot. But not too badly, right?" I looked to Nate for confirmation.

"Felipe's shoulder was the worst. He'll need physio after the wound closes up to get his full range of movement back. Dan's thigh was only a flesh wound. She's hoping it won't scar too much. You know how much she loves to wear indecently short skirts."

"Should I remember Felipe?" Black asked.

"He's one of Eduardo's men," I explained.

"Are we talking about the same Eduardo who the DEA would have a heart attack over if they realised you spent a few weekends a year living it up by his pool?"

"The one and only. I should introduce you."

"We need to get Jane comfortable first." He turned back to her. "Can you walk to the house? Should we get a golf cart or something? Or Emmy could land the helicopter closer now we're not in danger of getting shot at."

"I think I can walk there."

Black hooked her arm over his and supported her as they made their way slowly across the vast lawn. The place was a hive of activity now, and Eduardo's men had joined the party.

Eduardo himself came bounding out of his villa, wearing a burgundy warm-up suit and sunglasses, a gold-plated revolver stuck in his waistband. He grabbed hold of me and swung me around, a big grin on his face. Well, at least one of the men in my life was happy to see me.

"Oh, angel, you're late. Alejandro made dinner, but I'm afraid it may be ruined. I will have him start again."

"I'm not sure we can stay that long. I want to get out of here before someone notices the carnage down the road and puts two and two together."

"You must eat. I will tell him to hurry up. Where is

this husband of yours? I'm intrigued to meet the man who has managed to keep a wild cat like you tied down for so long."

I looped my arm through his and led him towards Black. "What's with the tracksuit?"

"Floriana bought it. She's always telling me to relax more. It's comfortable, but my gun keeps slipping."

"Probably you could put the gun down for a little while."

"I like to carry the gun. It makes me feel secure."

"I'm standing next to you, and I've got a gun. Secure enough?"

Eduardo shrugged and gave the shiny gold gun to his butler, who walked off with it held aloft on a tray. I tapped Black on the shoulder and introduced them. "Eduardo, Black. Black, this is Eduardo."

"It's good to finally meet you." Black sized Eduardo up then relaxed a touch. "I need to thank you for looking after Emmy while I wasn't here."

Eduardo dismissed that with a wave of his hand. "She looks after herself. Emerson is a strong woman."

If that was true, why did I feel so broken inside?

"I know, but thank you anyway."

Eduardo looked Black over, taking in his "wild man" look. "Would you like to borrow some clothes? I have spare warm-up suits."

I coughed to cover up the snort of laughter that threatened to escape, and Black tried to hide his smile. I didn't dare to meet his eyes. Black was about nine inches taller than Eduardo and even in his current state, twice as wide. He'd split the seams trying to get into the older man's clothes.

"I'm not sure anything in your wardrobe would be

big enough." I tried to be diplomatic, a rare occurrence for me. "Nick or Nate'll have something spare."

Although even now, the filthy little bitch inside me was enjoying the sight of Black wandering around shirtless. Fuck, had I missed that.

In the end, we compromised over Alejandro's food. Some of us grabbed mouthfuls on the go, and Eduardo's household staff packed us a couple of picnic baskets to take on the plane. Floriana led Jane into the house and helped her to clean up while I rinsed the soot out of my hair. Once I had a pair of jeans and a tank on, I felt more human.

Outside, the flurry of activity continued as we finished packing our gear into the helicopters, ready for the short hop to the airstrip. We'd brought the larger of the two company planes, but even after leaving the boats behind, it promised to be a tight fit. Why was it when you packed to go on a trip, everything fitted perfectly, but when you came back, your suitcase—or in our case, plane—seemed to have shrunk?

Things became clearer when we started transferring the contents over to the jet.

"Where are those trunks from?" I asked Eduardo.

He beamed at me. "Just a few gifts for my favourite girl."

I dreaded to imagine what was inside them. Clothes? Flowers? The contents of a small diamond mine?

Still, I smiled. "You're too damn sweet, you old brute. But don't worry, I won't tell anyone."

Dan hobbled around on a pair of crutches, trailing after Black as if she was afraid to let him out of her sight. They'd always had a soft spot for each other.

She'd be almost as happy as me that he was back.

Jane had been seen by the doctor, who said he didn't think flying would harm the baby, but suggested we do so fast if we didn't want the child to be born at forty thousand feet. I was only too happy to oblige. The thought of our plane doubling as a delivery room terrified me.

Finally, it was time to leave. I hugged Eduardo tightly, promising to come back and see him soon in slightly more relaxed circumstances.

As he embraced me, I leaned in close to whisper in his ear. "If I ever had a father, I'd be proud if you were him."

He squeezed me harder for a second then quickly waved me off, and as he turned away, I was sure his eyes were glistening.

Shit, mine were too.

Black had managed to fit in a shower and looked more at home in a pair of Nate's cargo pants and Nick's Guns N' Roses T-shirt. I still hadn't had a chance to speak to him alone. Even on the trip over, he'd ridden in one chopper with Jane while I squashed into the other between Dan and Nick.

Inside, I felt all wrong.

I knew I should be happy. Deliriously so. I mean, hadn't Black just come back into my life? If somebody had asked me yesterday to name the one thing I wanted more than anything, that would have been it.

But things just weren't right between us. How on earth was I supposed to fix them?

CHAPTER 21

A MIXTURE OF emotions flooded my soul. Anger led the charge, closely followed by sadness and, I hated to admit, jealousy.

Yes, I was furious at the Ramos clan, but I directed most of the venom at myself. Why the hell hadn't I stuck around after Black's apparent death and got to the bottom of this then? All that time I'd been trying to protect my friends, but I'd ended up consigning the person I loved most to months of suffering.

The sadness was over my relationship with Black. Would it ever be the same again? We'd always been able to talk to each other about anything. Well, almost anything, my true feelings for him aside. But today, the atmosphere had been strained. He seemed to be avoiding me, and his silence twisted my sanity.

Then there was the shame I felt at the green-eyed monster standing between me and Jane. She'd been with Black during the time I hadn't, and it was clear he cared for her. Where did that leave me?

With that in mind, I resorted to my usual tactic: avoidance. When we arrived at the plane and Jed asked for a volunteer to co-pilot, I stuck my hand up.

"I'll do it."

At least it would be Jed sitting next to me. If it had been Nick or Nate, they'd have seen right through the smile plastered on my face and an interrogation would most certainly have followed. Especially because when Nick asked me earlier if I was okay, he seemed unconvinced by my answer of, "Fine."

"Who's that woman?" he'd asked, nodding at Jane.

"I don't really know."

Black's hand had been splayed out on the small of her back, guiding her through the crowd of people, and Nick's eyes cut down to it. "Are they together?"

I'd shrugged. Why couldn't he leave me alone? "I've barely spoken to him, okay?"

"You want me to try?"

"No."

If Black did have something going on with Jane, I figured I'd rather put off the agony of knowing for a few more hours. Fortunately, Eduardo had picked that moment to drag me into the dining room, insisting I try Alejandro's petits fours.

Jed might suspect there was a problem, but unlike Nick, he'd never dig any deeper. If I told him things were good, he wouldn't push it.

Once the gear was neatly stowed on board, trunks and all, we trooped up the steps, and I turned left towards the cockpit while Black turned right towards the back of the plane with Jane. Towards the fucking bedroom. Tell me they weren't going to spend the whole flight in there together?

Jed settled next to me and stretched out.

"How's your leg?" I asked.

"It didn't feel so good, but the doctor gave me some pills, and it's a lot better now."

Pills? What pills? "Should you be flying?"

He laughed. "Yeah, I'm okay. Now the little green

men have taken off in their spaceship, I feel almost normal."

I gave him a sharp look.

"Don't worry, they were only painkillers. Why are you so uptight? I thought you'd be ecstatic."

"I am," I lied through gritted teeth.

The takeoff was always my favourite part of a flight, and today was no different. I loved the feeling of sheer power as we roared along the runway and the wings lifted the plane into the air. After we were airborne, Jed climbed steadily, and we soon broke through the clouds and settled into our cruising altitude of forty thousand feet. The clear blue sky stretched out in front of us as we headed for home.

I yelled to the passengers that they could take their seat belts off, and a minute later, Nick stuck his head through the door.

"You guys want coffee?"

"Please, I could do with a pick-me-up."

A few minutes later I felt a presence behind me and turned around, hoping Nick had managed to find some biscuits because my appetite had returned with a vengeance. I'd only eaten a couple of sandwiches and a handful of tiny cakes at Eduardo's, and I was ravenous.

"Thanks, you're a..." I trailed off as I realised it was Black standing there and not Nick. And he didn't even have my coffee. "Oh, it's you."

Something flared in his eyes, and for a second I thought it was hurt. But that didn't match his tone.

"Bedroom, now," he growled.

"Er, I'm flying the plane?"

"Diamond, we have seven other people out in the cabin who're more than adequately qualified to pilot this thing. Get back there."

Jed took the controls as I stomped down the aisle behind Black. Nick handed me a plastic cup of coffee on the way.

"Good luck," he whispered, then headed forward to take my place on the flight deck.

I didn't need luck. I needed a bloody time machine.

Jane was propped up against the headboard with all the pillows stuffed under her. Even with those, and the duvet tucked around to keep her warm, she looked uncomfortable.

"Do you need another cushion?" I edged towards the door. "I'm sure we have—"

"Don't even think about it," Black told me.

He sat at Jane's side, leaving me to perch awkwardly on the other end of the bed, my arms and legs crossed. Well, this was fun.

For a plane, the double room was quite spacious. But with me, Kitty sprawled on the floor asleep, Black and Jane, plus the elephant in the room that was our relationship, I started to feel claustrophobic.

"What?" I asked, sounding petulant and hating myself even more for it.

"I'm hoping you might care to enlighten me about what the hell's been going on? Because I've been in the dark for the last eight months, both literally and figuratively."

"Oh. That."

He closed his eyes for a beat and sucked in a breath, exasperated. "Yes, that. I thought you were dead, but when I heard the explosions above ground, I knew there was only one person crazy enough to have turned up."

"Hang on, back up a bit. You thought *I* was dead?"

"Diego Ramos told me they'd killed you in the same operation where they took me."

I almost said, "And you believed the asshole?" but I bit my tongue. Hadn't I assumed exactly the same thing? I settled for a shrug.

"Throw me to the wolves, and I'll return leading the pack." And not only that, I'd teach them how to use assault weapons too.

"I always thought that, but then months passed and you didn't come, and..." he trailed off.

"I didn't know you were alive, that's why," I said quietly.

"What?"

"I thought you were gone, and after that, my hands were tied. But the Ramos family crossed a line, and I couldn't let it go."

His voice dropped to the dangerous level that meant he was getting properly pissed. "What line?"

"Look, why don't we start at the beginning? You tell me what happened to you then I'll fill in my bits." I didn't know where to start with my side of the story. Actually, that wasn't right. I knew where to start. I just didn't want to put it into words.

Black sighed and leaned back. "I suppose that's sensible."

Then he started to tell his tale.

"It was that meeting at the Green Mountain hotel last year." He shook his head slightly. "Fuck. Last year. I can't believe it was so long ago."

I couldn't either, and the thought made me feel nauseous.

He stared at the far wall of the cramped cabin, eyes

unfocused. "I arrived a few minutes early, told the receptionist who I was there to see, and she gave me a key and said to go straight up."

"Who *were* we there to see?" That was one of the big mysteries in the investigation. Black had entered the appointment in his calendar himself, and it just said "New client."

"A guy called me up, said he'd been given my number by Patrick Johnson. You know, he of the wandering hands?"

"I'm hardly likely to forget that creep."

"Of course. Stupid question. Anyway, it wasn't the first time Patrick had sent a client our way, so I said I'd stop by for a quick preliminary while he was in town."

"And who was it?"

"No idea. He'd undoubtedly given me a false name, and the room was empty when I got up there. When I heard a knock on the door, I thought it was you and opened it. Next thing I knew, some asshole shot me with a Taser, and I woke up in the room you found me in."

"Carlos made the appointment." Jane's voice was soft and timid. "He wanted to meet you."

"Who the hell is Carlos?" Black asked.

Jane and I looked at each other. Which of us was going to tell him? She fixed her gaze on her hands as she twisted them on her lap, and I knew it wouldn't be her.

I swallowed, my mouth dry as a bar in Saudi Arabia. I hated conversations like this. "He was your brother."

"I don't have a brother. You know that."

"It's true."

"Emmy, my parents tried for years to have another child but they couldn't. I found the paperwork when they died. My mother went through eight rounds of IVF before I was born and four more afterwards."

He'd never told me that part. It all happened before I came on the scene, and I'd never wanted to reopen old wounds. Talking about his family hurt him.

"You look the same." Jane started crying. "You're twins."

I grabbed a box of tissues off the tiny nightstand and passed her a handful. She wiped the tears away but kept sniffling.

Black raised an eyebrow. "Just because he looked similar, that doesn't make us related."

"Jane's right. I only saw him once, and I could have sworn he was you."

"You're both mistaken." Strong words, but Black's voice lacked its usual conviction.

"DNA doesn't lie, and his came back as yours."

Already pale, he lost the last bit of colour in his cheeks. "You had a DNA test done, and you're using the past tense. Emmy, what the hell happened?"

"I arrived at the hotel bang on time, and I couldn't see you in the parking lot so I was heading inside to look for you. Then a cab pulled up with you in it. Well, I thought it was you. Obviously, I know better now. I was waiting for you to pay and get out when two dudes in a van shot a couple of RPGs at it."

"Except it was this Carlos inside, not me." Black filled in the missing piece.

"Yeah. Fuck, he didn't stand a chance. The whole thing went up like the Fourth of July. The cab driver bought it too."

Jane burst into tears, big racking sobs that shook her whole body. Black pulled her into his lap and wrapped his arms around her, stroking her hair while she cried her heart out.

"It's okay," he murmured, holding her tightly. "It's okay."

Why was she so upset? What had I said? Then I realised.

Shit.

When she stopped crying quite so hard, I reached over and took her hand. She tried to pull it away, then went limp.

"He meant something to you, didn't he?"

"All this time I hoped Carlos was alive somewhere, that he would come back. He *promised* he'd take care of us. And now he'll never see his baby."

Her face crumpled as she dissolved into tears again.

Chapter 22

MY EYES SAUCERED and met Black's. He shrugged, a tiny movement that told me he didn't have a clue the baby belonged to Carlos either. And I'd just told Jane he'd exploded. *Tactful, Emmy, real tactful.* She must have been devastated. I knew this because I'd gone through the same thing nearly nine months ago, except for Carlos there would be no miracle comeback.

And Black had just found out he'd lost his brother. He may never have known him, but in some ways, I guessed that made it worse because now he never would. And the part of me I hated was pleased Carlos had died, and pleased Carlos was the father of Jane's child, because that meant it wasn't Black.

Jane recovered slightly and spoke again. "Carlos was kind. Not like the others at the compound."

"Can you tell us more about him?" I asked gently.

She dabbed at her eyes with a tissue again, but nodded. "He saved me. Evil filled that family, pure evil, and he was the only good thing in it. At first, he didn't speak much, but then he learned. We talked for hours when nobody was watching, about our lives and what we wished they could be. For years, we both dreamed of escaping from that terrible place."

"Hang on, hold up a minute. Carlos was a prisoner too?"

"Not behind bars maybe, but Hector and Diego controlled him. They were cruel men. I'm glad they're dead."

"Do you know why Hector favoured Diego?"

"Because Diego was his biological son and Carlos wasn't; that's what Carlos told me. Every time he did something wrong, they would throw it back in his face."

That fitted with Diego's "stepbrother" comment. "So if Carlos wasn't Hector's son, why did he tell people he was?"

"Hector and his first wife adopted him. She'd always wanted a baby, and they tried for years and couldn't have one. So one day, Hector came home with Carlos as a surprise for her. She adored him. Carlos said his early years were wonderful, but Hector changed when she died."

I'd read about that in the research notes Mack and Luke put together. "She got shot in a drive-by, didn't she?"

"Yes. Shot. And without her there, Hector pushed Carlos away and left him to the servants to raise. Things only got worse when Hector remarried and had another son."

"Diego."

"Yes. He doted on Diego. They did the whole father/son bonding thing. Hector took him out shooting and fishing while Carlos got left at home. If he asked to go too, Hector would tell him it was a family outing, and he didn't consider him family."

"What a cruel thing to do to a child."

"Hector was a monster." Jane shuddered as she remembered. "But as Carlos got older, Hector put him to work doing the accounts. He'd spend all day with the spreadsheets, and then in the evenings he would come to me."

"So he wasn't allowed to leave the compound either?"

"Occasionally he left. He had meetings with lawyers, accountants, suppliers, people like that. Usually, one of Hector's henchmen would fly or drive him wherever he needed to go."

"Any idea why Carlos went to America?"

"I think so. He wanted to leave Colombia, and for the last few years, he kept telling me he had a plan to get us both out of there but it would take time."

"What was the plan?"

"I didn't know all of it. He said it was better that way, but if things went as they were supposed to, we would have enough money to escape and hide from Hector and Diego."

"Where was the money coming from?"

"Carlos didn't say, and I was afraid to ask. The whole idea of escaping seemed too good to be true."

"Do you think he was serious?"

"I didn't at first. Then one evening about a year ago, he came to my room. I'd never seen him so...animated. He had this light in his eyes. Hope."

"Why? Did he tell you?"

"Hector had sent him on a trip overseas. He didn't usually do that, but they'd been having some problems with that government program, the one where they spray the coca plants with something that kills them, and Diego and most of the men were busy dealing with that."

"I bet they were." Eduardo had told me all about Plan Colombia. It had caused him a headache too, at least until he found the right people to bribe. Government officials flew over the fields, spraying herbicide over the coca. Unfortunately, the chemicals also killed any other plants they touched, destroying crops and causing health problems for the people living in the targeted areas.

"Hector received a report from someone in his sales network that the DEA was nosing around. He sent Carlos over to find out who and shut them down. Except when Carlos got back, he told me he'd found his brother. I didn't believe him at first, but he insisted, over and over, and I began to think it might be true."

"It must have been me," said Black. "I was working for the DEA a year ago."

Jane nodded, and another tear slipped down her cheek. "He promised Hector he'd fix the problem, but when he went back to America, he was really going to meet you. He planned to ask you for help to get us out of Colombia. Even though it seemed impossible, he was convinced you would be able to set us free. Except he never came back."

"But I did," Black said.

"Yes. Even though Carlos said there was a good chance he wouldn't return, I kept hoping."

Black shifted her closer in his arms. "And you couldn't grieve either, could you? Because nobody knew about the two of you?"

Her tears fell harder as she shook her head. "I was supposed to try and escape. He left some money and a memory stick in the hut."

"That's what's in the envelope?"

"I need to post the stick to Blackwood Security in Virginia. Can you help me?"

"Sure." I pointed at Black. "You're sitting next to the Black part of Blackwood Security. That's where we're from."

"Really?"

I rummaged in the wardrobe until I found one of my business cards in a jacket pocket, then flipped it over to her.

She held it in both hands and read, then took the memory stick from the envelope and handed it to me.

"Do you know what's on it?" I asked.

Hair flopped across her face as she shook her head again, and she pushed the stray strands behind one ear. "Carlos said I was better off not knowing. And then it didn't matter because I was stuck at the compound. The thought of leaving on my own scared me more than staying."

"Do you have any idea what Carlos did while he was away?"

"No, but Hector was furious when he found out. His phone rang, and five minutes later, he started shouting about money and lawyers and trust accounts. Diego was angry too. He put his fist through a wall when he got out of the meeting with his father."

"Short fuse, then."

"What does that mean?"

"He loses his temper easily."

She bobbed her head. "Always. I knew it was something to do with Carlos when Hector stormed past and yelled at his security chief to get him back to Colombia immediately, no matter how difficult that might be. I didn't have any way of warning him. All I could do was pray."

"Money. It was about money," Black cut in. "In the

time I was there, they only let me out of the cell once a month, and Diego drugged me first. The little shit stood at the door and shot me with a tranquillizer dart. He was too much of a coward to just open it."

"Knowing that makes me wish I'd drawn out his death a bit longer. Really had fun with him."

"Much as I like you to be professional, it's a nice thought. Anyway, before he let me out for the first time, he made me practise imitating some guy's voice. He played recordings over and over for hours. Always in Spanish, his end of mundane phone conversations about money transfers and profit margins. I started hearing the damn voice in my sleep. That must have been Carlos."

A cruel punishment, made all the worse by it being Black's unknown brother. "Most probably."

"After Diego doped me, he'd wait just long enough for me to become coherent again, then we'd meet with some lawyer. I had to speak in Carlos's voice, and Diego told me to agree with everything he said and sign when I was instructed. Whatever cocktail he gave me messed with my head, so I didn't follow everything, but the gist was that the lawyer needed my signature to transfer assets back to Diego."

"I bet Carlos tied the money up to protect himself, knowing they couldn't kill him as the money would be lost. Except they did, accidentally, so they had to use the next best thing."

Black leaned his head back and closed his eyes. "Me."

"Yep."

"Diego was an evil fucker. As well as the drugs, he said if I didn't do exactly as he asked, he'd kill Jane in front of me."

The colour drained from Jane's face. Black noticed and held her tighter.

"That's what happened to Lorena, isn't it?" she whispered.

"I didn't answer one of the lawyer's questions fast enough. Diego pulled me through to the room opposite and made me watch from the window while one of his henchmen shot her." His voice dropped to a whisper. "I'm sorry."

"So you went along with him?" I asked, then immediately regretted it. I'd made it sound like I disapproved.

"What else was I supposed to do? I was stuck there, so spaced-out I could barely walk let alone take on his army. I didn't give a fuck about whatever I was signing for, but I needed to keep Jane alive. She was the only person left who wasn't loyal to Hector. Nobody else was around to help me."

I winced as that dig at me hit home. But Black was right; I hadn't helped him. Instead, I'd been off gallivanting around England and Syria and Jordan and Egypt and Japan and America. If only I could turn the clock back, I'd have done everything in my power to find him sooner. I'd also have inflicted a hell of a lot more pain on Hector and Diego. Death by a thousand cuts, maybe. I'd always wondered if that worked. An old friend of mine once got up to eight hundred and three, but then the dude quit on him.

My thoughts were interrupted by Jane's trembling voice. "What happens now?"

I remembered her earlier comment about her family, or rather, not knowing whether she had one.

"You can come home with us."

"Of course." Black gave her that smile again. "We've got two houses in Richmond. You can stay in either one."

"Actually, it's just one at the moment," I told him.

"What do you mean one? Just one house? Did you sell mine already?" He sounded surprised and a bit disappointed.

"No! Of course I didn't sell it. I'd never do that. In fact, I'm living in it. It's mine that's uninhabitable."

"What's wrong with it?"

Where did I start? "Well, there was a fire, but the sprinklers put that out. So there's water damage. And some bullet holes, a lot of bloodstains, the kitchen got taken out by a grenade, and quite a few of the doors and windows are missing. Oh, and the guardhouse is flattened."

His fists clenched. "Fuck. Ramos?"

"That was the line he crossed."

"How bad was it?"

"Mick died, and Seth's in the hospital with third-degree burns to his face, arms, and torso. Hector lost fourteen men. I'm officially dead, and the FBI is trying to work out what to do with the bodies. Agent Stone said the medical examiner's complaining we've taken up all his morgue space."

"Fuck," Black said again, rubbing his temples. "Are the police going to cause problems?"

"I doubt it. We shot as many as possible from the front. Plus, on the bright side, for the past eight months, they've been convinced I killed you or at least hired someone else to, so I can prove they're wrong on that."

He groaned and leaned back against the wall. "Did they arrest you?"

"They didn't have enough evidence. There were witnesses to say I didn't pull the trigger, and the lawyers fought them over access to our bank accounts."

Black clenched his teeth as I turned back to Jane.

"So that means there's one house left. But it's quite big, so we've got plenty of spare rooms. Do you want us to help look for your family?"

"It was so long ago that I saw them. I don't even know if my parents are still alive."

"How long?" I asked.

"Fifteen years."

"Fifteen years? You were in that place for fifteen years?"

Holy fuck. I'd had more than I could stand after fifteen seconds.

CHAPTER 23

JANE TOOK A second to gather her thoughts then answered, her voice soft. "I think it's fifteen years, although I lost track of time. I counted the days to start off with, but when I lost hope, time didn't matter anymore."

"How did you end up at the compound?"

"They took me when I was walking home from school in Tokyo."

"Who did? The Ramos family?"

Jane gave a small shake of her head. "No, others. I barely remember their faces now. A car pulled up next to me, and a man asked for directions. I was trying to help when someone put a cloth over my face from behind. When I woke up, I was on a boat. Not a big ship. It had a few rooms underneath the deck where they kept the girls." She paused for a second to compose herself.

"You don't have to talk about this if you don't want to."

But once she'd started, it seemed she wanted to carry on. Maybe, like me, she needed to get things off her chest.

"The men on the boat, they did things to me. Things I didn't understand at the time. I only knew it hurt. They made me bleed, and many times I wished I would die. Once, I tried to throw myself over the side, but they caught me and locked me back up in one of the bedrooms, handcuffed to a rail. After that, they left me in Colombia."

"At the Ramos compound?"

"Yes. At first, I was a plaything for the guards, but they lost interest in me as I got older. I was more use to them for cleaning and doing the laundry." Her eyes closed and she gave a tiny smile. "Then I met Carlos, and I didn't want to die so much anymore."

I felt like crying myself at what she'd been through. Men had forced themselves on me twice in my life and the feeling of dirtiness, of being defective, of having done something wrong, still overwhelmed me when I thought about it. To withstand fifteen years of that proved she had a strength few others possessed. There and then, I promised myself I'd do anything I could to help her. She was still in Black's arms, but I felt no jealousy now. If Black hadn't been comforting her, I'd have done it myself.

"Jane, I'm so sorry." Words were inadequate, but they were all I had. "What can I do? Anything, just name it."

"Only look for my family. Nothing else. My parents and my little brother. He's two years younger than me."

"Of course. When we get back, you can tell us everything you remember about your family. Our firm has a branch in Japan, and we'll get them onto the search."

Her voice faded, so quiet I had to lean forward to hear it. "My name isn't really Jane. When they took me, they asked me what I was called, but I didn't tell them. They stole everything else from me. My name was the only thing I could keep." She looked up at me from under long, black eyelashes. "That probably sounds crazy."

"No, not at all."

"At school, I loved English classes, and I read every American detective story I could get my hands on. So when they wanted to know my name, I said it was Jane Doe."

Jane Doe. The girl nobody knew. At least until Carlos came along and found her the way Black had found me.

"So what's your real name?" I asked.

"Akari," she whispered. "Akari Takeda. I haven't spoken it since I left Tokyo."

And when she did, it rang a bell. Why did it sound familiar? I thought back to my last trip to Japan, when I flew over to interview potential new recruits. I'd found two good people and enjoyed one raucous night at a karaoke bar before I'd come home. But that wasn't what stirred my memory.

In my mind, I went through my days there. The trip from Narita airport to my apartment, a sleepless night, then onto the Metro at Azabu-Juban. I exited at Shinjuku, close to our office in the business district.

I paused. Backtracked. That was it! Each Saturday, at the entrance to Shinjuku station, an old man stood wearing a sandwich board. Every weekend I'd been there, since my first trip to the country almost a decade ago, he'd been outside, come rain, come shine. And every time I saw him, the light in his eyes had grown a little dimmer, his posture, once proud, stooped a bit more.

It wasn't until five years ago, when I started to learn

Japanese rather than relying on an interpreter, that I'd finally found out what the words on the board said.

Have you seen my daughter?

Akari Takeda disappeared on her way home from school ten years ago.

A faded picture of a young girl in her school uniform smiled out at the passing commuters.

I will never stop looking for her.

If you have any information, please contact...

Dammit! I couldn't remember the whole number, only the first few digits.

One day a couple of years ago, I'd stopped to talk to him and offered him money, but he'd politely declined. "I only want people's help to find my Akari, nothing more."

I'd watched the number of years on his sign creep up from ten to fifteen, and still he stood there. Strong, determined, much like his daughter. Could I finally stop the clock?

"Excuse me a second." I needed to make a call.

Thankfully, the plane was equipped with all sorts of electronic goodies, so I popped out to the main cabin and gathered up a laptop, camera, and phone, earning myself some curious looks from those still awake.

"Later." I held up a hand and went back to the bedroom.

"Jane... Akari, can you smile for the camera?"

"What do you need a picture for?"

"I'll tell you in a minute; I promise."

I snapped a photo then fired off an email to the Tokyo office. The message was simple: *Find me the phone number of the old man from Shinjuku station.*

I looked at my watch. Japan was fourteen hours

ahead of Colombia and thirteen ahead of Richmond, and we were somewhere between the two. It would already be the next morning in Tokyo.

And my Japanese team was good. By the time I'd made myself a cup of coffee, the satellite phone had pinged with the information I needed.

I didn't want to get Akari's hopes up, but neither did I fancy having this conversation in the main cabin. Partly because it was likely to get emotional, and partly because I didn't want anyone to hear how shit my Japanese still was. Instead, I wedged myself into the tiny bathroom at the back of the plane and sat on the closed toilet. My coffee was still too hot to drink, so I balanced the cup in the basin and dialled.

On the other side of the world, the phone rang once, twice.

A man answered, his tone clipped yet polite. "*Kon'nichiwa.*"

"Hi," I answered in Japanese then took a deep breath. "Are you the person who stands at the station looking for Akari Takeda?"

A pause. "No, that is my father."

"Can I speak to him?"

"If it is about my sister, I would rather you speak to me. My father is not well, and every time he receives false hope, only to have it dashed, it takes another fragment of his soul."

"Sure, I can talk to you. What's your name?"

"Hiro."

"Well, Hiro, I'm Emmy. I think I might have found Akari."

I left out most of the detail, but explained to Hiro that we'd come across our extra passenger in Colombia.

Then I emailed him her photo, and I knew the instant he saw it because his voice cracked.

"It's her. I'm sure of it. Is this a joke? Please, tell me the truth."

"No joke. Do you want to speak to her?"

It took a few seconds before he replied in the affirmative, his voice wobbly.

I unfolded myself from my cramped quarters and walked back through to the bedroom, not forgetting the coffee. Akari was still curled up on Black's lap, sobbing softly as he stroked her hair.

I held the phone out. "Hiro wants to speak to you."

Her expression changed from shock to amazement to happiness. She reached out and took the phone, gripping it as if she was afraid it might vanish.

"*Moshi moshi*?" Hello? Her smile grew so wide I feared for her jawbone.

We'd both had reunions today. I only wished I could feel the same joy I saw in Akari as she greeted her brother. My own feelings were bittersweet, my elation at having Black back tinged with worry that our relationship was irreparable.

No, I didn't want to think about it.

Nursing my fractured heart, I left Akari and my husband to themselves and retreated to the safety of the crowd, where I sat to the side and typed out a message to Hiro so I wouldn't interrupt his conversation with his sister.

Emmy: We're on our way to Richmond, Virginia. I can make arrangements for you to travel over to meet us, and your parents too. Let me know?

Then I called Sloane to give her a heads-up. She squealed with delight when I told her we were all on our way home, mostly in one piece. She'd already heard about Dan's injury, but I reassured her it wasn't too bad. I also asked her to keep Black's return to herself. Reintroducing him would take a bit of thought.

As we sped over the ocean, fluffy clouds drifted past below. Evan snored, and I threw a packet of peanuts at him, then several bread rolls until he turned over and shut up. I settled back into my seat and stared out the window at nothing. Time and space flew past, ten minutes, then twenty. The world looked so tranquil from up there, a far cry from the storm brewing in my head.

When I could take it no more, I crept back to look in on Black. He'd taken off his borrowed shoes and fallen asleep with his feet hanging off the edge of the bed. His face twitched as he dreamed, and I hoped he was thinking of the good things in life. Akari was still awake, smiling to herself. I motioned to her and she quietly shuffled off his lap, still clutching the phone, then curled up beside him.

With one last backwards glance, I left them to their peace and went to land the plane.

CHAPTER 24

SLOANE HAD CLEARLY been busy, because when we landed at Silver Springs, a local private airfield, there was a convoy of SUVs waiting to pick us up. We took the weapons and any sensitive equipment off the plane with us and left the rest. Everything else could wait until tomorrow.

Akari rode in the back of one of the vehicles with Black again, but this time I didn't mind. I was just pleased she didn't look as miserable as she had on the first leg of the journey. I hopped into the second car beside Jed, practising my anti-interrogation technique once more. It was a good plan until I remembered he snored worse than Evan, although a well-placed elbow to his ribs soon solved that problem.

The grandfather clock in the hallway was striking midnight when we got back to Riverley Hall. I'd only had a couple of hours' sleep in the last two days, and I was dead on my feet. Looking around, it seemed I wasn't alone.

"Do you want to find Akari a bed, or shall I?" I asked Black. What I really meant was, "Is she sleeping in the same room as you?"

I forced myself to breathe while I waited for his answer. Each tick of the clock felt like a pin being pushed into my heart.

"The lavender room's small but it's got the nicest view, as long as nobody's in it already." Yes, his house was posh enough that the rooms were named.

Relief washed over me. "It's empty. You get some rest, and I'll make sure she's settled."

Black started to yawn then snapped his mouth shut. "Thanks. I'll see you in the morning."

The adrenaline of our Colombian adventure had worn off, and around us, the rest of the team stumbled like zombies as they headed for their beds. I motioned for Akari to follow me up to her room and rummaged in the wardrobe for sleepwear. "Use what you want from the bathroom and press speed-dial one on the phone to get through to the night-time security team if you need anything."

She nodded, and I half walked, half crawled through to my own bed and passed out.

For once, I slept without dreaming—a blessed gift. Had my subconscious, which had replayed Black's death for me so many times, finally understood he was alive and decided to shut the hell up? I sincerely hoped so.

In the morning, I woke feeling refreshed, but it was only seconds before a wave of panic crashed over me. What if the whole Colombian episode had been a figment of my overactive night-time imagination?

I crept along the corridor to Black's room and snuck inside, breathing a sigh of relief when I saw him laid out on the bed in front of me. His top half was naked. I didn't know whether he was wearing anything on the bottom half because a sheet covered it, but the dirty part of my mind wanted to imagine not.

As if sensing me there, he stirred, lazily opening one eye and then the other.

"What's up?"

Fuck, I'd missed his husky voice in the mornings.

"Just checking I wasn't imagining things."

"I've pinched myself a couple of times, but I'm definitely here. And fuck am I glad to be home. I've spent months sleeping on a dirty floor, so having a mattress back is a luxury." He stretched his arms out then peered over at the clock on his nightstand. "I'm not sure I've ever slept for twelve hours before. I'd better get out of bed seeing as I've got eight months to catch up on."

My pulse raced. It was my fault he'd spent so long locked up. *Mine.*

And now he was looking at me, waiting for me to leave. The old Black wouldn't have done that. He'd have got up and dressed in front of me while I pretended not to look.

Things *so* weren't right between us.

I didn't know what to say, and coward that I was, I backed towards the door instead.

"Okay, I'll see you downstairs."

A little wave, and I closed the door without waiting for an answer, then cursed myself. Why did I always lose the words?

Dammit, Emmy.

As I walked through the downstairs hallway, I almost tripped over the pile of boxes from Eduardo. Sloane must have got someone to unload them. Curiosity got the better of me, and I flipped the lids open. Flowers, ball gowns, and enough sparkles to start my own jewellery shop nestled neatly in packing foam. I had a rummage. Bless him, he'd even put in a pair of matching silver pistols. His and hers? Nope, mine and mine. I decided I could get used to shiny things, but I'd never tell Bradley that.

I carried on to the kitchen and fixed myself a bowl of cereal and a glass of orange juice. As I sat down to eat, Nick walked in, dressed in a pair of boxer shorts and a wrinkled T-shirt, closely followed by Luke and Mack, who looked a bit dishevelled.

"Good night?" I smiled, and she turned red. I couldn't help chuckling.

According to Bradley, he'd had to start buying extra condoms for the supply closet since they'd moved in. At least somebody was getting some, even if it wasn't me anymore. No chance I'd be hopping back into bed with Jed now that Black was home.

Luke didn't share Mack's embarrassment, but he did seem slightly nervous when he greeted me. He hadn't yet met Black, I realised. Hell, that had the potential to be awkward. I needed to fill Black in on the story there before he worked it out for himself.

They all joined me at the breakfast bar, with the two lovebirds opting for toast and Nick pouring out a bowl of Coco Krispies. I didn't even know those were in the house, and I very much doubted Toby did either, or he'd have had a heart attack.

"Where did you get those?"

"Cupboard," Nick answered.

"Any idea how they got there?"

"I asked Bradley to bring them. You want some? I've got Frosted Flakes as well."

"No, I'm good with muesli."

Now Black was back, I wanted things to return to normal, or as close to normal as possible given everything that had happened. That included sorting out my diet, getting my exercise regime on track, and going back to work. Black deserved some time off, so that left Nate, Nick, and me to run things.

I was raising another spoonful of muesli to my mouth when Akari appeared in the doorway, dressed in the pair of pyjamas and robe I'd found for her last night.

"I've got a pain." She clutched at her stomach.

Oh, shit. We had a pregnant woman with stomach pain! Now what? A doctor. She needed a doctor.

"Hospital. Yes, hospital."

I jumped up to get a car.

Black appeared behind her, dressed by now although he still hadn't shaved. I couldn't get used to him with a beard and long hair.

"What's going on?"

"Akari's got stomach pains. We're going to the hospital. You should come too, for a checkup."

"I'm fine."

"You don't know that. You've been drugged with goodness knows what and stuck in a dungeon for the best part of a year. Stop arguing and get in the car."

He opened his mouth, and I thought he was going to say something, but he acquiesced and came outside with us. The Explorers were on the drive where we'd abandoned them last night, and I yanked open the driver's side door of the nearest one. Black helped Akari into the back then Mack, who'd decided she didn't want to be left behind, rushed out of the house carrying her coffee in an insulated cup and leapt in beside her. That left Black to take the seat next to me, and we were off.

We made it to the hospital in record time, leaving a trail of disgruntled drivers in our wake. Mack was hyperventilating by the time we got there, and even Black had pressed his foot on an imaginary brake pedal at a couple of points during the trip.

"Your driving hasn't improved, I see," he said wryly.

Neither had my parking. I abandoned the vehicle right outside the front doors. It was easier to have it towed and get Bradley to bring me another one than to try and find a free space in that place. There were some perks to being rich. Just sue me.

Inside, I herded everyone up to the desk where the receptionist peered over her ugly-ass glasses and asked my name.

"Emerson Black."

I tried to explain that I wasn't the one needing treatment, but she held up her hand, stopping me.

"Address?"

I told her.

"We've got you down as dead."

"Well, clearly I'm not."

"The computer says you are." Her tone said the computer didn't lie.

"Fine, have it your way. I don't need a doctor anyway. It's Charles Black and..."

More typing. I tried to finish my sentence, and the hand came up again.

"He's dead too. Look, if this is some kind of joke..."

"Okay, okay, leave that one. Let's go with Akari Takeda."

"Male or female?"

Bloody hell, why me?

"As Charles Black, dead or alive, is obviously a man, and the rest of us are women, I'm gonna go with female."

"There's no need to get snippy."

I bit my tongue as her fingers pecked at the keyboard again.

"She's not on the system."

"I know. Can you please add her and get a fu...get a doctor?"

"I'll need her insurance details." The woman was going to breathe fire in a minute.

"She hasn't got insurance. I'll pay cash."

"I'll have to do a credit check."

"Look, lady, I just bought you a new paediatric wing. I think I'm good for a bloody checkup."

She glared at me, sucking in a breath. "Well..."

I gave up and marched past, heading towards the ER. She leapt out of her seat to follow me, but Black slowed her down by leaning on the lift-up section of her desk so she couldn't get past. Oh, the joys of teamwork.

I left them arguing and went to find somebody who could actually help.

CHAPTER 25

FORTUNATELY, THE FIRST member of staff I saw was Dr. Beech, my favourite death-certificate-signing, press-conference-holding ER doctor.

"Hey, Doc."

"Hi, Emerson. You're looking in remarkably good health for a corpse." He laughed at his own joke. "Great funeral, by the way. Bradley really pushed the boat out. Even had a live band at the wake. It was a shame you missed it."

Fucking Bradley. Honestly, he'd use anything as an excuse for a party. I needed to have a word with him.

"It might have looked odd if I'd turned up, don't you think?"

"Oh. Yes, I guess it would."

"I've got two people who need to be checked out. Can you help? The receptionist out there's convinced I'm dead, and she's acting like Cerberus. Fuck knows how anybody ever gets medical treatment around here."

"She can be a bit of a jobsworth, can't she? I'll come right out. What are we dealing with?"

"One pregnant lady, might well be about to pop, and one man who needs a thorough check over."

"No problem. Did I tell you about our new fundraising campaign? We want to put in a sensory room for some of the long-term patients."

"I'm sure I can be persuaded to make a donation."

"Excellent. Nurses! Come with me."

It was amazing how much red tape could be bypassed when a person had just been press-ganged into buying another addition to the children's unit. Within a couple of hours, Black had been tested for everything under the sun, including glaucoma and West Nile Virus, "just to be on the safe side." He'd been CAT-scanned and MRI-ed, and the nurse took so much blood he threatened to report her under the Geneva Conventions. And at the end of it all, thankfully, Dr. Beech pronounced him in good health, apart from a mild case of anaemia and a vitamin D deficiency.

After that, we went to find Akari, who was in a private room with a midwife sitting by her side.

"Miss Takeda here is in labour, isn't that great news?"

It appeared Akari didn't share the midwife's sentiment. In fact, she looked downright terrified.

"Are you Daddy?" the midwife asked Black.

He seemed as freaked out as Akari. "No! I'm...well...Uncle, I guess. The baby's father isn't around."

"Never mind, at least she's got someone to help. Have you been going to prenatal classes with her?"

"No, no classes."

"That's not ideal." She shook her head and tutted. "But not to worry, I can help you to prepare for the birth."

Honestly, Black went white. I'd seen him in gunfights and I'd seen him in knife fights, but I'd never seen him look worried like he did when the nurse mentioned childbirth.

"I need some water." He dashed from the room. Wimp.

Then the nurse turned on me. "Men! Just haven't got the stomach for it. You'll be staying though?"

"Me? Fu...er, no!"

"Well, somebody should really be with her. Does she have any other family?"

"Yes." Thank goodness. "Her brother and parents are on their way." Sloane had arranged everything. The Takedas were in the air right now.

"Well, that's great. Do they have far to come?"

"Uh, from Japan."

"I hate to tell you this, missy, but the baby won't wait for them to arrive all the way from there."

Oh, shit. Right, I could do this. Childbirth was supposed to be a natural, beautiful thing, wasn't it? I thought back to when Carmen's son was born. Afterwards, she'd told Nate if he ever got her pregnant again, she was going to castrate him. Maybe not so beautiful, then.

Akari started panting, and the nurse reached out to hold her hand. She screamed and batted the woman away then grabbed mine instead. Oh, this was horrible. And Black had bloody abandoned me.

The midwife peered under the sheet covering Akari's bottom half and muttered something about dilation. With my free hand, I got my phone out and checked the calendar. My last contraceptive shot was a month ago. I'd be good for another eight weeks. No way was I ever going through this.

Akari shrieked again as another contraction came, and I dropped my phone. The doctor dashed through the door, ran around the bed, and trod on it. Little bits of screen scattered across the floor. Bollocks.

The midwife encouraged Akari to push, and she nearly broke all the bones in my hand. Would it be frowned upon if I asked for some painkillers?

Akari relaxed enough for me to wriggle free, and I moved my fingers, checking they still worked. The contractions must have been coming thick and fast because then she grabbed my arm instead, cutting off all circulation. The scream that followed probably reached Tokyo, and my ears were still ringing long after she shut her mouth.

There was a flurry of activity from the medical staff. Akari's face went a disturbing shade of purple, and then I heard crying. Was it over? Please say it was over.

The midwife held up a gunk-covered baby, which was bawling its eyes out. "It's a beautiful baby boy."

Thank goodness for that. I wouldn't have cared if it was a baby Frankenstein as long as I could get out of there.

The midwife wrapped him in a towel and placed him in Akari's arms, and she gazed at him with love-filled eyes. It was kind of cute, I guess, but my heartbeat still hadn't calmed down. I needed a drink. Gin, preferably, but water would have to do. After muttering a hasty, "Congratulations," I made a swift exit and found Black leaning against the wall outside.

"You're a shit." I thumped him in the chest as I walked past.

"Yeah, sorry about that. What are those marks on your arm?"

"Bruises. From Akari's fingers. That's what happens when you sit next to a woman in labour."

"So you saw the baby being born?"

"No, I closed my eyes for the gruesome part. And let me tell you now, I am never, ever putting myself through that."

A twinge of regret crossed his face, but only for a second and then it was gone. Well, it was his own fault he'd missed the birth. He should have manned up and gone in there.

"Good. Yes, that's good. Trying to find a replacement for you while you took maternity leave would be impossible."

"I'm one of a kind, all right."

Seconds later, reinforcements arrived in the form of Mack, Nate, Carmen, Nick, and Dan.

"Did we miss it? Did we miss it?" Carmen squealed.

"Yes. The baby came a few minutes ago."

"Is it a boy or a girl?"

"A boy. He's really tiny."

"Sweet! Bradley's gone out to buy a nursery, by the way."

"Where's he planning to put that?"

"I have no idea. I'm not sure he does either. He just saw a shopping opportunity that was too valuable to pass up."

Shopping, parties. Oh, Bradley. "What's all this I hear about a funeral?"

"You mean yours?" Dan asked.

"Yes, mine."

"Bradley did an excellent job with that on such short notice. He even had one of those airplanes towing a banner that said 'RIP Emerson.' There was a great turnout too."

I. Was. Going. To. Kill. Him.

Luckily for Bradley, Nate broke in. "Sloane called. She said Hiro Takeda's plane just landed and you'd know what that meant. And she also said you're not answering your phone?"

"I know what she means, and the doctor trod on my phone."

"I'm not even going to ask."

Probably for the best. I borrowed Nate's phone to get Hiro redirected to the hospital then went to find Black. He was sitting next to Akari, looking down at the baby.

"He has my nose and jawline, don't you think?" he asked me.

I stared at the tiny little person, who'd thankfully been cleaned up by now.

"Yeah, I can see that. He's going to look a lot like you and Carlos when he grows up."

"I can't believe he's here," Akari whispered. "They were going to kill him."

"Who?"

"Diego and Hector. I heard them talking. Diego said he didn't want a crying child around the place."

"Well, they can't do that now. Things'll be okay; I promise. Your brother's just landed in the States, and he's on his way here."

"It will be strange to see him after so many years. What should I say? It was difficult talking to him on the phone."

"I don't think it matters. He loves you so much he'll be happy if you simply sit there."

The nurse came back with a doctor in tow. "We need to give you a checkup, Miss Takeda."

She reached out, but Akari shrank away. "Don't

touch me. Please."

The sheet shifted off her legs, and I saw what I'd missed earlier. Deep scars marred her flesh, all the way up her calf. She followed my gaze and quickly tugged the sheet back.

"Please don't let them touch me." She turned her eyes on Black, pleading.

"We won't. I promise." He focused on the medical staff. "Handle with care. Got it?"

The nurse gulped, and the doctor nodded and took a step backwards. Black had that effect on people.

We got Dan's leg seen by a colleague of Dr. Beech's and a reconstructive surgeon, and Hiro arrived half an hour later. He looked nervous, nothing like the badass cop the dossier Sloane had sent over suggested.

I met him in the corridor and shook his hand, then as an afterthought he bowed. "You will have to excuse my manners," he said, speaking English this time. "I still can't believe this is happening."

"Yeah, sorry about the short notice. It's been one hell of a day. But congratulations, you're an uncle now. And you must be the grandparents?" I spotted an elderly Japanese couple standing behind Hiro.

The woman nodded, clutching onto her husband's arm for support, and I led them through to Akari. Tears flowed, as was only to be expected after so long apart, so Black and I left them alone to get used to being a family again.

When we got outside, the parking jobsworth had just finished writing my ticket. I gave him a hundred bucks and the finger as I walked to the driver's door.

"I'll drive," Black said. "My heart might be healthy at the moment, but a few more trips like this morning's and that could change."

"I didn't go that fast."

"You left skid marks when you turned into the parking lot." He held out his hand for the keys.

Fine. I had to message Hiro anyway, so I tossed them over and took the passenger seat. Dan's muttered, "Thank goodness," as she climbed into the back didn't escape my notice.

As Black drove off, not a hell of a lot slower than me, I hasten to add, I borrowed his phone and told Hiro to call when he and his family were ready to leave. We'd find somewhere for them all to stay. Bradley would just have to interrupt whatever havoc he was busy wreaking and sort out rooms for them. It was going to be a full house at Riverley tonight.

CHAPTER 26

LUKE STAYED BEHIND at the house while everyone else went to the hospital. He still didn't know exactly how or why, but Emmy's husband had somehow turned up in Colombia and flown back with her.

Mack's grin hadn't wavered since she realised Black's resurrection wasn't a cruel prank. "I still can't believe it, but it's the best news ever," she kept saying over and over.

Luke didn't share her enthusiasm. Not only was he staying in the man's house, but he'd also been sleeping with his wife. How would Black react if he found out? Normally, escape to Mack's place would be the obvious solution, but a few days ago, the concierge of the smart apartment block she lived in had called with news of a burst pipe on the floor above. Cascading water had left Mack's home flooded. As they were in the middle of the Colombia job, Mack just asked the guy to turn the water off and mop up the mess as best he could. They'd yet to take a trip over to see how bad the damage was.

Since Emmy had offered a room at Riverley Hall for as long as they wanted it, Mack's housing situation hadn't seemed like such a problem. But now its owner was back, and by all accounts, he was quite scary.

Luke considered hopping on a plane to England, but he didn't want to leave Mack behind. Not to mention the meetings he had set up for the expansion of his own company, and the fit-out of the new office he needed to oversee. No, returning to Lower Foxford wasn't a viable option.

His phone rang, and he glanced at the screen. Tia. "Hey, little sis."

"Ryan said Emmy sorted everything out. Is that true?"

"Yes, everything got dealt with."

"Is she back?"

"She arrived yesterday, but she's gone to the hospital."

"Oh no!" Tia paused then her voice dropped to a whisper. "Did she get hurt?"

"No, Emmy's fine, but she rescued a pregnant lady while she was away, and she went into labour early this morning."

"Ooh, a baby! How fab! Can I come over and see? My exams are all finished now."

"Uh..."

"Please, I promise I won't get in the way," Tia wheedled.

"I suppose so." Luke didn't reckon Emmy would mind. She got on with Tia better than he did.

"And Ryan too?"

"I'm not sure about that. Isn't he supposed to be working?"

"Emmy said he wasn't to leave my side."

"I think she meant until she fixed the problem, which she's done now. So he can probably go home."

"Oh." Tia sounded disappointed. Too disappointed.

"Is there something going on with Ryan that I should know about?"

"What? Uh, no."

Yes, there was. His sister's lying skills hadn't improved, even with the master around to learn from. Suddenly, Luke wanted her close, and if Ryan had to come too, so be it. He'd rather have the pair of them nearby than alone in a house doing who knows what together.

"Okay, bring him over. I'll tell Emmy."

Technically, Ryan would only be following her instructions so she couldn't get too upset, right? Luke just hoped he'd still be alive when Tia got there. What if he ended up having a run-in with Emmy's husband?

A commotion in the hallway indicated somebody had returned. Luke recognised Mack's voice straight away, then Nate and Carmen's.

"The baby's so cute, isn't he?" Mack said as she walked into the room. "Don't you think he looks like Black?"

Luke slid an arm around her waist. "Hang on, is the baby Black's?"

The man had only been away for eight and a bit months. To have a baby with another woman in that time would have been fast work.

"No, it's his twin brother's, but you know—genetics. And the baby has such tiny hands. Strong though. He gripped onto my finger and refused to let go."

"Sounds fascinating. Are Emmy and Black back?" Luke had bigger worries than the baby.

"Not yet, Emmy insisted Dan get her leg checked out by a doctor here."

Okay, that bought Luke a little more time. "Not a bad idea."

"No, and also she's going to get Dan to see her

plastic surgeon to try and avoid scarring."

"Emmy has a plastic surgeon?"

"Yes, he's really good. You wouldn't know she'd been shot twice, would you?"

"No, where?" Luke had explored every inch of her body but couldn't recall seeing any evidence.

"Leg and shoulder. Both a few years back now."

"I had no idea."

Another small reprieve, but it was only putting off the inevitable. He took Mack aside.

"What do you think Black's going to say when he meets me?"

"He'll probably introduce himself and expect you to do the same?"

"I mean, what if he finds out about...you know. That I'm with you now, but I used to be with Emmy?"

"He might think it's a little odd, but if I assure him you're not messing me around, he'll be fine with it. He's always looked out for me and Dan as well as Emmy, so he might have some questions."

"I meant what if someone lets slip that I slept with his wife?" Luke's face flushed as he said the words. On the awkwardness scale, this conversation rated as an eleven.

Fortunately, Mack didn't seem to feel the same. "Oh, that. I doubt you need to worry about him finding out by accident. Emmy'll probably mention it herself. They tell each other everything."

"I think we should stay in a hotel tonight."

"Don't be silly; it'll be fine. He'll understand. Trust me."

Luke was still stewing over things when he got his first look at Black an hour later. Luke had been asleep when the others arrived back the day before, and he'd still been in bed when everyone left for the hospital. Now Dan limped in on crutches with a packet of painkillers in her hand, followed by Nick, with Emmy and Black bringing up the rear. Emmy gave Luke a shaky smile when she saw him leaning against the kitchen counter, and he returned one of his own.

Black was a big man. About six feet six, Luke guessed. His muscles stood out against his lean frame, and he moved with an easy grace belying his stature. Black hair reached almost to his shoulders, and his full beard gave him a menacing appearance.

But his eyes were the thing that worried Luke the most. So dark that the irises blended into the pupils, they scanned the scene in the kitchen, missing nothing. Black's gaze tore through everything it touched, like taking a potato peeler to a person's psyche.

His head swivelled towards Luke almost immediately, and Emmy stood on tiptoe to whisper something in his ear. He nodded, then walked over and stuck out his hand.

"Charles Black."

"Luke Halston-Cain." He went all formal, hating the quaver in his voice.

Black's handshake was dry and firm, but he made no attempt to crush Luke's hand as men sometimes did when they were trying to prove a point.

"I hear you're dating Mack. I hope you like shopping."

"I don't mind shopping, as long as it's with Mack."

"Good answer. Make sure you look after her." There was an implied threat behind the words.

"You don't need to worry about that."

Luke allowed himself to breathe again when Black walked over to the fridge and got out a carton of orange juice. He went to drink from it, and Emmy cleared her throat. He sighed and got a glass instead.

The tension buzzing through Luke dropped a notch as Black lost interest in him. Everyone in the kitchen surrounded the man like wasps to the honey jar. He exuded the same kind of magnetism that Emmy did, the certain something that made a crowd turn when she entered a room and drew people from all walks of life to crawl at her damn feet.

Black managed to eat lunch, ask his questions, and issue orders all at the same time. Sloane arrived from the office and began making notes, and soon so many people filled the kitchen it was standing room only.

Bradley bustled into the middle of things, laden with bags that he dropped on the floor the second he saw Black.

"You're back! You're really back! I've called your favourite designers to order you new clothes, but I'm afraid we've missed most of the summer collection."

"Have I got anything left to wear? Or did it all get thrown out?"

"Nothing's been thrown out. Emmy wouldn't let anybody touch your stuff. But it's from last season." Bradley's horrified expression showed he didn't understand how anybody could contemplate suffering that shame.

"I think I'll manage to find something then, Bradley."

"But..."

Black crossed the room until he stood over the smaller man. He was the darkness to Bradley's incessant sunshine, and Luke stepped to the side to get out of Black's shadow. Childish maybe, but he'd regressed, and the unnatural fear of being sucked into hell was very real.

Bradley gulped as he looked up. "Maybe I'll just have a look through and recycle anything that looks really awful. Although I'm not going to have much time what with creating a nursery for the baby and organising a homecoming party for you."

"My wardrobe's fine, and we're not having a party. I want to keep things low key. And I should warn you, Emmy's heard what you did at her funeral and she's not very happy about it."

"Why? It was an excellent funeral. Everybody said so."

"Perhaps because she wasn't actually dead?"

"Now she's just being picky."

"Instead of parties and clothes and nurseries, do you think you could get hold of the lawyers and find out how I get my death certificate revoked? And whether the transfers of my assets can be undone?" He paused for a second. "I don't care that my estate's gone to Emmy, but if anything got paid in tax, I want it back."

"Sure thing, boss. I'll call Oliver. And nothing got transferred to Emmy. She didn't even file the will for probate."

"Why the hell not? It's been nearly nine months."

"She didn't exactly need the money, did she? And Miriam was being such a witch about everything, Emmy told Oliver to hold off from filing for as long as he could."

"What exactly has Miriam been doing?" Black's voice turned low and dangerous, and his eyes narrowed.

Bradley seemed to shrink a couple of inches even though Black's anger wasn't aimed at him. "Miriam told Emmy she was contesting the will, and as your only living relative, she should be getting the lot. Oh, and she came round a few times and shouted at Emmy a bit."

"And Emmy let her?"

"Emmy hasn't been herself."

Luke tried to lighten the mood which had turned, well, black. "She looks happy today though, huh? I've never seen her smile so much."

When Black skewered him with his gaze, Luke wished he hadn't opened his mouth.

"Emmy's not happy. She's just pretending to be happy because she knows everyone expects her to be. No, she's not right at all. Where the hell is she, anyway?"

Black scanned the room, and Luke realised Emmy wasn't with them anymore. People around him shrugged. Nobody knew where she'd gone.

"Track her phone," Black ordered. "Assuming she's picked up a spare since the last one got trashed at the hospital."

Nate fiddled with an app on his own handset. "According to this, her yellow phone's in her house, somewhere around the lounge. The green one's turned off."

Black sighed, a heavy sound that settled over the room. The air turned viscous, and the volume of chatter dropped a notch further.

"It's time to talk some sense into my crazy wife."

The crowd parted, and he stalked off in the

direction of the basement.

CHAPTER 27

I FELT SURPLUS to requirements as everyone swarmed around Black, asking questions. Things were still tense between us, and guilt weighed on my shoulders as if Hercules himself was pushing down on them. Why hadn't I put the pieces together sooner?

Like when the initial warning call came in on my red phone? Hector or Diego must have got my number out of Black's. Why hadn't I questioned that? And while I was pissing around chasing Carlos's murderers on a motorbike, Black's abductors had used the chaos to sneak him out of the hotel. If I'd asked more questions at the time, I might have found a witness.

But I didn't.

Then, after all the mess with Luke and his half-brother, why hadn't something fired off in my brain? If my synapses had bothered to do their job, maybe the possibility of Black having an unknown sibling would have occurred to me, even if the odds of it were worse than beating the house in Vegas.

Two men. Two unknown brothers.

Hadn't Black taught me that anything was possible? That I should look at problems from every angle?

I laughed softly to myself. What if I had a sister out there? I might have. Especially as my father was most likely an asshole. Or a cousin? Or a— *Stop it, Emmy.*

No, I hadn't thought things through with Black. And I should have. Instead, I'd fallen victim to my own feelings and wallowed in self-pity like a selfish little bitch.

How could he ever forgive me for what I'd done when I couldn't forgive myself?

Dan laughed, and Nate popped the cork on the first bottle of champagne. Not to be outdone, Bradley lugged in a box of indoor fireworks and an entire vineyard. The atmosphere crackled with happiness, and excitement, and...fucking glitter. Oh, Bradley. My eyes cut to the window. Fat drops of rain plopped against it, the grey sky matching my mood.

I melted out of the room and made my way to the basement. The dusty cabinet slid to the side on hidden runners, and I slipped through the door behind, the darkness calling me. My footsteps echoed off the concrete as I walked and then ran through the tunnel.

When I emerged at the other end, scattered pizza boxes still lay on the table, the movie room untouched since the night Diego's men attacked. I didn't want to see the awful state I knew the rest of the place would be in. I'd designed and built that house from scratch, and although I kept telling myself that it was only stuff, and it could all be replaced, I still choked when I looked at the wreckage.

I'd needed to get out of the kitchen at Riverley Hall, though. It was easier to deal with the ruins of my home than the ruins of what I'd once had with Black.

Instead of dwelling on the past, I forced myself to think of something positive. While the doctor had been assessing Dan's leg earlier, I'd visited Seth in the specialist burns unit, and he'd improved markedly since I last saw him. Tomorrow, the doctors planned to undertake an experimental procedure with artificial skin grafts, and the medical team were hopeful he'd make a good recovery. Even better was the news that he didn't have any internal damage.

"Good thing I fell down that hole, wasn't it?" he said.

"These things are relative, but yes."

"And you got the bastards?"

I nodded.

"Saves Justin a job. Carla hasn't been able to get him out of that Batman costume."

"There are worse things he could be."

"You're right." He paused to cough, then his tone grew serious. "Mick's funeral's in ten days. Will you go? Reckon I'll still be stuck in here."

I squeezed his good hand. "Of course."

"Carla wants to go too. You'll look after her?"

"I promise."

Although I'd have to put on a brave face for everyone. I hated funerals.

And I hated the state of my home. As I wandered through downstairs, the damage was every bit as bad as I'd feared. The fire, hot and intense, had swept through several rooms before the sprinklers brought it under control. Although they'd done their job, the resulting trails of sooty water got everywhere. They'd dried into black streaks down the walls, the tears of a tortured abode. A macabre tribute to death.

The kitchen was worse, a mass of charred, splintered wood and chipped granite. Jagged bottles lay in the debris of the wine cooler, and the faint whiff of their contents permeated through the smoky atmosphere. The interior designer would have apoplexy when she saw it. Her jaw had dropped enough last time when I'd accidentally shot up the kitchen in my sleep.

Back then, there were bullet holes everywhere, and rather than tell the truth, I'd fibbed and said I woke up that morning and decided I simply couldn't live with the décor anymore. She'd looked at me like I'd grown another head. Still, it was better than admitting I didn't remember doing it.

Now there were craters in the walls upstairs and downstairs, blood on the carpet, blood on the furniture, and more holes in the dining table courtesy of Alex. In the downstairs hallway, I could tell someone had used a bigger gun than I did, because a mass of brain matter decorated the wall by the window. Alex and arsehole number thirteen? Thankfully I'd told Bradley to leave the place alone before I left for Colombia—he'd have flipped if he saw that.

I poked my head through the back door and found outside hadn't escaped either. Carmen had made a mess with her sniper rifle, and although the rain was making quite an effort, brownish stains still decorated the path.

Boards covered the broken windows and the electricity was turned off, making my normally bright and airy house dark and gloomy. I sank down on the remains of the couch and drew my legs up to my chest, wrapping my arms around them and resting my head on my knees.

"Why is everything such a great big bloody mess?" I asked aloud.

Black's voice came out of the darkness. I hadn't even heard him come in—yet more evidence of my incompetence.

"Because you had a great big bloody gunfight, Diamond."

He sat on the other end of the couch, perching on the edge as if he wasn't sure whether he wanted to stay or go. A sliver of light from outside highlighted his face.

"I think that end's still damp. And I wasn't just talking about the house, Black. I was talking about us."

"I know."

He sat back, staring into space, and let out a sigh. Then we turned to each other and our eyes locked briefly before we both looked away.

"I fucked up," we said in unison.

Our eyes met again. His showed surprise this time.

But I recovered first. "You fucked up? What are you on about?"

"I let my guard down and managed to get abducted. In a hotel, for fuck's sake. Then I couldn't find a way out. I put you through eight months of hell. Nate said you didn't cope very well."

"No, I didn't." That was the understatement of the millennium. "But I should have. Instead of trying to find you, I accepted you were dead and lost the plot."

"Emmy, the cops did a DNA test on a charred corpse. There was no reason either one of us should have suspected I had a twin brother."

I gripped the edge of the couch, and it flaked away in my hand. "But there were little inconsistencies. Looking back, I can see that now. I should have tried harder. And I hurt everyone else as well when I ran off without telling them where I was. Then when Luke helped me, I did nothing but lie to him."

"Luke? Are we talking about the same Luke who's

in my kitchen? The one who's dating Mack?"

"Yes."

He raised one gorgeous eyebrow. "I'm confused."

"I kind of had a thing with him for a couple of months." It seemed like a decade ago now. "I came out of hiding when his sister got kidnapped and I needed the team's help to find her. Two months I lived in his home, he gave me all of him, and I didn't tell him so much as my real name. I couldn't have got through that time without him. He was a rock. At least some good came out of this and he ended up meeting Mack. They're good together."

"When you were living with him, do you mean sleeping with him?"

"Yes."

His eyes darkened then turned curious. "Doesn't it feel odd now he's with Mack?"

"A little, but I don't feel as if it was really *me* with Luke. It was some strange, hollowed-out version of me. She looked like Emmy and sounded like Emmy, but there was nothing inside. He's not the type of man I'd go for at all if I was feeling myself."

"I'm glad he was there for you. I'm just sorry I wasn't."

"Stop apologising. It was my fault. At least you had Akari." I took a deep breath "You two seem close."

"Hers was the only friendly face I saw in that pit, but we barely got a chance to speak. The guards were always around, so it was just whispers when she brought my food. I tried to get her to find me a weapon, something I could use to get myself out of there, but she was too scared." He shook his head infinitesimally. "I'd have needed another eight months to convince her."

"I wonder if she's looking to you as a replacement for your brother?"

"It sounds odd when you say 'brother.'" He paused, turning things over in his mind. "I'll help her with money and moral support, but I'll never be a replacement for Carlos. She's sweet and compliant, and I need more of a challenge. I like a woman with a few sharp edges, Emmy. You must know that."

Okay, this conversation was weird. Black's preference in women wasn't something we'd made a habit of talking about, and I didn't relish the idea of starting now. Time to move on.

"So what now?"

He sat still for a long moment. He had that habit, the one of thinking things through. Not like me. Nine times out of ten, I'd jump in, foot in mouth, and say something inappropriate.

Eventually, he spoke. "Well, I think I fucked up, and you think you fucked up. But we got through it and we're both here now. Luke's happy with Mack, and Akari's got her family back. So can we just put the past eight and a half months behind us, go back home, and be fucked up together? Like we always used to? If we dwell on the past, it'll eat away at our sanity and destroy us."

"I don't know if I can. You were always the strong one, Black."

He shifted and looked at me, and my breath hitched. I was used to him delving into my soul, but at that moment, his guard came down and I could see into his.

"Because I had you. When we met, you completed a

part of me I didn't know was missing. I was always strong because you needed me to be, but I only had that strength because you gave it to me in the first place. So please, Emmy, understand how much I need you."

He turned away, and his hand came up to swipe at his cheek.

Fuck.

How should I react? He'd never said anything like that before. Never given any indication that he needed me as much as I needed him. I wanted more than anything to have the kind of life we used to have, though. And more. How could I tell him I wanted more?

He waited for me to say something.

I needed to say something.

Say something, Emmy.

"Well, when you put it like that, I'll try, okay? I want things to be how they were as well."

Gah! That was terrible. The words I really wanted to say were stuck in my throat. Three little words I'd never uttered to anybody.

Three little words, eight tiny letters, one big deal.

Because once I said them, I couldn't take them back.

Black's lips parted slightly, and for a moment, I thought he was going to say something else. But he didn't. Instead, he sat in silence for a minute or two, staring at the blackened wall. When my nerves had begun to stretch, stretch, stretch, he stood up.

"You're right; this couch is still damp. Let's go home. It's late, and we both need sleep."

He held out his hand, and I reached up and took it. Effortlessly, he pulled me to my feet, and I took my place at his side. I never wanted to be anywhere else. *Never*. As darkness fell, we walked back through the tunnel, our palms heating as they joined us.

Chapter 28

PEACE REIGNED IN Riverley Hall when we got back. Without Black around, people had drifted off. He led me straight upstairs, and when we got to the second floor, I trailed him into his bedroom. Our rooms were next to each other with an interconnecting door. We often stayed up late talking, and the last thing I insisted Black do each night was to lock that door so I couldn't get to him. Mainly in case I went sleepwalking, but also a tiny bit in case I ever got tempted to give in to my feelings, run in there, and throw myself at his sculpted, oh-so-delicious body.

Yes, I know I said if I ever saw him again, I'd confess all, but now that moment had miraculously arrived, I'd chickened out.

I was such a bloody coward.

While Black changed and brushed his teeth, I paid a visit to my bathroom and did the same, returning in one of his T-shirts with just my knickers underneath. The shirt was old and soft with the tour dates for some rock band we'd been to see years ago emblazoned across the chest. Except on me, the words ran across my stomach, because the shirt nearly reached my knees.

Dark eyes looked me up and down. "Some things never change, I see."

"What? I'm not really a lace and satin kind of girl."

He stalked towards me, speaking in a low voice. "Maybe one day I'll buy you something made from lace and satin." I held my breath. "Then I can reclaim my damn T-shirts. Your closet's like a black hole—once they disappear in there, I never see them again."

Okay, hormones, stand down. "Do you want this one back? I could take it off right now," I teased, taking hold of the edge and lifting it an inch or two.

He gave me a sharp look, and I dropped my hands.

Mr. Black, who stole your sense of humour tonight?

He climbed under the quilt and pulled it up to his waist. The sleigh-style bed had a high footboard, so I hopped up and settled back against it, nestling into the soft covers, my legs stretched out on top.

It was my first chance to study his face properly since we got back. The glow from the bedside lamp did nothing for his colour. It kinda surprised me that Bradley hadn't mentioned a spray tan when he'd been ranting about Black's wardrobe earlier. Black would have shot him down in flames, of course, but still... funny.

At least Black's eyes were starting to regain some of their familiar sparkle. They'd looked so tired on the plane yesterday. His mouth was half-hidden under his untrimmed beard, and if the light hit right, he could probably have been mistaken for Bigfoot.

He ran a hand through his hair, which may have been long, but since he'd had a shower, it no longer looked lank and greasy. I didn't love the look, but it wasn't awful, and a part of me itched to crawl over to him and tangle my own fingers in it.

The beard, though, that was a different story.

Yuck.

"What are you thinking?" he asked, breaking into my reverie.

"Just about your beard."

"Good things or bad things?"

"Bad." I'd never lie to him. Leave some things out, maybe, like the fact that I was completely and hopelessly in love with him, but never lie. "It looks like you have road kill stuck to your face," I added, just in case I hadn't been clear enough.

He nodded slightly, the way he often did when he came to a decision, and swung his legs out of bed.

"Well, let's do something about it." He grabbed my hand and pulled me up, then led me into his bathroom.

Now what?

"Get rid of it." He handed me a pair of scissors.

Oh, thank goodness. He sat up on the counter, and I angled his face so I could see properly. I stood between his legs, his hands resting on my waist, and started cutting. Bit by bit, the wiry hair fell to the floor, and bit by bit, my husband's beautiful face came back to me.

I cut off as much as I could with the scissors then picked up the shaving soap and cup he kept next to the sink. Working up a lather, I brushed the foam over his face, then reached for his straight razor. *Snick*. Our eyes met as I unfolded it, and the steel edge glinted under the lights. I leaned in and began to shave. I was the only person Black would let this close to him with a knife, and he knew with a flick of my wrist, I could kill him.

Neither of us said a word. I'd never done this

before, and being mere inches from his lips sent heat rushing through my body, most of it heading south. My pussy throbbed, and I tried to press my thighs together without him noticing. Awkward. His hands at my hips sent trails of fire across my skin every time I moved, napalm to my fucking libido. *Don't shudder, Emmy.* Losing my grip on the razor and maiming my husband would be kind of tricky to explain at the ER. I didn't dare to make eye contact either because if I had, I'd have been gone. Thank goodness he'd kept his shirt on.

Once I'd finished shaving, I couldn't resist running the backs of my fingers over his cheeks. Smooth. I stepped back, snapped the razor shut, and tried to bring my breathing under control.

Black sat there for a few more moments, seemingly caught in a trance.

"You okay?" I asked.

He snapped out of it and slid off the counter, turning to look at himself in the mirror. His fingers reached up to follow the same path mine had taken moments before.

"Thanks, Diamond," he said huskily, then trailed me through to the bedroom.

Okay, I needed to get out of there. Either that or I'd end up wrapping myself around him like a lovesick boa constrictor.

"I need to sleep. I'm really tired," I mumbled, heading for my room. My heart pounded harder than when I'd taken on a good-sized chunk of the Syrian army. "Don't forget to lock the door behind me."

He didn't move as I left the room, but a second after I'd thrown myself on the bed, the lock clicked. Thank goodness. A solid obstacle to my temptation.

"Fuck, fuck, fuck," I muttered to myself as I burrowed under the duvet and slammed my head back on the pillow.

He was back, my Black, and my feelings for him were stronger than ever. But how the hell was I supposed to tell him that? At this rate, I'd probably blurt it out over breakfast because my head was a wild jumble of mixed-up emotions.

Sleep was out of the question. How about taking a cold shower? Or going for a run?

Oh, what was the point?

Nothing short of a nuclear disaster would stop Black from dominating my every thought, and that vision of him sitting in front of me on the bathroom counter was burned into my brain. Another image for my mental spank bank.

Speaking of which... My knickers were soaked, and I needed to take care of myself to get the release I so desperately craved. I reached under the edge of the thin cotton, pressing down on my clit before I plunged two fingers deep inside, imagining it was Black's fingers sliding in and out of me, Black's thumb rubbing slow, tight circles over my most sensitive spot. A groan escaped my lips, and I closed my eyes. The big O was there waiting for me, hovering within reach as I pictured Black's lips doing all the things they never had.

Then the lock tumbled on the door between our rooms. I'd never stopped doing anything so fast in my life.

Or looked so guilty.

I pulled myself up the headboard as Black stormed into the room. Fuck, I was panting. Had I gone red?

Yes, undoubtedly. *Breathe, Emmy. Just breathe.* It didn't help that even in silhouette he still looked so damn hot.

This was bad. This was really, really bad.

I'd need to turn in an Oscar-winning performance to convince Black he'd woken me from a gentle snooze, kind of tricky because in my head I looked half-fucked. *Nonchalant. Go for nonchalant.*

"Is everything okay?"

Black stopped at the end of the bed, the outline of his left fist clenched. He waved something at me with his right.

"What the hell is this?" he growled.

Chapter 29

I SCRAMBLED OUT of bed and stood there, frozen, as Black stalked in my direction.

"What the hell is what? I can't see in this light."

In the faint glimmer from the half moon, all I could make out was the angry man striding across the room towards me. What on earth had got him so worked up? He was fine fifteen minutes ago.

He snapped on the light above my nightstand, and I blinked in the glare. *Focus, Emmy.* What was his damn problem?

Oh, fuck.

Fuck, fuck, fuck.

The letter. The bloody letter, the one I'd written months ago pouring out my feelings for him onto paper, something I never for one second dreamed he'd read. My heart was scrawled across that page in ink, and now he held it in his hand.

I glanced over at the balcony. What were the chances of me getting past him to jump off it?

Not good, I concluded. "Er, did you read that?"

"Of course I read it. It was addressed to me."

Oh. Yeah. I stayed silent. I had absolutely no clue what to say.

"Did you mean it?"

"I meant it at the time," I squeaked, shrinking back

against the wall.

Mack had tried to explain quantum tunnelling to me the other day, and theoretically, it was possible for me to pass right through the wall and come out on the other side, but guess what? It didn't happen.

"The time, Emmy, as you so helpfully included by putting the date at the top, was five months ago. Do you still mean it?" Black enunciated slowly and clearly as if speaking to a small child.

"Yes," I replied quietly, so quietly I wasn't sure at first whether he'd even heard.

But he must have because before I could repeat it, he hauled me up and slammed his mouth onto mine.

Holy hotness. I'd barely had time to process the fact that he was kissing me when he licked along the seam of my lips, softly at first then harder until I yielded. He tangled his hands in my hair, holding me against him as the kiss turned into a wild clash of tongues and teeth.

I'd been dreaming about that mouth for years, and it didn't disappoint.

"Told you I needed you, Diamond. I wasn't fucking kidding."

And I needed him.

But I couldn't speak because he'd stolen my breath and my mind and every ounce of sense I might have once possessed. All that was left were primal urges, and I shoved him backwards onto the bed, clawing at his clothes to get at the good bits underneath.

But the asshole flipped me. The sound of ripping filled the air as he shredded my T-shirt and tore off my knickers. Now I was naked and he wasn't.

"Not fair," I gasped.

"I never play fair."

He pinned my hands against the mattress, trapping me, only I didn't feel trapped. I was exactly where I wanted to be. Flat on the bed with my husband's lust-filled gaze raking up and down my body and his hot, hard, heavy cock pressed right where I needed it. I ground against it, shameless.

"Emmy..."

"Just give it to me."

"Good things come to those—"

"Don't you dare! Don't even think about finishing that sentence."

Tonight, I did *not* want to wait. I bucked my hips and twisted, forcing him onto his side. One quick move and he was the one who was stuck, although he didn't seem to care. The prick was laughing. I shut him up with a kiss.

"This isn't funny," I muttered against his lips.

He laughed harder. Oh, harder, harder. Fuck, I didn't care as long as I got some. I tore his shirt in half and shoved his boxer briefs down to his ankles. Better. I glanced downwards, and fuck me, I didn't know whether to lick it, stroke it, or sit on it. Or better still, tattoo my name on it because that thing was mine.

Black took advantage of my indecision and rolled me again. Arsehole. But he echoed my thoughts when he feathered kisses along my jaw, punctuating them with sweet words.

"So. Fucking. Beautiful." His hand inched downwards. "And. So. Fucking. Mine."

Always. I'd never belong to anyone else.

Over the years, I'd glimpsed Black naked on many occasions. It would have been difficult not to with the amount of time we spent together. But nothing compared to seeing him like this, stretched out above me with that delicious cock just waiting to bury itself inside my pussy.

He reached down with a hand first, ready to finish what I'd started, and I sucked in a gallon of air as one long finger skated over my clit. Circling, circling, circling before it slid in up to the knuckle.

"So wet." He raised one eyebrow. "Did I interrupt something?"

"Possibly."

"And while you were touching yourself, what were you thinking about?"

His low, silky voice turned me to mush, and he added another digit, stretching me as he stroked inside.

"Emmy?"

"Huh? What?"

"*Who* were you thinking about?"

"You. It's only ever you."

"Good."

In one smooth motion, he removed his fingers and slammed into me, burying himself to the hilt, taking what little breath I had left away. Holy shit, he was big. You know what they say about the size of a man's vehicle being inversely proportional to the size of his cock? Well, Black should have been driving one of those tiny clown cars.

I stifled a giggle at the thought.

"Now what?" he asked, flexing his hips.

"Nothing."

Honk honk. Fuck.

Black gave his head a small shake of exasperation, a movement he'd perfected over the years, then focused on the task at hand.

Eyes fixed on mine, he began to move, and I found out what I'd been missing. There was nothing kind about him tonight. He exuded a raw, animalistic strength as his wild side came through, bordering on savage. And I matched him thrust for thrust. This wasn't making love. You could barely even call it sex. This was two people satisfying a desperate need for each other in the most primitive way. I felt my release building and bit down hard on his shoulder to stop myself from screaming. I didn't particularly want everyone in the house running to see what the matter was, guns drawn.

As I clenched around his cock, Black came too, his heat erupting into me. He slumped forward, spent, supporting himself on his elbows as he peppered tiny, gentle kisses across my cheek.

"Diamond, you have no idea how long I've been waiting to do that."

"Enlighten me."

His lips flickered, and he hesitated. Why did he suddenly look nervous?

"Remember the day when a crowd of Jimmy's finest wanted to lynch me? And you stepped between us?"

I closed my eyes and groaned. "How could I forget?"

"Well, since then."

My eyes sprang open again. "That was the day after we met!"

"Yeah, I know. I didn't like you so much on day one." He rubbed his nose, reminding me once more how I'd broken it.

Oops.

Black slid out and rolled to the side, propping himself up on one arm. I pressed my thighs together and blushed as warmth trickled out of me. What would the housekeeper say? Oh well, she'd have to get used to it.

Now, how could I get out of sleeping in the wet patch?

Black ran one finger from my collarbone to my belly button, then lower, lower, and a shudder ran through me. Once it subsided, I properly took in what he'd just said.

"Hang on, you mean...that long... What?"

"There were two reasons I wanted you to come back to Virginia with me. One because you were perfect for Blackwood. The other was because I just...wanted you."

All that time? I was speechless, and that took some doing.

He dipped his head and kissed me, and a glow spread through my insides, warming me from my fingertips to my toes.

"But why didn't you say something?"

"Jimmy was right. At first, you were too young, even when I thought you were eighteen. Then, as we got older, and I got to understand you better, I knew you weren't ready."

"But when you kissed me, when we danced in that bar, the next morning you said it was a mistake."

"I lied."

"But why? I came back to tell you I wanted to make a go of things. Why did you tell me you were drunk and you hadn't meant it?"

"You still weren't ready."

"But..."

Black silenced me with another kiss, sweeter this time, and I melted into him. Even when I hooked a leg over his hips, I couldn't get close enough. I didn't even care about the sweat.

Time went all screwy, and my lips tingled when he pulled back.

"Why'd you stop?"

"Back then, your first reaction when my lips touched yours was to run. Trust me, you weren't ready." He ran his fingers through my hair and bent his forehead down to mine. "I wanted you to want me as much as I wanted you."

"I'm ready now," I whispered.

He slid a hand between my legs and flashed a grin. "I'd noticed."

Before he made me lose my damn mind completely, I had one thing I needed to get off my chest.

"Black, I love you."

My heart thumped as I said the words, and I could feel his answer before he spoke.

"I love you too, Diamond. Always have, always will." His hand snaked around my back and pulled me tighter against him. "If we weren't already married, right now, I'd be asking you to be my wife."

"Just for the record, my answer would be yes."

He traced my new tattoo with a finger, four words in curling black script on my left side, level with my breast.

"Always by my side," he murmured.

"You were, you are, and I hope you always will be."

"Always."

He kissed me again, and then we moved onto round two, which was a lot less frantic but every bit as good.

He didn't stop there, either. When he'd filled me for the second time, he cleaned up the mess with a washcloth, smirked, and hooked my legs over his shoulders. Turned out he knew exactly what to do with his tongue as well.

At that point, I lost the ability to speak again, but I managed to use my mouth for other things instead. It was Black's turn to clap the pillow over his face as hot cum hit the back of my throat. Guess I wouldn't need to creep downstairs for a midnight snack ever again.

"We need to make some modifications to this room. And yours," I said once I'd crawled up his body and kissed him stupid, tasting myself as well as him when our mouths met.

"Extra soundproofing?"

"Walls, floor, and ceiling. Might as well do the bathrooms too while we're at it."

"And upgrade the music room."

"Huh?"

"I've always wanted to fuck you over my grand piano."

Once we'd spent a couple of minutes getting our breath back, we went for round three. Then round four, because we had a ton of lost time to make up. Although Black had explained why he didn't push for an "us" earlier, I couldn't help rueing all the wasted years. Years of lying alone wondering *what if?* Years when I could have been muttering filth as I traced his perfectly defined hip-grooves with my tongue. Years where we could have locked ourselves in the music room while he strummed my clit and came up with new uses for his drumsticks.

We'd never get that time back.

But tonight, Black wrapped his arms around me as I lay half on top of him, my head resting on his chest. I may have been dead, but at least I'd gone to heaven.

"Diamond, we need to get some sleep. It's been a long few days."

His words made me yawn, which would have been an invitation earlier, but now it was just exhaustion. "I know. I'm tired too."

I tried to wriggle off so he could go back to his room, but his arms tightened.

"What are you doing?" he asked.

"You need to go back to your bed."

"No, I do not. I've waited long enough to get you in my arms, and this is exactly where you're staying."

"But what if I hurt you?"

"I'll be holding onto you so tightly you won't be able to swing a punch. From now on, if we're in the same house, we're in the same bed. Understand?"

"Yes, I understand."

His heart beat under my palm as my eyes closed. This was strange, so strange. But a good strange.

The *best* kind of strange.

CHAPTER 30

A SOFT KISS on my shoulder woke me from possibly the best night's sleep of my life. Then another kiss, and another. Stubble tickled my skin as Black spooned me, and I was hovering in that strange limbo between sleep and wakefulness when he slipped his cock inside.

Definitely the best wake-up call I'd ever had.

He barely moved at first, just a slow rocking of his hips, but I groaned as he hit the right spot, and his arms tightened.

"You awake, Diamond?"

"Nope, still dreaming."

I twisted to kiss him, but all I got was a brush of his lips.

"Shh. I'm doing the work this morning."

"Why? Are you gonna make me go to the gym afterwards?"

"You're not going anywhere near Alex today. Maybe ever. Yes, I'll train you myself. You can work out in my bed."

"Lead from the front, Chuck."

He thrust harder and helped me into the land of the living. Sloppy morning sex—I hadn't realised how much I'd missed it. When had it last been? A decade ago with Nick? And Nick was no Black. One of my husband's hands came around my front and reached between my legs, stroking in exactly the right spot.

"You nearly there, Diamond?" he whispered.

I didn't get a chance to answer before I came, trying to stifle a scream and letting out a long, drawn out moan instead. Then it was Black's turn to bite down on my shoulder and quiet his own cry, which erupted as he found his release seconds later.

I turned so he could see my smile. "That's the nicest thing I've ever woken up to."

"Better than the time Dan hired a stripper to serve you breakfast in bed on your twenty-fifth birthday?"

"Definitely." Although that dude sure had been pretty. "Maybe even better than coffee."

"That's some compliment coming from you." Black nuzzled my neck. "And it'll only improve with practice."

Practice makes perfect, that's what they say. Although in my eyes, he already was.

Since Black had given me a reprieve from the gym, I snuggled back against him and closed my eyes. Last night was seared into my memory, filed under F for Fucking amazing. Or possibly A for Amazing fucking. I only regretted that we'd taken so long to do it, but Black was right—before, I hadn't been ready. And I couldn't deny he was worth the wait.

With that thought, I made him a promise. "I'm going to try really hard not to run away from things from now on."

"I'll handcuff you to the bed if you even consider it. Although the running away option seems attractive this morning. How many people were in the house last night? Were they all planning to stay?"

"The handcuffing option seems quite attractive, too." I grinned at him then wrinkled my nose at the thought of the guests. "I expect most of them will have slept here. There was a river of champagne flowing."

"Just when I want you all to myself."

I shared his sentiment, but we were shit out of luck. "That won't happen for weeks. Mack's apartment got flooded, so she'll be here for a while. And if she's here, Luke will be too. And the Takedas, at least until the baby's old enough to fly back to Japan."

"Plan B." He disentangled his arms and rolled out of bed. "Come on. It's not light yet, so nobody else'll be up. We can sneak out."

I got momentarily distracted by his abs and, er, other things. "What?"

"You, me, and a pair of handcuffs. Just for a few days. We can start unravelling what's left of this mess when we get back."

"What did I say two seconds ago about not running away?"

"I prefer to think of this as a strategic retreat."

"Nate's gonna go mental. I promised him I wouldn't take off again."

"I'll tell him it's my fault. Are you coming?"

I certainly hoped so. Of all the decisions I'd ever made, that one was the easiest. "Of course I am. What do I need to pack?"

Most of the time, we stayed in one of our other homes, and I didn't need to pack a thing. But the idea of a quiet hotel somewhere, a little privacy, nobody knowing who we were... Yeah, that appealed.

"Don't pack much. I'm not planning on either of us wearing many clothes."

This trip sounded better and better. I climbed out of bed, relishing the ache between my legs. "Where are we going?"

"Did you get your birthday present?"

"The car? Yes, it was amazing. Such a surprise. I nearly told the bloke delivering it to sod off because I wasn't expecting it." I stood on tiptoes and kissed Black. "Thank you."

"Oh, yeah, the car. Glad you liked it."

"What's that got to do with packing though? Are we going somewhere hot or cold?"

I dropped onto the edge of the bed as Black stopped in front of the window and stretched. That ass. I'd never, never get sick of the sight of it. Unsurprisingly, Black caught me looking and turned around.

"Like what you see?"

"Sure do, honey. You can send me dick pics any day."

"Fuck that. You're getting the real thing." He took a step towards me. Stopped. "Later, you distracting little minx. If we don't leave now, we'll end up downstairs eating waffles and cooing over the baby."

Waffles, yes. Baby, no. Tiny little people scared the crap out of me.

"Fine. But you still haven't given me a clue where we're going."

"I need some sun. That okay with you?"

I'd spend a week in a cave as long as Black was with me, but somewhere hot sounded perfect.

"Bikinis it is."

CHAPTER 31

IT ONLY TOOK me five minutes to grab the essentials. Bradley kept my bags packed for a variety of climates, everything from the Antarctic to the Sahara, so I just shoved a few extra bits in. Okay, I shoved sex toys and fancy underwear in. Black tossed his dive computer and a pair of handcuffs into his duffel before disappearing onto the balcony with his phone. Now, where had I left my favourite flip-flops?

I was rummaging in the closet when Black smacked me on the arse. "Ready?"

No problem, I'd go barefoot.

"Stingray?" I asked as we ran down the stairs.

"Why not?"

I'd only driven the thing a couple of times, so I took the driver's seat and off we went. But where to?

"Which direction?"

"Silver Springs. We need the jet. They're refuelling it at the moment."

When we got to the airfield, the ground crew was milling around our Lear. The Bombardier we'd taken to Colombia stood next to it on the tarmac, the early morning sun reflecting off one wing. Had our trip to South America really only been two days ago? My whole life had changed since then.

Black went to file a flight plan while I carried the

luggage on board and started the pre-flight checks. And finished them too. What was the hold-up?

Finally, he strolled up the stairs, and my heart skipped. Probably it would keep doing that for a while, but I wasn't complaining.

"That took a while. They were somewhat alarmed to see me."

"It's not every day a dead man walks through the door. Are you flying or are you going to tell me where we're going?"

"I'm flying, and it's a surprise."

Great. Another surprise. Because I hadn't had enough of those this year.

Three and a half hours later, we began our descent, and I saw Killarney Lake below as we approached Lynden Pindling International Airport. We'd arrived in Nassau. Last time I visited the Bahamas, I'd almost got shot rescuing a kidnap victim, but it could have been worse. At least it wasn't Colombia.

Black landed smoothly and parked the jet, then we each grabbed a bag and held hands in the middle. Such a small thing, but it meant so much. The warmth that spread through me was nothing to do with the sun. A black Mercedes waited by the plane, engine running, and Black tucked me against his side in the back seat for what turned out to be a short drive to the marina. Who knew Black would turn out to be a cuddler?

"We're going sailing?"

He didn't answer, just led me down the jetty until we reached one of the larger yachts. I read the name on the hull: Black Diamond.

"You bought a new boat!" I squealed, sounding like a complete girl.

Each of Black's boats was named after a gemstone. There was the Black Emerald in Egypt, the Black Sapphire in the South of France, and the Black Ruby in Florida. This new Sunseeker was bigger than all of them, even the one in Nice.

"I haven't been on board yet. It got delivered right before I... Before I left. The only person who knew was Oliver, but as I understand you never did anything with my estate, I guess he didn't tell you."

"No, I didn't know. I didn't *want* to know. Having to deal with all that would have made it even more real."

"Bradley also mentioned problems with Miriam?"

"There were some issues, yes."

"How bad?"

"Put it this way, if I had two bullets and ended up in a room with Hitler, Hector Ramos, and Miriam, I'd shoot Miriam twice."

Black wrapped his arms around me. "Diamond, I'm so sorry. I'll fix everything when we get back. And what's more, I'll enjoy doing it. I suppose if something good's come out of this, it's the realisation I'm not genetically related to that bitch."

"We still need to talk about that, about who your real family might be. If you want to, that is."

"Later. We'll do all of that later. I just want to enjoy being 'us' for a few days first, okay?"

That sounded great to me.

We jumped on board the Black Diamond, kicked off our shoes, and started exploring. I loved boats.

Something about the way they were put together appealed to my inner sense of order. Basically, they were really expensive jigsaws.

Below were four double bedrooms, two with ensuites, and a separate bathroom. The main deck housed the galley plus a large salon and dining area. Oh good—someone had stocked the drinks cabinet. Behind the bridge on the top deck lay more seating and sunbeds. Tell me Bradley had remembered to pack my sunblock? Now that Black had washed the dirt off, he was pale as fuck, and he wasn't the only one who needed some colour.

The swim platform at the stern held a small zodiac boat, and when I poked around in the lockers beside it, I found a dive compressor and a full set of scuba gear. This holiday got better and better. I hadn't dived since my accidental trip to Dahab earlier in the year, and I couldn't wait to get back underwater.

I found Black poking around below decks, checking the bilge pumps and the seacocks. While others might look at the massive engines and wonder how fast the boat went, Black's mind worked differently. As always, he wanted to know how he could disable the boat and sink it if necessary. Old habits died hard.

"Are we setting sail?" I asked. "Or do you want to christen the bed first?"

Black's answer was to toss me over his shoulder and carry me to the stateroom.

Two hours passed before we came up for air, and by then we were starving. So much for the whole sailing thing. We found a little café at the edge of the marina and ordered a lunch of fresh fish and grilled vegetables. Black ate two portions. He'd lost at least twenty kilos, and he needed to bulk up again.

"I guess the food wasn't great in Colombia," I said.

"Could have been better. There wasn't a lot to do in my cell except exercise, so I stayed fit, but I also got hungry. Getting enough to eat was the problem, despite Akari's best efforts."

She'd kept him alive. That was what mattered. I reached out and squeezed both of his hands in mine, amazed my cherry-red manicure had survived a gunfight intact. Whatever Bradley's pet manicurist had put on my nails, they'd probably survive an atomic bomb.

"Are we having dessert?"

Black picked up the menu. "I could be tempted."

After lunch, I took a shower to rinse away the sticky remains of the chocolate gateaux Black had eaten off my stomach, while he studied the operating manual for the yacht. Typical. No sense of adventure.

"Ready?" I asked once I got back to the salon, flicking the damp ends of my hair over my shoulder.

He gave me a look. *That* look. One day into the new us, and I'd already become well acquainted with what it meant. I shook my head and pointed at the bridge.

"No. Sail first. Sex after."

"You drive a hard bargain, Mrs. Black."

"I think you'll find the hard parts are all yours."

"Not helping."

We eventually got around to taking the yacht for a sail. As neither of us had driven the thing before, Black hired a pilot to take us out of the marina, and then we were on our own.

"Have a good day, ma'am," the pilot said as I waved him off.

"Oh, I will."

Black steered while I sat on his lap, his arms reaching around me to the wheel. He punched coordinates into the navigation unit, and we headed out to sea.

"Are we going somewhere in particular?"

"It's a surprise."

Oh boy, another surprise. But the last few surprises had been good, so I could live with that.

In fact, I still couldn't believe I was there, with Black, closer than we ever were before. The yacht cut through the waves, and I pinched myself as I gazed at the crystal blue water twinkling on the horizon. Ouch.

"Stop that," he growled in my ear.

"Stop what?"

"Fidgeting."

"Why?"

He shifted, and I felt he was hard again. "Because if you don't, we'll have to stop, and then we'll never get to where we're going."

"How is that a bad thing?"

"You're bloody insatiable, aren't you? There'll be plenty of time later, believe me. At least I don't need to try and hide this anymore." He wrapped my hand around the impressive bulge in his shorts. "I've had to take a lot of cold showers over the years."

"Really?"

"You have no idea of the effect you've had on me, do you? I couldn't even get out of bed yesterday morning because you could have hung a flag on it."

"Oh." I'd had no idea. "I thought you just didn't want me near you."

"Glad we cleared that up."

I twisted around and kissed him softly on the lips. "I love you."

"I love you too, Mrs. Black."

Two hours later, Black slowed the boat as we approached a small island. A harbour with a wooden jetty lay straight ahead of us, a single boat bobbing gently in the current. Not a yacht, just a small runabout that had seen better days.

Long white beaches stretched out on either side, backed by lush vegetation, and three hills rose in the centre. What was this place? A resort? Apart from a hut on the beach, I could only see one building, a large white house nestled in a dip near the top of the highest hill.

Where were all the people?

"It's beautiful," I breathed. "Are we staying here tonight?"

"We're staying here until we decide to go home. It's called Lorelei Cay."

Wow. I'd never seen anywhere quite so idyllic. Or so deserted. "Did you rent the whole island?"

"No."

A sigh threatened to escape, but I stopped it. The selfish part of me wanted Black and the island all to myself, but I'd have to live with it and share the island part. It looked pretty quiet, anyway, and we also had the boat if we wanted to hide out.

"I bought it," Black said.

"Sorry, you did what?"

"This place. I bought it."

"You bought a freaking island?"

"We both had big birthdays coming up. You were about to hit thirty, and I'll be forty soon. So I decided to buy us something special. I was going to bring you here for your real birthday last December."

That was it. I burst into tears.

"What's the matter?" His arms tightened around me. "Oh hell, Emmy, what's wrong? Do you hate it? I can always sell it again."

"No," I blubbed. "It's perfect. You're perfect. I'm just so fucking happy."

He angled my face towards him. "Then why are you crying? You never cry."

"I don't bloody know."

Black chuckled and wiped my tears away with his thumbs. I liked this new, tender side of him.

An elderly black man in a pair of Bermuda shorts and a worn T-shirt emerged from the trees near the jetty, and I made an effort to stop leaking and help Black to moor the boat instead. A quick hop up the gangplank, and Black introduced us.

"Emmy, this is Wilson. He and his wife are the caretakers here."

I shook hands. "Nice to meet you, Wilson."

"It's good to finally meet you too, ma'am."

"Emmy, please."

"Emmy. I'll take care of the boat, ma'am. You and Mr. Black go take a look at this beautiful island."

Black led me along a path through the trees. Yes, I could definitely get used to this hand-holding thing.

"Last time I came here, this was more of an animal track," he said. "They had to widen it when they renovated the villa."

"When was that?"

"A year ago, while you were in Paris. I bought it six months before that."

"It's beautiful." So was his smile.

"The only person I told was Oliver. He helped to organise the building work, even though it was outside his usual remit."

I snorted at the thought of Oliver picking out sofas. "Bet he loved that. Bradley will be devastated he missed out."

"Can you imagine what would have happened if I'd told Bradley? You'd have known within a day, and we'd never have managed a quiet getaway. He'd probably have flown a circus troupe out to welcome us."

I laughed because that was exactly what Bradley would have done.

The house itself was stunning. Part brick, part wood, with airy, open rooms, huge windows, and a wide deck that looked out over the sea. The furniture was sleek and modern, but when I dropped onto the massive bed in the master suite, surprisingly comfortable. Black had decorated this place to my tastes rather than his own. Fuck. This man was everything.

"Want to take this mattress for a test run?" I asked.

"Later." He held out a hand. "First, I want to show you something."

He led me up a narrow staircase in the corner of the room, and we emerged into the sun on a hidden roof terrace. Waist-high walls hid the double sun lounger at one end from wandering eyes.

"Look at the view." Black waved an arm at the trees, the swath of white sand, and the crystal blue sea twinkling all the way to the horizon. "This was what made me buy the place. Once I came up here, I knew I had to have it." He leaned down and kissed me. "A bit like you, really."

I stepped to the edge and leaned forward, hands on top of the wall. Up there, I felt like the queen of the damn world, and I had my king by my side. He stared off into the distance, a tiny smile playing across his lips.

"What are you thinking?" I asked.

"I'm thinking you're wearing too many clothes."

I peeled off my T-shirt. "A situation easily rectified, Mr. Black."

Before I could blink, I was underneath him on the sun lounger and my shorts had disappeared too.

"I might just keep you up here naked, Mrs. Black."

"As a sex slave?"

"Why do you think I brought the handcuffs?"

"How long have you been at Lorelei Cay, Wilson?" I asked over dinner that evening.

Wilson's wife, Marcie, had cooked us up a feast of rice, vegetables, and grilled snapper. Apparently, Wilson liked to fish in his spare time.

"Ten years, now. We came here under the previous owner, and we don't ever want to leave."

"Don't you get lonely?"

"Spent my twenties in New York, working as a broker. Destroys a man's soul. One day, I stood at the window to my office, staring out at the lights, and I figured there must be more to life. I quit on the spot and moved to Nassau. Met Marcie and worked as a barber for twenty years before we came here. No, we don't get lonely. The other islands are just a boat ride away, and friends stop by to visit."

"You know how to cut hair?"

"Sure I do. Not that I've got much left myself."

"Could you do me a favour?" I pointed at Black. "Fix that?"

"What?" Black asked. "The hippie-surfer look doesn't suit me?"

"Sorry, honey."

"She's right. Can you fix it?"

Wilson laughed. "I'll just find a pair of scissors."

An hour later, Black had short hair again, and all was right with the world.

On Lorelei Cay, I discovered another new side of my husband. Black was utterly, delightfully, perfectly filthy.

"What do you want to do today?" I asked his backside as he stood naked on the bedroom balcony.

"You."

"Honey, you just did me. Anything else? And please don't say walking because I'm not sure I can."

"Then how about swimming? A lap of the island?"

"As long as you don't turn it into a race."

Oh, who was I kidding? This was me and Black. Of course it turned into a race. I got ahead at one point when I pulled his swim shorts down so he couldn't kick with his legs anymore, but the asshole yanked them up again and he still beat me.

"Fuck."

I crawled up the beach, sucking in air. Black reached a hand down and pulled me to my feet.

"My kind of fun, Diamond."

"Sometimes, I hate you."

"No, you don't. Five minutes, and we'll head out again. I saw another nice beach on the other side of the island."

What? How did he even have time to look? "Perhaps I'll walk."

"Perhaps I'll walk behind you."

"Don't be such a pervy old man."

"You like me that way."

I liked my husband any way I could get him.

My husband.

Mine.

In the afternoon, we went diving, and let me tell you, scuba sex is not as easy as it might appear. First, you have to get the buoyancy just right. Secondly, you have to keep an eye on your air because believe me, it goes down fast in the throes of passion. And thirdly, this yellowmouth grouper kept staring at us and it felt kind of awkward. We both finished, but...yeah.

"If that fish was human, it'd be watching porn in a booth at an adult video store," Black grumbled as we hauled our equipment onto the Black Diamond.

"The piscatory equivalent of a third wheel."

He hefted a pole spear from the equipment locker at the stern. "Maybe I'll catch him for dinner."

"Yeah, and if I distract him with my tits, I bet the asshole wouldn't even swim away."

Black's eyes turned predatory. "Or perhaps you could distract me instead?"

Wilson and Marcie had sailed off for provisions,

and a barrier reef kept other boats away from the island. Black untied my bikini and lay me down on the sun deck, which right now, seemed pretty close to paradise.

He knelt in front of me, stroking himself, and I didn't dare to blink. I wanted to remember every second of this trip. A drop of pre-cum appeared, and I leaned forward to suck it away.

"They say every man has a weakness, Diamond, but I don't. You're my strength."

"Don't make me cry again, you arsehole."

He chuckled as he eased into me, slowly, so slowly. "I mean it. I'd do anything for you."

"Bring me a donut?"

"Are you serious?" He pulled out an inch. "Because I could—"

My turn to laugh. "Just fuck me, Mr. Black."

"Not today, Diamond. Today, I'll make love to you."

If he got any sweeter, my heart would explode and I'd die from shrapnel wounds, so I shut him up with a kiss. What if we stayed here forever? I'd found my paradise, and I never wanted to leave.

CHAPTER 32

WE'D BEEN ON Lorelei Cay for four days when Nate emailed me. Four glorious days of sea, sun, sand, and sex. Not the last two together, I hasten to add. They didn't mix well. Black hadn't managed to leave his control freakish ways behind entirely, but the punishments for ignoring all his orders had suddenly got a lot more entertaining.

Anyhow, after Nate got over his initial snit at us taking off, he promised not to disturb us unless it couldn't be helped. So when the message popped up, I saw the attachment and groaned. What was more important than the four S's?

Black put his book down and glanced over at me. I'd like to say he was relaxing with some trashy novel, but he never did that. No, he was reading a well-thumbed copy of Sun Tzu's *The Art of War*. He liked to refresh his memory every so often.

"What's up?"

"Nate." I waved my iPad at him.

"Turn it off."

"I can't. It might be something important."

"Up to you." He looked at his watch. "But I'm still fucking you before lunch, and that's in an hour."

I stuck my tongue out and undid my bikini top, just to give him something to think about.

"Bitch."

I grinned at Black and lay back on the sun lounger, then opened up the message and began to read.

Ems,

We finally managed to break through the encryption on the memory stick Akari gave you. Took Mack and Luke two days, and they were banging their heads off the desk at one point.

It's full of the good stuff—all the Ramos family's dealings for the last decade. The DEA are gonna wet themselves over it. Thousands of files, but one was addressed to Black. I didn't want to open it—that's for him to do, not me—but I've scanned it for viruses, and it's safe.

I'm sending it to you because I don't know what frame of mind he's in. If you think he's up to it, can you tell him?

Nate.

P.S. Don't worry about us. We're only busting our asses dealing with all the shit you left behind. You carry on enjoying yourselves.

I looked over at Black. He'd shifted slightly to keep the sun off his face, and now he was watching me from behind his sunglasses. I might not have been able to see his eyes, but I could feel them.

"The temperature on this section of beach just dropped ten degrees," he said. "Bad news?"

"I'm not sure."

He gave me space to think. He always did. It was just one of the many reasons I loved him.

And the question was, would he want to know? We

hadn't spoken much about Carlos or his time as a prisoner in Colombia, which didn't surprise me. I was the one who talked about my problems. Black, now more than ever, locked them up inside. Should I add to his burden? I was kind of tempted to open the damn file so I knew what it said, but Nate was right. It was for Black to read, not us.

A bird flew past on the horizon, and for a moment I envied its freedom. No difficult decisions to make, no impossible missions to plan. Just hour after hour, day after day, soaring on the breeze and planning what to shit on next. But I didn't have that luxury. After turning things over in my head for a few minutes, I decided to tell Black. Whenever we'd been on jobs in the past, he'd always liked to have all the information available to him, even if it wasn't what he'd hoped to hear. This may not have been work, but I applied the same principle.

"Nate forwarded me a document. It's for you, from Carlos. If you don't want to read it, then you don't have to, but at least you know it's there now."

Now it was his turn to mull things over, and he wasn't happy about the news. I could see it from the tension in his muscles, the way his hands formed into fists at his sides. I reached over and uncurled the fingers closest to me then brought them to my lips. At least that got me a hint of a smile.

He sat up, one leg either side of his sun lounger, hands on his thighs and his head hanging low. What was he thinking?

"Open it," he said.

"Are you sure?"

"I don't want to know, but at the same time, I need to."

Silently, I called up the file. It looked like a letter, from the quick glimpse I got before I handed it over. Black took the iPad but patted the seat in front of him. He wanted me there.

"You read it too. No secrets."

I nestled between his thighs, and he held the iPad in front of us. His chin rested on my shoulder, and we both read what Carlos had to say.

Charles, or is it Black?

I'm not even sure what to call you. But then, I guess at this stage, it doesn't really matter. If you're reading this letter, it means I'm dead and Jane's alive. I've got a favour to ask there, but before I get to that, I'd better start at the beginning.

First of all, congratulations to Mackenzie for breaking through my encryption. I had every confidence that she would. From what I've seen, you only hire the best.

So...

My name is Carlos Ramos. At least that's the one I've always known myself by. I was brought up as a Ramos, I lived as a Ramos, and now I've died as one. But I wasn't born a Ramos.

I was five years old before I found out the truth. It started out like any other Saturday, at least until I twisted my ankle playing hide-and-seek with Mama. My foot swelled up, and yes, I cried. Mama never liked to see me sad, so she promised to buy me a gift. A surprise, she said, but I knew what it would be: a keyboard. I used to sit beside her when she played the piano, and I'd been asking for my own for weeks.

That afternoon, she went into town and came back

in a casket.

The man I thought was my father told me it was my fault. That my mama died because I wanted a new toy, and if I hadn't been such a difficult child, she'd still be alive. It wasn't until years later I found out the bullet was meant for him. She'd died because she borrowed his car. The day I realised that was the day I promised myself I would bring him down.

Every day I lived in Hector's house, I hated him more. And my stepbrother, Diego. Every night, I dreamed of escape, but before I left, I wanted to give the fuckers something to think about. And I did. Now I'm dead, and I'm lying six feet under with a smile on my face. Because I took their money. Twelve years of their work, countless laws broken, too many lives lost, six hundred million dollars, and I took every last dime.

The money's locked away in various funds. One matures every three months, and will continue to do so for the next thirty years. If I don't sign the release forms personally within a week of each anniversary date, the money goes to charity. Drugs rehab. I thought that was a nice touch.

So, you're probably asking, why has this man sent a rambling letter when we haven't even met? Well, look in the mirror. Literally, just do it. See the man staring back at you? There I am. Believe me, I was as surprised about it as you would have been if we'd ever come face to face.

I found out about you a couple of years ago when Hector sent me to New York to fix up a problem. Normally, Diego would have gone, but he'd accidentally killed his girlfriend and Hector told him he had to clean up his own mess for once. That argument was something to behold. Anyway, I digress.

I asked around to find out who was interfering in Hector's business. Not so I could do Hector's dirty work, but because I was tempted to send a congratulations card. Imagine my surprise when my informant sent me a surveillance photo of myself. Clean shaven, a little paler, but me nonetheless. Only it was you. I covered up your meddling and started finding out everything I could about Charles Edward Black. It wasn't easy, I'm sure you'll be pleased to hear. Congratulations on everything you've achieved with Blackwood—building a behemoth like that out of nothing took some doing.

Months passed, and I decided I had to meet you. After I finished this letter, I was leaving for the United States to do exactly that. Obviously, I never made it. That's my biggest regret, I think, that I had a brother out there, and I never got to know him. From what I saw of you, you're a man I'd have liked spending time with.

So, that's the story. Now onto the things I need to ask of you.

Firstly, Jane. You'll have met her by now, and maybe you'll see why I fell in love with her. She's quiet, but once you get to know her, you'll find a sweetness like no other. Please, look after her for me. She doesn't have anyone else.

I've set up a bank account for her. You're the signatory. The account details are at the bottom of this letter, and the passcode is in her head. I used to say it to her every time we parted. Flip it backwards and match each letter to the alphabet.

The second thing I ask is that you carry on where I left off against Hector and Diego. I've copied everything I can get hold of onto this memory stick—details of their supply routes, dealers, money laundering strategies, suppliers. Pass it to someone you can trust to bring them down.

Finally, in case you want to know, I found my mama's diary a year back. We came from a village called Valento on the banks of the Amazon, about a hundred miles east of Hector's compound. With your resources, I'm sure you can find out where that is, but I've included a map just in case. Mama wrote that Hector brought me home as a surprise and said he picked the one that was smiling. When Mama found out he'd left you behind, she made him go back, but you were gone. In her words, she withheld conjugal rights for a month until he apologised properly. But she couldn't turn back the clock.

I don't know what's left of the village now; I was always too scared to find out. I'd hoped one day we might go together.

So, that's it. Not much of a letter is it, for a lifetime? Then again, I never was good with words.

Got to go.

I have a plane to catch.

C.

Black took a shuddering breath behind me, and his arms tightened around my stomach.

"Shit," I whispered. A tear ran down my cheek. I'd spent twenty years not crying, and this was twice in a week. Was I making up for lost time or something?

Black took my "shit" and raised me.

"Fuck." He let out a sigh.

Neither of us spoke for a full minute, then I turned around and hugged him tightly. He buried his head in my shoulder. All I could do was hang on while he battled with his emotions.

"I'm sorry," I whispered. "I'm so sorry."

His face was wet against me as he broke, and we clung together as we tried to heal each other's pain. Neither of us said a word. We didn't need to.

Movement at the far end of the beach caught my eye, and I waved Marcie away. No, we didn't need dinner, not right now. My appetite had deserted me, and Black's would have too.

"Just take whatever you need," I whispered to him.

Vanity had driven me to take my watch off, so I wasn't sure how long we spent like that. Enough time for the sun to start its downwards descent, the horizon calling it in for the night.

Black moved first. He stood, still silent, and held out his hand. I put mine into it, and he led me across the beach, into the house, up the stairs, and into bed. That afternoon, as he slid into me, his eyes were endless pools of darkness. I saw his pain, his hurt, and his sadness as he tried to lose himself in me.

And under it, as he reached his climax and I reached mine, there was something else.

Love.

Years ago, I'd doubted he could feel that emotion, but I knew the truth now.

We both did.

Once we were both lost, then we found each other, and now we'd each give ourselves to mend the other's soul. It wouldn't be an easy road, but we'd walk it together.

Until the day one of us died.

CHAPTER 33

LUKE WOKE WITH the same headache that had dogged him for the past week. The fear of Black finding out about him and Emmy was still very real although he'd won a brief reprieve. Because when he'd risked going downstairs the day after Akari had her baby, Emmy had disappeared again, and this time, she'd taken Black with her.

Nate had been sitting at the kitchen counter when he found out. Black sent a text message saying *Need some time to talk, back in a few days.*

That was it.

Nate had read the message aloud, calmly set down his mug of coffee, then flung his phone across the table and put his head in his hands.

"Black's taken a leaf out of Emmy's book. She's corrupted him."

"They could probably do with a bit of space," Carmen said, the voice of reason. "They've both been through a lot."

"I suppose," he'd grudgingly agreed. "An extra week won't make much difference."

At least they hadn't completely disappeared like on previous occasions. After five days of wondering, Mack had tracked their phones to the Caribbean. Jed wheedled someone he knew into sending a satellite photo, and as he zoomed in, those clustered around the screen saw a tropical island several miles from the nearest land.

"Reckon that's the place?" Jed asked.

"Definitely." Mack pointed to one end of the beach.

Beside two sunbathing figures, someone had written "FOXTROT OSCAR" in giant letters in the sand.

"She knows us so well."

Mack turned off the monitor. "Let's leave them in peace."

Emails went back and forth, and Black agreed to the Takedas temporarily moving into the guesthouse at the back of his property. Bradley flew into action, converting one of the three bedrooms into a nursery faster than Luke could iron a shirt.

Watching the man do his thing was something to behold. Emmy may have claimed he drove her up the wall, but Bradley could certainly organise the shit out of stuff. In less than a day, he'd got a team of workmen in to make the cottage child-proof and install new furniture. Akari would sleep in the newly decorated nursery with the baby while her parents and brother took the other two bedrooms.

Kitty would be moving in with the Takedas too, much to Luke's relief. He'd got used to the big cat now, but while it adored all the women in the house, it didn't seem so keen on the men. Luke had been giving it a wide berth. Kitty also seemed quite taken with Emmy's dog, Lucy, and the fact that a jaguar wandering through the house with a Doberman seemed quite normal now showed just how accustomed Luke had become to the crazy lives Emmy and her friends led.

Which was good, since it looked as if he and Mack would be staying at Riverley Hall for a while. The whole ceiling at Mack's apartment needed replacing. Bradley was sorting that out, as well as the renovations on Emmy's house, which had just been started. A lesser man might have had a breakdown, but Bradley simply donned a pair of sparkly dungarees and got on with things.

Then Tia arrived with Ryan in tow, and Luke had to admit he seemed a decent enough chap. They weren't sharing a bed, Tia claimed, but they'd chosen adjoining rooms on the third floor. Luke could guess from his own experiences exactly what happened after the lights went out.

He should act like a responsible brother, shouldn't he? He'd spent too many years ignoring his sister, and now that Emmy had helped to repair their relationship, it was time for him to step up to the plate. He needed to speak to Ryan about the rules, although he dreaded the thought of doing so. What should he say?

Google was little help, but when he caught Ryan on his own the day after he arrived, Luke decided to wing it.

"Have you got a minute?"

"Sure."

Luke ushered him into an empty room on the first floor. Some sort of office by the looks of it.

And after a few words of mumbled small talk came the difficult part. "Ryan, tell me honestly, are you and Tia seeing each other?"

Ryan looked him steadily in the eye. "Yes, we are. I care about her, and I promise you she's not just some hook-up."

Now what? He'd half expected Ryan to deny it, although he appreciated the man's honesty. Hell, someone should write a manual for these discussions.

"As her brother, I feel I should say..."

Ryan held up a hand. "Let me save you the trouble. Emmy's already phoned and had this talk with me, and quite frankly, there's nothing you could say or do that would scare me more than she does."

"Oh, in that case... Well, good."

"Can I go now?"

"Almost. Just one more thing. If I stood watching the door to your room each night, would I see you sneaking into Tia's?"

The other hand came up too. "No, I swear."

"In that case, I think we'll get on fine," Luke said, tension seeping away.

He should speak to Tia too, but he had even less idea what to say to her than he did to Ryan. Could he get Emmy to help out there as well? Or Mack?

Speaking of Mack, she was the girl he wanted to spend the rest of his life with. The One. Luke loved everything about her, and he was sure she felt the same way about him. He'd never even dreamed of meeting a woman who shared his love of electronics as well as his sense of adventure in the way she did. That she was beautiful and completely uninterested in his money was an added bonus.

And this week, he'd seen how Mack behaved with Akari's baby. She adored the little boy and spent hours helping Akari with him. Luke wanted children one day, and more than anything, he wanted them with Mack.

So he'd gone and done it. One day while Mack was out at work, he'd bought a ring. It came from Cartier, impressive but not huge, a simple three-carat diamond set in platinum. It was like Mack: stunning and uncomplicated. Nothing like Emmy. Emmy was as confusing as women got. Good to have as a friend, terrifying to have as an enemy, and as a wife? He shuddered at the thought. No, he didn't envy her husband that job.

Luke hadn't worked out the proposal thing yet, but he planned to do it soon. He wanted his ring on Mack's finger to make sure every other man knew she was off limits. Permanently.

Today was out of the question. He wanted to come up with something special, something memorable, and that would take time he didn't have right now. Because after a full day of meetings, they were going to a charity ball in the evening.

The last Blackwood Foundation fundraiser he'd attended had left a bad taste in his mouth, but Mack wanted to go and so he'd take her. Luke had learned that Emmy's pet charity operated on both sides of the Atlantic, and for reasons he didn't fully understand yet, it was close to her heart.

Still, Luke had made a half-hearted attempt to get out of going. "I'm not sure my tuxedo fits," he'd told Mack.

"Oh, that's fine. You don't need to wear one."

"It's not black tie?"

"No, it's fancy dress."

"Fancy dress?"

"Bradley decided to go with a theme this year—The Heroes and Villains ball."

"I heard a rumour a nasty computer virus is going to hit that day." Luke might even write it.

"Don't be such a stick-in-the-mud. Bradley's organising costumes for both of us."

"Super. Fantastic."

"I'm going as Poison Ivy."

"Remind me not to get on your bad side."

Mack leaned in to kiss him, and suddenly the potential embarrassment didn't matter so much anymore. As long as she was happy. Luke still dreaded to think what costume he'd end up in, but before he found out, he needed to go to his new office.

The Richmond subsidiary of HC Systems was almost ready to open, despite distractions of the Colombian variety. Blackwood's people had assisted to no end, with Sloane helping some of Luke's London staff to relocate and Emmy tasking her HR department to headhunt suitable candidates for the other roles. The fledgeling company had even landed its first two contracts, thanks to Emmy's recommendations.

Luke's investment in video conferencing technology meant meetings with his London team were easy, and apart from a few late nights and early mornings due to the time difference, running HC's head office remotely was going smoothly. And that meant he was free to spend most of his spare time in Virginia with Mack. A year ago, the commitment would have given him palpitations, but everything had changed. He'd changed. Mack had changed him. Next up was house hunting, and the thought made him heady with anticipation.

Meeting Ash had been the start of a rollercoaster ride—scary, exhilarating, and fun—but now he was about to step off into the next stage of the adventure. He couldn't wait.

Early evening found Luke dressed to kill in the Joker's purple suit while Bradley fussed around, organising last-minute alterations and a multitude of stylists. Honestly, was make-up really necessary?

"I thought we'd go with Heath Ledger's Joker rather than the Jack Nicholson version, so much more malevolent, don't you think?" Bradley asked as he rushed past with his arms full of yet more costumes.

Luke didn't have time to agree before he was gone.

Apparently, the make-up was "absolutely vital. How can you even think of going without?" and by the time Bradley's team had finished, Luke looked in the mirror and didn't recognise himself. His hair had a greenish tinge and added extensions, and his face? Whoa. The man never did things by halves, did he?

Then Mack walked in wearing a green leotard covered in sparkly ivy leaves, green tights, green stilettos, and a floor-length cape. Her hair was even redder than usual, and her eyebrows had been replaced with leaves.

Luke took one look at her and groaned. "Bradley, Mack needs a different costume."

"What do you mean? She looks amazing!"

"I know. That's the problem. I don't want every man in the place staring at her for the entire evening."

Bradley shrugged. "They won't all be staring. I expect some of them'll be gay."

Oh, that made all the difference.

Mack rolled her eyes. "Luke, it doesn't matter. I'm not going home with any of them. I'm going home with you, and I love this costume."

"Fine. But I'm not leaving your side all night."

"Even better."

CHAPTER 34

OUR DAYS ON Lorelei Cay were the best of my life, but all too soon, the time came to leave. Mick's funeral was coming up, and I planned to go with Black. Plus, I had a meeting at the White House with our Dear Leader himself, and he'd get grumpy if I cancelled. Something about the Middle East, apparently, and Nate was coming too.

And this evening was the annual Blackwood Foundation Ball in Richmond. If we left now and didn't hit any delays, we could make it back in time to attend. Bradley had gone with a theme again to make the event more fun. Or excruciatingly painful, depending which way you decided to look at it.

At least in our time away, we'd sorted out a story for Black's absence. Oliver and his team had been busy while the pair of us lounged on the beach. The DEA had kindly confirmed that Black had been on a top-secret undercover assignment for them, which resulted in the death of a primo drug lord and a successful operation to shut down his empire. Senator Trent was happy, Stone and Belcourt were happy, and their PR team was busy writing bullshit for the media. Oh, and the DEA had also smoothed things over with the local police department, which hopefully meant the cops would leave me alone until the next time I pissed them off.

As part of the deal, we'd passed all our intelligence on the Ramos family over to Agent Belcourt, and the DEA was busy shutting down his network on the East Coast. The files Carlos provided meant the number of favours the agency owed us sat comfortably in double figures.

Happy days.

And my death? Well, that was an administrative mix-up. Dr. Beech had done a shiny new press release, and apparently the sofas delivered that morning for the staff room at the hospital were very comfortable, thank you. Oliver got both of our death certificates revoked, and since I'd never filed Black's will, he should be able to slot back into his old life when we returned.

"What are we going to tell people about us?" I asked.

"What, you mean about our change in sleeping arrangements?"

"Something like that."

"I haven't thought about it. I guess we'll just have to pick the right moment," was his incredibly insightful reply.

"Which is when?"

"You're full of difficult questions, aren't you?"

"Always, but you wouldn't want me any other way."

We sailed back to Nassau on the Black Diamond, and although I was sad to leave the Caribbean, our parting would only be temporary thanks to Black's extravagance.

"I still can't believe you bought an island," I said as we tied the boat up in the marina.

He shrugged. "My investments made enough money to cover it while I was locked up. Didn't even make a dent in my finances."

"Good. You can buy me plenty of new bikinis for our next trip."

"I could, but you won't be needing them."

He slipped a hand under my T-shirt and pulled me towards him for a kiss. I'd had the man naked for a week, and I still couldn't get enough of him. I never would. I could drink from him forever and I'd crave more. One touch made me shiver, and a single brush of his lips made me melt. It was more than just physical— our souls were joined, bound together into one, and even death couldn't force them apart. I was his. Forever Black.

We only spent a few minutes at the airport, but a headwind on the flight back meant we touched down in Virginia later than planned.

"Bradley said he'd leave our costumes out in our bedrooms," I told Black. "Everyone else will have left by the time we get back."

"What are we going as?"

"I dread to think, but he promised my costume would have more fabric than last time."

Two years ago, I'd arrived back from a meeting just in time to change into my belly-dancing outfit, while Black had suffered the indignity of gladiator sandals.

"If it doesn't, we're not going."

As we hurried from the plane, Black held out his hand. "Keys. I want to try the Stingray."

Why not? If I didn't have to watch the road, I could spend more time staring at him like a hypnosis victim.

Thank goodness I didn't have to hide it anymore.

I might have gazed for longer if Black hadn't tested the car to the limit of its capabilities. Did I want to see death coming? A tough decision.

"And you complain I drive too fast?" I asked when we reached Riverley. The smell of burned rubber lined the driveway, and I needed new tyres.

"We're late."

I'd remember that excuse next time he told me off.

Apart from the ticking of the grandfather clock, the house was silent, the limos having departed fifteen minutes earlier. Black pinned me against the wall in the hallway before I could blink. Asshole. I kicked his legs out from under him, and we both ended up on the floor. Fuck, he was so tempting.

"We can't. We're late," I said.

He flexed his hips and I groaned. Not helping. The ball momentarily forgotten, I leaned forward and kissed him, whispering dirty thoughts as I did so. He did something magical with his fingers, and I'd turned into a quivering mess by the time he lifted me up and set me on the floor.

"For fuck's sake, you can't leave it there," I gasped.

"As you said, we're late." He grinned, most un-Black like. "You need to learn some self-control, Diamond."

Oh, I had self-control. If I didn't, I'd have booted him in the shin for that little trick. Instead, I trailed him up the stairs where, as promised, Bradley had laid out costumes on our beds.

Black grimaced. "Batman?"

"You're my hero," I said sweetly, fluttering my eyelashes in pretend adoration.

"And what's he given you?"

"I'd better check."

Hero or villain? Batgirl, maybe? Oh, I forgot, this was Bradley's doing.

Catwoman. I got Catwoman.

I muttered curses as I squeezed myself into the skintight suit. This was going to be horribly sweaty and it bloody squeaked. I was glad we were late now. The less time I had to wear this abomination, the better. I walked back into Black's bedroom to find him standing in front of the mirror.

"I'm not sure about the cape," he said. "I feel like an idiot wearing it."

"*You* feel like an idiot? At least you don't look as if you got lost on the way to a fetish club."

He turned around and let out a low whistle. "We could go to a fetish club instead if you want."

"Do you enjoy that kind of thing?" I asked, remembering the rope and the pair of handcuffs I'd found in his room when we first met.

"Like most things in life, I've tried it, but it's not for me. And there's no way I'm sharing you with another man."

Thank goodness for that. No other man would cut it now. "Woman?"

He raised an eyebrow and laughed. "If you don't get in the car right now, we're not going, because as much as I like you in that outfit, I'd like you out of it more."

I didn't bother to silence my groan. "We did come all the way back from the Caribbean to go."

And we only needed to put in a quick appearance, right? Then we could write our own comic strip, one where Catwoman came out on top.

It was my turn to drive, and I stuck religiously to the speed limit. I didn't want to explain to the highway patrol why two recently deceased comic book characters were driving too fast in a Corvette Stingray. Trying to save mankind probably wouldn't be an acceptable excuse.

When we arrived, everyone had just sat down for dinner. Team Blackwood occupied three tables, and I spotted our two empty seats. Time to surprise everybody.

On second thoughts... I motioned to Black to hold back. Why? Because I'd heard someone mention my name, and I was inherently nosy.

Wonder Woman, also known as Dan, knocked back a glass of champagne. "I hope she comes back like the old Emmy. She's been a shadow of her former self. It's not natural."

"I like the new Emmy," Iron Man said. "We have a meeting next week at the White House, and if she's reverted to old Emmy, then Black can take her. Old Emmy and the White House was not a good mix."

Oh, Nate. He'd said that many times before.

"Why?" Luke asked.

"Let's see, there was the time she decided to test out how well guarded the president was and managed to walk into his private apartment and inform him, just as he sat down to breakfast with the first lady, that his security was shit. Although perhaps my particular favourite was when, in a meeting involving the president, the vice president, the Joint Chiefs, and six senators, she asked the state senator for Oklahoma whether he'd been smoking crack. The president snorted coffee out of his nose."

I couldn't keep my mouth shut any longer. "The president saw the funny side. He told me afterwards he'd been wanting to ask that for ages."

"Emmy!"

Dan leapt up and hugged me, swiftly followed by Mack, Carmen as Harley Quinn, and Tia.

"I can't believe you're here," I muttered into her hair. "That make-up must have taken ages."

She gave me a twirl, blue from head to foot as Mystique.

"Half the day, but it was worth it."

And who was that next to her? Ryan? Yes, I recognised the eyes through his Spider-Man mask. He'd better be behaving himself.

Nick gave me a little wave from the other side of the table. "Nice outfit."

"At least I managed to get my underwear on the inside."

"Hey, everybody loves Superman."

Despite the sweating and a slight inability to breathe because my costume was so tight, I had a great evening. All my best friends in one place, some old, some new. We'd survived the trials and tribulations of the past eight-and-a-bit months, and the future looked...okay, it looked kind of blurry right now, but that was the champagne's fault. Tomorrow, things would look rosy.

"Ooh!" Bradley started clapping, and his Cruella de Vil wig slipped. Apparently, Nate had talked him out of bringing a real Dalmatian. "It's auction time!"

Dan, Mack, and Tia got up on stage to help sell the lots, which had the men in the room emptying their wallets. A fist fight threatened to start over a bottle of whisky as the bidding reached five figures, and Catwoman waded in to sort things out. I couldn't resist doing a backflip on the way. That shut them up.

The auction raised just shy of a million dollars, and I knew how far that money would go. The streets of Richmond would be a better place for people like teenage me. I leaned back in my seat with a well-deserved gin and tonic, but then I noticed Luke opposite, staring into a glass of whisky. He'd been quiet all evening. Why? Because Mack was up on stage falling out of her leotard? Or something else?

He didn't say anything, and I didn't want to get into a heavy conversation. Not this evening. But as always, the universe had other plans.

I'd just survived an epic trip to the ladies room and been passed in the corridor by Thor, also known as Jed, who gave me a thumbs-up as he trailed a slutty vampire upstairs. Honestly, the man was a walking cock. Then I saw Luke.

"Have you got a second?" he asked.

"Sure." I swallowed down a sigh. "Cheer up, it might never happen."

We found a quiet corner near the bar, and he fidgeted with his collar while I waited for him to speak.

"Come on, spit it out," I said.

"I'm worried."

I reached out to smooth the wrinkles on his forehead. "It's okay, the Joker's supposed to have lines." He didn't smile. "What's worrying you?"

"What happens if Black finds out about us? I mean

that we used to be an item?"

"Oh, he already knows."

"How?"

"I told him."

"Really? Mack thought you might, but I wasn't sure. Is he upset?"

"Of course not. He's grateful you looked after me when he couldn't."

"Are you sure? I mean you were still married to him when we..."

"Relax, it's fine." Giggles came from behind, and I glanced over his shoulder. "But you might want to help Mack. I think she's had one glass of wine too many."

Luke dashed off, looking happier than he had all evening, and I went to find Black. He was talking to a congressman as I slipped my hand under his cape and squeezed his ass. Taut, firm, mine.

The politician droned on about the constitution while I stifled a yawn, and Black worked his jaw from side to side as he did the same. Dull, dull, dull.

When I could take no more, I stood on tiptoes and whispered into his ear. "I lied to Nick earlier. I'm not wearing any underwear."

Black's expression didn't change as he interrupted the man. "I'm afraid my wife's just reminded me I have a pressing matter to attend to."

The pervert looked at me and licked his lips. "Of course. Good to talk to you, Mr. Black."

"What a prick," Black muttered as we walked away. Then he leaned a little closer. "Why do you smell like baby powder?"

"Because when I took a bathroom break, my costume got stuck and two strangers had to help me back into it. Luckily, one of them had kids. And stop laughing. It's not funny."

"Yeah, it is."

"Next year, the theme is a pyjama party."

"You don't wear pyjamas."

"Then I guess we'll have to stay at home."

Black's hand squeaked over my arse as he pulled me closer. "Don't worry, Catwoman. I'll free your pussy."

"Such a fucking gentleman. Uh, how quick can you do it?"

Ever efficient, Bradley had arranged a limo to take us back to Riverley. Someone would fetch the Stingray tomorrow. The driver of the Mercedes opened the door as we approached, and Black practically shoved me inside. I glanced at the privacy screen as I tumbled across the seat. Was it up? Yes. Good, because it wasn't the only thing up. We'd barely got a mile down the road before Batman demonstrated the importance of loving your enemies.

CHAPTER 35

WHAT A BEAUTIFUL, crisp, clear start to a delightful Sunday. I stood on Black's balcony with a cup of coffee, leaning forward over the stone balustrade. The sun was shining, the birds were singing, I didn't have a hangover, and Black had fucked me twice last night and once this morning.

Happy days.

I took a deep breath of cool air then looked up sharply as I heard a noise from above. I was just in time to see Ryan leap the five-foot gap between Tia's balcony and the one outside the bedroom he was allegedly sleeping in.

"You'd better be keeping your clothes on," I yelled.

He grinned over the edge and gave me a cheeky salute. "Yes, ma'am."

Well, Tia could do worse. I went back inside to find the love of my life sprawled naked on the bed.

"Poor baby, did I wear you out?" I asked.

"Mmm hmm."

"Do you want breakfast?"

"Mmm hmm."

"Any preferences?"

"Bacon roll."

So he could still speak English then, just about.

Downstairs in the kitchen, a small group of zombies

had gathered around the coffee machine, worshipping it like a shrine to sobriety.

"Are you all auditioning as extras for *Dawn of the Dead?*" I asked.

Nothing. Only grunts.

I rummaged through the fridge and got the bacon out, then found some ready-to-bake baguettes in a cupboard. Those would do. Surely even I couldn't screw up cooking part-baked bread?

Nick wandered in as I shoved them into the oven.

"I need to get to the office. Has anybody got spare socks I can borrow?"

"I bought you two new packets last week," Bradley said.

"Yeah, I know, but I think I wore those, and I can't find any clean ones."

"There's this thing called a washing machine..."

"I can't find that either."

"Nicky, why don't you get a housekeeper?" I asked. "Your whole house is a tip."

"Maybe I should. At least then I'd have socks."

"Is that a definite yes?"

"I guess."

"Great. Bradley, can you find Nick a housekeeper? He'll never manage it by himself."

"Sure, I'll start looking for candidates. This'll be awesome." Bradley already had his iPad out, hangover forgotten. "I won't need to keep buying socks and boxers and shirts every week. Somewhere in Nick's house, there's a black hole they disappear into."

Nick's whole property was a wrinkle in the space-time continuum. He'd stopped caring about it years ago, and merely thinking of the interior made me shudder.

I shoved that mess to the back of my mind as Akari and Hiro came through the back door, Hiro flashing a grin and Akari giving us her sweet smile. She was still incredibly shy and hated to be touched by anyone except Black, but I had hopes that once she got to know us all better, she'd let her personality shine through.

Nate had sorted out her money situation, at least. He'd given me an update yesterday.

"Carlos used to tell Akari, 'Dreams are the future's way of telling us what's waiting.'"

I hoped that wasn't true in my case. "You found the cash, then?"

"We followed his instructions, and it was right where he said it would be."

So Carlos had done his best for her, right until the end. She'd be looked after. The remainder of the Ramos fortune would go to charity, just as he'd intended. Black could have imitated him again and got it back, but he didn't want to.

"It's blood money," he'd said. "I don't want a dime of it."

A sentiment I totally agreed with.

Meanwhile, Hiro settled Akari into a seat and poured her some juice.

"How's the baby?" I asked her.

"He's sleeping. My mother is watching him."

"Have you decided on a name yet?"

She nodded. "Hisashi. It means 'always with you.'"

"That's perfect."

A ringing phone interrupted our conversation, and I realised the guard from the gatehouse was calling me. Great. It was too early for visitors.

"Emmy, Miriam Black's here. I told her she's not allowed in, but she won't take no for an answer. I don't think she knows you're alive, and she's demanding to speak to whoever's in charge. Should I call someone to remove her?"

Oh boy, this morning just got better and better.

"It's okay, bring her up. Can you show her through to the kitchen? I'll be waiting in there." Then I dialled Black. "Miriam's on her way up the drive."

Suddenly, he was awake. "Be there in five."

Miriam was yelling before she got fully through the kitchen door, all red-faced and probably drunk.

"I demand to speak to someone with some authority in this place."

Nick moved out of the way, and she did a double take when she saw me leaning against the counter.

I couldn't help smiling. "That would be me."

Her colour dropped a shade. "I was told you'd died."

"Then I guess you were misinformed."

"You nasty, lying little bitch. I should have known you'd resort to playing dirty. My lawyer says you're deliberately stalling everything."

"Yep." The grin was stuck on my face.

"Is that all you've got to say for yourself? You just don't want to give me what's rightfully mine, do you? That money's my birthright, not yours, you scheming little gold-digger. You're nothing but a little slut who married Charles for his wealth. I insist you file that will right now so I can contest it."

"Not going to happen."

"Then I'll force you to do it. My lawyer's preparing papers to take you to court as we speak."

"Then he's even more stupid and greedy than you are."

"Did you just insult me?"

"I sincerely hope so."

"You... You..."

"Bitch?"

"Yes! You stand here in what should be my house and call me names..."

She didn't get any further because Black, who'd been standing in the doorway since she called me a gold-digger and a slut, interrupted her. And he was absolutely, gloriously, unreservedly fucking furious.

"I think you'll find this is *my* house."

Miriam turned slowly and all the colour drained out of her face. She clutched at her chest but unfortunately stayed standing.

"But...but...but you're dead."

"Do I look like I'm fucking dead?"

"Well, no, but..."

"How dare you come into my house and insult my wife? The wife I've been married to for twelve damn years, which is longer than you've been with your prick of a husband. That seem like a flash in the pan to you?"

"W-w-when you put it that way..."

"Emmy's never taken a cent from me that wasn't freely given. You, on the other hand, put your hand out the minute you need cash."

"It's not like that. We're family."

"Not anymore. You're dead to me the same as I was dead to you. Now get out and don't set foot on this property again."

Miriam backed through the kitchen door and practically sprinted from the house. I was sure we hadn't seen the last of her, but hopefully she'd leave us alone for a while.

Black walked over and high-fived me. "Fuck, that was satisfying."

"I can't believe the gall of the woman, walking in here like that. And she called me a gold-digger. And a slut! Last time I checked, my bank account was comfortably into nine figures, and I've slept with less than ten men in my life."

"Although you do have to admit there's a certain irony that four of them are in this room."

I couldn't believe Black had just outed us. I threw an orange at him, but he caught it and began peeling.

It was Dan who did the maths first. "So, going on the assumption you haven't slept with Nate or Hiro, that leaves five men."

She glanced at Nate, and he nodded his confirmation. Why did he look so horrified?

"And I'm going to count Ryan out too because you're not that much of a cougar. So that leaves Nick, Jed, Luke and... Oh my gosh! You two are together! Like together-together?"

Two steps, and Black had wrapped me up in his arms, his chin resting on top of my head. That didn't make me feel short at all.

"Oh, you guys, this is so great!"

"This calls for a party!" Bradley tried.

"No!" Black and I both shouted at him in perfect unison.

"Not even a small one?"

Time to change the subject. "Who wants a bacon roll?"

There was a chorus of yeses, and Mack, who didn't

look as if she was on the same planet as the rest of us, raised her hand. Something glinted in the sunlight coming in through the window.

"Mack, what's that on your finger? Is that a ring?" I peered closer, and it was. A great big diamond ring on the third finger of her left hand. "Did you get engaged?"

"Uh..." Mack looked at it in amazement.

Luke had been slumped over the breakfast bar, but now he sat up with his eyes wide in horror.

"Luke, where did this ring come from?" Mack asked.

"I don't know. Well, I sort of do. It came from Cartier. But I'm not sure how it got onto your finger. I left it in my sock drawer."

"I don't think I was wearing it at the ball. Was I?" She looked to me for confirmation, and I shook my head.

"So are you guys getting married?" Dan asked.

Luke looked panic-stricken with a hint of what-the-fuck-have-I-done. "Are we? Did I ask you to marry me? I mean, I was going to, but I don't remember."

Mack rubbed her temples, and her colour matched her costume from last night. "Everything after that last round of cocktails is a blank. Did you really ask? What did I say?"

Seriously? Oh, this was gold. "I always thought Black's proposal was the worst ever, but this might actually have beaten it."

"Diamond, I didn't really propose. As I recall, Nate suggested we get married, and we were drunk enough to go along with it."

"Exactly my point."

Dan leaned forwards on her elbows. "Well, if you're

wearing the ring, Luke must have put it on your finger because you said yes."

"I guess."

"So are you getting married or not?" Bradley asked, ever the impatient one.

"Er, Mack, will you marry me? And for the record, this wasn't how I'd envisaged asking you."

The wail of the smoke alarm interrupted before Mack could answer, and I leapt sideways to yank the oven door open. Bradley pushed me out of the way, grabbed the charred baguettes with a tea-towel, and threw them out of the window Nate had just opened. See? Teamwork. Always a good thing.

"Okay, as you were." I re-took my position in front of Black. Guess we'd be ordering in for breakfast. "Mack, he needs an answer."

She looked as if she was about to puke, but managed a quick smile. "Yes, all right."

"Thank goodness for that," Luke said, then slumped over the table again.

"Who won the pool?" Carmen asked.

"Luther. Again. *Now* can we have a party?" Bradley wasn't giving up.

"Maybe something low key," Mack conceded. "With no alcohol."

"Can I be a bridesmaid?" Tia asked.

"Sure."

Everybody began chattering at once, congratulating Mack and Luke. I twisted around and smiled at Black.

"There've been some horrible moments, but things are going to be okay, aren't they?"

He stroked a thumb over the wedding ring on my own finger, now there to stay after our recent adventures.

"No, Diamond. Things are going to be a lot better than okay."

Mr. Black

After finishing the Black trilogy, I couldn't resist taking a look into the mind of Mr. Black in a short story, BLACK.

As it contains so many spoilers for the first three books, it's not available for sale, but everyone who's read Forever Black can get a copy for FREE from the following link:

www.elise-noble.com/614ck

Happy Reading!

Elise

What's next?

Due to the author's inability to make up her mind, the Blackwood Security series continues in two directions, both of which are standalone novels.

Gold Rush

Lara Reynolds has a lot of things she wants to escape. An asshole of an ex-boyfriend and a stalker are just two of them. Becoming housekeeper to Nick Goldman, a man whose house is as filthy as his mind, is far from her dream job but she's out of other options.

She tries to flee from her past, but when you have a weakness for high heels, there are bound to be a few stumbles along the way. Will Lara run out of luck or fall into love?

You can find out more about Gold Rush here:
www.elise-noble.com/gold-rush

Oxygen

Sometimes love can be found when you least expect it...

Akari Takeda walked on the dark side for fifteen years until death gave her the chance at a new life. Determined not to waste the time she has left, she moves to Boston with her young son to follow her dream of becoming a pianist.

But three men get in her way—Jansen, the skilled but uptight violinist, easygoing Jude, who understands how important coffee is to a girl, and Lincoln, the smooth-talking janitor who looks good in leather.Which of them will steal her heart, and who isn't everything he seems?

You can find out more about Oxygen here:
www.elise-noble.com/oxygen

If you enjoyed Forever Black, please consider leaving a review.

For an author, every review is incredibly important. Not only do they make us feel warm and fuzzy inside, readers consider them when making their decision whether or not to buy a book. Even a line saying you enjoyed the book or what your favourite part was helps a lot.

Want to stalk me?

For updates on my new releases, giveaways, and other random stuff, you can sign up for my newsletter on my website:
www.elise-noble.com

Facebook:
www.facebook.com/EliseNobleAuthor

Twitter: @EliseANoble

Instagram: @elise_noble

I also have a group on Facebook for my fans to hang out. They love the characters from my books almost as much as I do, and they're the first to find out about my new stories as well as throwing in their own ideas that sometimes make it into print!

And if you'd like to read my books for FREE, you can also find details of how to join my review team.

Would you like to join Team Blackwood?

www.elise-noble.com/team-blackwood

END OF BOOK STUFF

When I first started writing Emmy's story, I had no idea it would turn out this way. Originally, Ash was a secretary who lived happily ever after with Luke, but the more of Pitch Black I wrote, the more pissed off she got with that scenario. She needed a different man, so I gave him to her.

I like to think it's worked out okay.

Thank you so much to everyone who read the draft versions of my books, who told me what they liked and disliked about the characters, which parts didn't work, and pointed out all my mistakes. I didn't cry much, honest.

Huge thanks again to Abigail and Amanda, artist and editor extraordinaire, for all your help with bringing the characters to life.

And thanks to you for reading—I hope you stick around to meet some of the other characters fighting to get out of my head. Nick's next. All six feet two of tanned, dark-haired gorgeousness. If I had to lick the abs of one of my fictional characters, Nick would probably be the man...

Other books by Elise Noble

The Blackwood Security Series
Black is my Heart (prequel)
Pitch Black
Into the Black
Forever Black
Gold Rush
Gray is my Heart
Neon (novella)
Out of the Blue
Ultraviolet
Red Alert
White Hot
The Scarlet Affair
Quicksilver
The Girl with the Emerald Ring (TBA)
For the Love of Animals (Nate & Carmen)

The Blackwood Elements Series
Oxygen
Lithium
Carbon
Rhodium
Platinum
Lead
Copper (2019)

Bronze (2019)
Nickel (TBA)

The Blackwood UK Series
Joker in the Pack
Cherry on Top (novella)
Roses are Dead
Shallow Graves
Indigo Rain (2019)

Blackwood Casefiles
Stolen Hearts (2019)

Blackstone House
Hard Lines (TBA)

The Electi Series
Cursed
Spooked
Possessed
Demented (TBA)

The Trouble Series
Trouble in Paradise
Nothing but Trouble
24 Hours of Trouble

Standalone
Life
Twisted (short stories)
A Very Happy Christmas (novella)